Margaret Maron is a past president of the Sisters in Crime organisation and a long-standing member of the Mystery Writers of America and the Carolina Crime Writers Association. Her novels have been nominated for the Anthony, the Agatha, the Macavity, and the American mystery awards. She won an Agatha Award for the short story that first introduced Deborah Knott, the character featured in this first Deborah Knott novel. Margaret Maron is also known for her stories featuring Lieutenant Sigrid Harald of the NYPD. She lives with her artist husband near Raleigh, North Carolina.

Bootlegger's Daughter

Margaret Maron

HEADLINE

First published in Great Britain in 1994
by HEADLINE BOOK PUBLISHING

10 9 8 7 6 5 4 3 2 1

ISBN 0 7472 4650 5

Typeset by
CBS, Felixstowe, Suffolk

Printed and bound in Great Britain by
Cox & Wyman Ltd, Reading, Berks

HEADLINE BOOK PUBLISHING
A division of Hodder Headline PLC
338 Euston Road
London NW1 3BH

To Carl Jackson and Sue Stephenson Honeycutt –
for friendship and kinship rooted two hundred years
in eastern North Carolina's sandy loam

ACKNOWLEDGMENTS

My sincere thanks to the professional men and women of the North Carolina State Bureau of Investigation, especially Special Agents Henry Poole and Shirley Burch; to the attorneys and judges of the Second Judicial Division, especially Ms Joy Temple, and the late Judge Edwin S. Preston, Jr; and most of all to Elizabeth Wells Anderson, whose memories 'kept me between the ditches' when I started traveling down roads where she once lived. They patiently answered my questions with candor and honesty, and if there are errors, the fault lies not in the things they told me but in my transmutation of their answers.

DISCLAIMER

MAY 1972

Prologue

Possum Creek trickles out of a swampy waste a little south of Raleigh. By the time it gets down to Cotton Grove, in the western part of Colleton County, it's a respectable stream, deep enough to float rafts and canoes for several miles at a stretch.

The town keeps the banks mowed where the creek edges on Front Street, and it makes a pretty place to stroll in the spring, the nearest thing Cotton Grove has to a park, but the creek itself has never had much economic value. Kids and old men and an occasional woman still fish its quiet pools for sun perch or catfish, but the most work it's ever done for Cotton Grove was to turn a small gristmill built back in the 1870s a few miles south of town.

When cheap electricity came to the area in the thirties, even that stopped. The mill was abandoned and its shallow dam was left for the creek to dismantle rock by rock through forty-odd spring crestings.

These days, Virginia creeper and honeysuckle fight it out in the dooryard with blackberry brambles and poison ivy. Hunters and anglers may shelter beneath its rusty tin roof from unexpected thunderstorms, teenage lovers may park in the overgrown lane on warm moonlit nights, but for years the mill has sat alone out there in the woods, tenanted only by the coons and foxes that den beneath its stone walls.

The creek does serve as boundary marker between several farms, and the opposite bank is Dancy land, though no Dancy's actually dirtied his hand there in fifty years.

Until this spring.

About two-tenths of a mile upstream from the mill is a surprisingly sturdy old hay barn that Michael Vickery, a Dancy grandson, has recently claimed for a ceramics studio. He's a pretty fair painter, and ceramic sculptures will be the latest in a string of artistic endeavors since he came home from New York in January. He's making the spacious hayloft into a comfortable modern apartment, doing most of the work himself, and the two middle-aged black laborers that he's hired to clear out the underbrush around it have heard it's going to be a real fancy living place all right. They'd give a pretty to see it, but things being how they are, they'd never ask flat out, and it hasn't occurred to Michael to show it to a pair of black 'boys' even though he's been off to Yale and does support the civil rights movement.

(He never uses the word *nigger* anymore except when he's knocking back a Schlitz down at the local beer joint and he honestly doesn't feel that counts. *It's just to keep the home boys thinking I'm still one of them*, he tells himself with conscious cynicism. *Like a sweet-faced woman feels she has to say 'fuck' once in a while when she's out with the girls so they won't think she's too prissy. Means nothing.)*

After three days of chilly fogs and rain that made working outdoors miserable, the low-pressure system has finally moved on out to sea, and proper spring weather has filled in behind with hot sunshine and a warm west wind. Michael Vickery's got those two day laborers back clearing the slope down by the edge of the water while he stacks bricks for an outdoor kiln on the other side of the barn.

Of course, there are chemical weedkillers that would knock out the poison oak, briars, and bullace vines, but Michael's troubled by fish kills in other North Carolina creeks and rivers and he wants to mend the damage done to Possum Creek by Dancy tenants who laced these fields with chemical fertilizers and pesticides and never had a minute's uneasiness for what might be happening to the water table.

The hired men would spray if Mr Michael told them to, but grubbing roots by hand stretches out the pay at a time of year when farm work's thin. Too late to plant tobacco, too early to start suckering it. So it's *yessuh*, Mr Michael. Whatever you say, Mr Michael. Want us to work up from the creek today, 'stead of down from the barn where we started? Sure thing, Mr Michael.

Sweat pours off their bodies and drenches their shirts as they toil in the steamy morning sunlight, and each time they pause to get a drink of water, they seem to hear something downwind across the creek. A baby pig maybe?

'Ain't no pigs over yonder,' says one. 'Closest place with pigs is probably Mr Kezzie and he ain't got but a couple of fattening hogs. Might be a cat. Or a mockingbird. Used to be

5

one'd set up on our chimney and sound like the rusty hinge on our screen door.'

They swing bush knife and mattock and talk about some of the odd noises they've heard mockingbirds mimic.

'Only that don't sound like no mockingbird,' says the first man stubbornly.

The sound drifts fitfully on the soft western breeze, never lasting really long enough to get a good fix on it. When Michael Vickery comes down to see what they want him to bring them from the store for a midmorning snack, they tell him to listen.

He does, but naturally the bird or cat or whatever it is chooses that time to go silent.

The white man shrugs, takes their drink orders, and says he'll be back in about thirty minutes, 'cause he has to run by the brickyard before they close for the weekend.

As the roar of his pickup fades over the rise, heading for the highway, both men ease off on their tools. A drowsy humid stillness hangs over the creek bank. Even the birds are mute in this hot morning air. Just when they've decided that whatever it was is gone for good, it comes again, a high thin note floating back up the quiet water.

The first workman drops his mattock and heads for the creek. 'Some little creature's in trouble,' he says.

For some reason, it's a pitiful noise to him, halfway between a kitten and a young piglet so hopelessly entangled in barbed wire that it's almost resigned itself to death, and the older man just can't let it go.

Together, the two track the thin mews downstream to the mill. They splash across the broken spillway and finally follow their ears into the old millhouse itself.

And that's when they abruptly connect the cries with what's been occupying the hearts and souls of half of Cotton Grove ever since Wednesday.

They look at each other fearfully. One of them is still carrying his axe-handled bush knife, and he holds the sharp hooked blade in readiness as they enter the dim stone building. The other grabs up a couple of potato-sized rocks, and he, too, is on guard. Field mice rustle among the debris near the door, but the two men barely notice. The crying comes from overhead and sounds exhausted to them now.

'Who's up there?' they shout. 'Anybody there?'

The mewing cries continue, and it almost breaks the heart of the older man because now he's surer than ever what it is up there crying. Half a lifetime ago, he listened to cries just that pitiful as his only baby son wasted away from diphtheria in his cradle.

As he mounts the steps, a stench meets his nose.

Carrion. And body wastes.

Part of the tin roof has collapsed at the gable end of the loft overlooking the creek, so there's enough light to see clearly.

The cries come from a very young infant strapped in a molded plastic carrier. She's soaked in her own urine and stinks of putrid diapers, but that's not what makes the men want to retch.

It's the white woman who lies on the stone floor beside the baby.

She's face up. Her body is clad in the long-sleeved black jersey, white jeans, and flat-heeled slippers the radio said

7

she'd been wearing when she disappeared three days ago.

Blowflies are thick all over her pretty face and maggots are already working the clots of blood and brains beneath her long dark hair.

APRIL 1990

1

Rainy Days And Mondays
Always Get Me Down

His green-and-vermilion topknot was as colorful as a parrot's, and in Colleton County's courtroom that afternoon, with its stripped-down modern light oak benches and pale navy carpet, a cherryhead parrot couldn't have looked much more exotic than this Michael Czarnecki.

Nineteen years old. Tattooed eyeliner on bloodshot eyes. Stainless steel skull-and-crossbones dangling from his left earlobe. His jaw was purple from where it'd banged the steering wheel when he ran off the road a little past three that morning, and he was still wearing black skinny-legged jeans and the electric orange-and-green 'Boogie On Down To Florida' sweatshirt he'd had on when the state troopers plucked him off I-95 and perched him in our brand-new jail.

From his own perch, the black-robed judge frowned down at Czarnecki like an elderly cowbird while Assistant District Attorney Kevin Foster read the charges: speeding 74 in a 65 zone, driving while impaired, simple possession of marijuana.

'You got an attorney?' asked Judge Hobart, who knew quite well that he'd appointed me that morning when the calendar was first called and that this was why I was now seated at the same table with the defendant.

I stood up. 'Your Honor, I represent Mr—' I glanced again at the court calendar in my hand and tackled the unfamiliar name with more confidence than I felt. 'Mr Zar-*neck*-ee.'

'*Zar*-n'kee,' my client corrected me shyly.

'Not representing him too well, Miss Knott, if you can't even say his name right,' the judge sniffed. 'How does he plead?'

I'd worked it out with Kevin before lunch. He'd knocked a 78 down to 74 and had thrown out a piddling seat belt violation and two charges of reckless and endangering, but we were stuck with DWI and simple possession. And I was stuck with punk hair, 'Boogie On Down To Florida,' and a judge with many, many axes to grind.

I-95 passes straight through the middle of Colleton County, North Carolina, linking Miami to New York. I've never actually looked into the wording of the billboard law that regulates signs along a federally funded highway, but it's lax enough that farmers here can rent their roadside land to advertise the locations of factory outlets that sell towels and sheets, name-brand clothing, and, of course, cheap cigarettes.

Despite the tourist dollars, our stretch of I-95 would be a no-exit tunnel if Harrison Hobart had his druthers, and he normally throws the book at any Yankees who stray off the interstate and into his court. Fortunately, it was only a week till the May primary, so Czarnecki, who was boogie-ing on back up to Teaneck, New Jersey, got lucky. His outlandish hair, his satanic earring, and his smartass sweatshirt afforded so many opportunities to zing me, that Hobart finally let the kid off with a ninety-day suspended and a two-fifty fine.

Did I mention that Harrison Hobart's seat is up for election? Or that I'm one of the candidates?

I hadn't really planned to run for judge. Not consciously anyhow, but it must have been lurking down deep in my subconscious because something snapped last winter. It wasn't even my case. I was sitting there on the lawyers' bench at the front of Courtroom #2 that rainy January morning, waiting to try and keep Luellen Martin out of jail one more time even though she was nearly seven months behind in her restitution payments and her probation officer was ticked because she'd skipped a couple of reporting sessions as well. Luellen works out at the towel factory and makes enough money to get her hair fixed every week, keep up car payments on a Hyundai, and trundle her kids down to Disney World over the Christmas holidays; but she couldn't ever seem to get up the monthly hundred dollars she was supposed to be paying various complainants after bouncing checks all over town last spring.

A jury case was in session; Reid Stephenson defending an impassive-looking black man.

'What's the charge?' I whispered to Ambrose Daughtridge, who was also waiting for a case to be called. I should have known. After all, Reid was not only my cousin, he was also one of my partners.

'DWI, wouldn't take the Breathalyzer,' Ambrose whispered back.

Refusal to take a Breathalyzer test's not a real smart decision under the usual circumstances. As the examining officer explained, 'I tried to tell him that if he didn't take the test, God himself couldn't let him drive for twelve months in the State of North Carolina.'

'And did he understand?' asked Tracy Johnson, who was prosecuting the calendar that day in a navy blazer and red wool skirt. She's tall and slender with blonde hair clipped shorter than most men's. Quite pretty actually, except that she keeps the good bones of her face obscured by businesslike horn-rimmed glasses.

'Objection,' said Mel. 'Calls for a conclusion.'

'Sustained.'

Tracy had graduated from law school only six months earlier, and it still needled her a bit whenever an objection to one of her questions was sustained. She pushed her oversized glasses up on her nose and hurriedly restated: 'Did you ask Mr Gilchrist if he understood that if he didn't take the test and was found guilty, he'd automatically lose his license for a year?'

'Yes, ma'am,' said the officer. Sanderson. Late twenties, spit and polish uniform. Always sits at attention. Even when he's trying to convey more-in-sorrow-than-anger earnestness. 'I did everything but *beg* him to take that test. I told him even if he didn't pass, he could probably get a limited permit. But if he didn't take it, he was going to be walking for twelve months. He didn't say nothing 'cept "Huh!"'

'"Huh"?' asked the judge. Perry Byrd that day. Well into his third term of office.

'That's all he'd say, Your Honor,' Sanderson said. 'Every

14

time we asked him anything, that's all he'd say: "Huh!" Real cocky-like.'

No law officer says *uppity* anymore. Not in open court anyhow. *Cocky*'s the new code word in the New South.

Judge Byrd nodded and laboriously made a notation on the legal pad in front of him. At fifty-two, Perry Byrd's peppery red hair had a hefty sprinkle of salt in it. Broad strapping shoulders on a six-foot-two build, and the florid face of an incipient stroke victim. He also had a prissy little high-pitched voice and, even talking under his breath, everyone sitting near the front, including the jury, could hear his absent-minded 'cocky-like' as he wrote.

Reid looked over at the lawyers' bench and he rolled his eyes at Ambrose and me.

Judge Byrd finished writing and looked up. 'Well, get on with it, Miss Johnson,' he told Tracy, fussily.

Some judges enjoy bossing brand-new ADAs and it's not always a male/female thing, although the two years I'd worked in the DA's office, there'd been this one white-haired little bastard who rode me like a dog-fly, never lighting, always just out of swatting distance.

Tracy quickly finished her examination of Trooper Sanderson, and Reid's cross-examination explored the possibility that he and the arresting trooper might have maybe, 'unintentionally of course,' denied his client permission to call his lawyer.

'No, sir,' said Sanderson, displaying a copy of the Alcohol Influence Report form he'd filled out earlier and which Gilchrist had signed. 'We go right down the list and when we got to "Is there anyone you now wish to notify?" he said "No."'

'But hadn't he earlier asked to call his lawyer?'

'Not to my knowledge, sir,' Sanderson said blandly.

Even though Reid is my mother's first cousin, he's four years younger than me. He's got the Stephenson good looks, too: tall, blond, melting blue eyes. When he wants to, he can look like a Wall Street broker; most of the time though, he tries to act like a good old country lawyer. He leaned back in his swivel chair and wheedled around every way he knew, but Sanderson sat up straight in the witness box and wouldn't admit that Gilchrist had been denied any of his constitutional rights.

'No further questions,' Reid finally said.

'State rests, Your Honor,' said Tracy.

The jury looked at Reid expectantly, but Judge Byrd motioned to the bailiff. 'Head 'em out, Mr Faircloth.'

Eight women, three of them black, and four men, one black, stood up and followed the elderly bailiff out through the right rear door. I was interested to see that the one black man was James Greene, formerly a deputy on the town police force and now head of his own small security service.

Why in God's name, I wondered, had Reid left him on the jury? I could tell it was likely to be after lunch before the court would get to Luellen's case, but a freezing rain was falling outside and there was nowhere else I needed to be right then, so I settled back on the bench.

When the door closed behind the last juror, Judge Byrd called for motions and Reid asked for dismissal for lack of evidence. I'd come in late, so I couldn't tell if there was merit to what would be an automatic motion on Reid's part, even had his client been falling-down drunk.

'Denied,' Byrd squeaked in his little high voice. 'Will there be evidence for the defense?'

'Yes, Your Honor, there'll be evidence.' Reid sat down and conferred with his client until the bailiff had finished bringing the jury back in.

Ambrose looked at his watch, sighed, and wandered out to the hall where other lawyers paused to exchange pleasantries as they passed from one courtroom to another, keeping check on how much longer it'd be before one of their cases was called. Earlier that morning in Courtroom #3, I'd pled two young men guilty to taking a deer illegally and got them off with a $150 fine and ninety days suspension of their hunting licenses. ('They were real respectful and cooperative,' the game warden testified.) And I'd helped an elderly grandmother avoid a fine for writing worthless checks on what she'd thought was still a joint account with her sailor grandson. (He'd gotten married in San Diego and had closed the account without telling her.) Nothing else was on my court schedule that day except Luellen Martin's hearing.

While I sat there, her probation officer came in with a steaming white foam cup and sat down at the end of the bench beside me. The smell of hot chocolate mingled with the sweet floral perfume she wore. Either I'm getting older or probation officers are getting younger. I know they have to be twenty-one and college graduates, but in her blue print jersey with its broad, white, lace-edge collar, this one looked like a yuppie teenager. No wonder Luellen kept skipping her probation meetings.

'Call your first witness, Mr Stephenson,' Judge Byrd directed.

17

Reid had only one, the defendant himself.

Gilchrist appeared to be in his midthirties, quite dark, close-clipped wiry hair, neatly dressed in a blue turtleneck sweater, a brown corduroy jacket, and blue jeans. A self-employed plumber who lives here in Dobbs, he told his story quietly and with no apparent emotion, almost as if he were describing something that had happened to a stranger.

But his eyes were wary.

On the Thursday in question, he said, he'd worked all day on some frozen pipes over in the next county. He'd had a bad cold all week and was running a fever; so before he went to bed that night, he'd mixed himself a homemade toddy.

'I waited till after my three daughters had gone to bed because my wife and me, we don't hold with drinking in front of the girls.'

At Reid's prodding, Gilchrist indicated that he'd poured about two fingers of Georgia Moon Corn Whiskey into a pint Mason jar, then added honey and lemon juice. (Too bad he hadn't bought George Dickle or Jim Beam, some brand name that didn't carry such a load of drunken images.)

He'd sipped the toddy while watching the late-evening news and had then gone to bed. Two hours later, he'd been awakened by a phone call from his sister, who worked a night shift at a convenience store over in Widdington, about twenty miles away. Her car wouldn't start and there was no one else she could call, so Gilchrist had hauled himself out of bed, sleep-drugged, stuffy head, low-grade fever and yes, a debatable quantity of that homemade toddy, and had driven over to pick her up. He'd taken her to her house out in the country about three miles from Dobbs and was on his way back to his own house when the trooper pulled him.

According to his testimony, he'd cooperated up to the point they tried to administer the Breathalyzer. 'I walked the line, touched my nose and did all that stuff, but when they wanted me to blow on the tube, I said I wanted to call my lawyer and they said they'd get to that.'

He then described how Sanderson and the arresting officer, Davis, kept pressing him to take the test. When he refused and repeated his request to call a lawyer, they started filling out the Alcohol Influence Report. 'That's when I just quit talking and said whatever I thought they wanted me to say because I didn't want to get them mad at me.'

It sounded logical. On the AIR form, the question about calling someone is down near the end. If Gilchrist had gone into a passive mode of answering yes or no according to what he thought the troopers wanted to hear, it was quite likely that he'd automatically answered no at that point.

Gilchrist's testimony also disputed Sanderson's version of filling out the report. According to him, Davis had read the questions and Sanderson had filled in the blanks. 'They said I had that paper and was reading along with 'em, but they never gave it to me till they said I had to sign it, so I did.'

On cross-examination, Tracy tried to rattle Gilchrist about how many inches of Georgia Moon he'd actually poured into that Mason jar, but nothing got beneath the unemotional surface the black plumber had learned to present to white officialdom.

'I bought that bottle at the ABC store back before Christmas,' he said, quietly underlining the assertion that he was no habitual drinker. 'It's still got almost a third left in it.'

On redirect, Reid said, 'How old are you, Mr Gilchrist?'

'Thirty-seven.'

'How long you been driving?'

'Since I was sixteen.'

'Ever been arrested before?'

'No.'

'No speeding tickets, no DWIs?'

'No.'

'Defense rests, Your Honor.'

The jury was taken out again. Once more Reid asked Judge Byrd to dismiss and once more the motion was denied. Then Perry Byrd mechanically ran over the usual points he planned to touch on in his instructions to the jury. 'Any requests for further instructions?'

'No, Your Honor,' Tracy said.

'No further requests,' said Reid.

The jury filed back in and seated themselves with a friendly, interested air. This was only Tuesday, the first day they'd actually sat on a case, and they weren't yet jaded. Reid had a warm avuncular smile on his face as he went over to address them, and several smiled back tentatively.

'Now's when we bring out our closing arguments,' he said and delivered a short and eloquent speech about the burden of proof being on the state. His argument, of course, was that all the state really had was the defendant's refusal to take the Breathalyzer and the account of the arresting trooper who'd stopped Gilchrist at 2:30 in the morning, a sick man on his way back to bed after performing a Good Samaritan deed for his sister.

'A dark moonless night, ladies and gentlemen, on a winding

stretch of deserted highway. Two cars meeting each other. Trooper Davis says he observed my client weaving back and forth over the center line and he had what? Fifteen seconds? Twenty seconds to observe all this?'

'Don't forget, ladies and gentlemen, that Trooper Davis is an experienced officer with nearly ten years as a North Carolina highway patrolman,' said Tracy Johnson. I decided those ugly glasses were a smart touch. They neutralized both her prettiness and her inexperience and lent a tone of judicial competency as she ran over the case again and asked for a guilty decision.

In persnickety tones more suited to explaining Parcheesi rules, Judge Byrd instructed along predictable lines: the jury was not to consider what they'd *like* the law to be, but what it is; yes, there's a presumption of innocence and the state must prove guilt, but not beyond *all* doubt, he told them, leaning heavily on the *all*, merely beyond reasonable doubt. He read them the law on DWI, told them their possible verdicts, then sent them off to deliberate.

It was 12:15.

I'd hoped to slide Luellen's case in before the lunch recess, but Ambrose Daughtridge had poor-mouthed about his schedule enough that Tracy called his case next, so Reid and I splashed across the street in the freezing rain to Sue's Soup 'n' Sandwich Shop for a bowl of her homemade Brunswick stew. The little shop was crowded and steamy and permeated with the wonderful smells of hot coffee, toasted bread, and fragrant meats. We had to wait a few minutes for one of the tiny booths that line the wall opposite the long Formica lunch counter.

Reid was torn between optimism for his client's case and disgust that Gilchrist had even been charged. He'd managed to keep on the panel a sharp-eyed middle-aged woman who'd worked as an auto insurance adjuster, and he seemed to think that she was the natural choice for foreperson, someone who'd see this case for what it was and bring in a quick not guilty.

I hate to lick the red off anybody's candy cane and kept my mouth shut.

'What?' he asked.

'She's never going to get elected foreperson,' I told him. 'James Greene is.'

'What you talking? She's white, she's educated, she's sharp—'

'She's a woman,' I interrupted. 'And a civilian.' Our stew arrived, hot and thick, and I added a heavy sprinkle of black pepper. 'James Greene may be a black man, but he's still a man *and* an ex-police officer. The other men'll vote for him to show they're not bigots and he'll toss around enough jargon that the women will defer to his expertise.'

'Yeah?' Reid crumbled saltine crackers over his bowl and stirred them in as he considered how Greene's being foreperson would affect Gilchrist's chances. 'Well, hell, he knows even better than the Webster woman that it's all a crock of shit. Everybody sitting in that courtroom knows that Davis wouldn't have pulled Gilchrist that night if he'd been white. Greene's just some extra insurance I slipped past little Tracy.'

'God takes care of fools, drunkards and brand-new ADAs.' I reached for the pepper shaker again, but Reid pushed it away.

22

'You're gonna wreck your stomach,' he warned. 'What'd I forget?'

'There's talk that James Greene wants the security contract for that new pharmaceutical plant over in Cotton Grove.'

'Yeah, I've heard that, too. So?'

I swallowed a meltingly tender chunk of beef. 'So Owen Barfield's one of the owners.'

Dismayed enlightenment broke on Reid's face. 'And Owen Barfield is Judge Perry Byrd's brother-in-law,' he groaned.

'Bingo!' I said. 'What better way to get the word to Owen that Greene's Security Agency is absolutely colorblind when it comes to providing security than for James Greene to be foreman of a jury that convicts a black man when there are good grounds to let him off?'

Reid pushed aside his stew. His appetite seemed to have suddenly disappeared. 'You've got a weird mind, Deborah,' he said, frowning at me. 'That's too goddamned Machiavellian. Greene wouldn't—'

'How 'bout a nice slice of pie?' asked our waitress as she paused at our booth to top off our cups with more coffee. 'We've got deep-dish apple or there's one piece of pecan left.'

Pecan pie's my absolute favorite and I do indulge in the wintertime – after all, what are bulky sweaters for? – but good as Sue's is, it doesn't hold a candle to my Aunt Zell's, and I don't squander those five hundred calories on anybody else's.

'I'll take the apple if you'll melt me a little cheddar on the top,' said Reid, who wore a bulky red sweater vest under his gray tweed sportscoat.

I was wearing a cropped green jacket over a soft challis skirt with a wide tight belt that registered every ounce I ate, so I passed.

The rain had slacked off by the time we got back to the courthouse, but it had washed away most of the sand that a janitor had sprinkled earlier and the wide marble steps were glazed in a thin coat of ice. Reid took my arm as we started up. 'How you gals walk around on those stilts in good weather beats me, but why you don't break your neck in winter . . .'

Since my beautiful black leather boots had sensible one-inch heels, I knew his grousing was just to cover his worry.

'Maybe the jury will come back as soon as court reconvenes,' I comforted, patting his hand. A quick return would mean acquittal.

It was nearly three before the jury brought in their verdict. I'd gotten Luellen another stay of active time, and though Judge Byrd gave her a stiff lecture – 'You know what *suspended* means, Miz Martin? You under some kind of impression you don't have to go to jail if you don't keep to the terms of the judgment on you?' – he did allow her one more chance to set up a regular schedule of restitution payments with her parole officer.

Machiavellian or not, James Greene *had* been chosen foreman and the jury did deliver a guilty verdict. Reid and I – and maybe the wary-eyed Gilchrist – were the only two not surprised. (Later, the bailiff showed Reid the ballots that had been thrown in the trash can. On the first vote, the count had been seven to five for acquittal.)

Perry Byrd tried hard not to beam as he sent for Gilchrist's driving record. Despite the plumber's testimony, he wanted to see for himself; and when it was brought to him, Byrd frowned and muttered to himself in those carrying undertones, 'I don't believe this man's gone twenty-one years with no tickets.'

Even under uniform sentencing, a judge has much leeway. The punishment for a first DWI conviction with no priors could be as light as court costs and a few hours of community service. Gilchrist's was near the maximum: 120 days suspended for three years upon payment of a $250 fine and court costs, plus forty-eight hours of active jail time.

Reid was appalled, but still game. 'Your Honor,' he said, 'my client operates a one-man business for his livelihood. We request that he be allowed to wait till the weekend to activate his jail time.'

'Denied!' said Judge Byrd. 'Bailiff, take the prisoner in custody.'

Okay, so Gilchrist probably would've blown a ten. Big damn deal. It wasn't his choice to go out that night and it wasn't like he'd deliberately gone and driven recklessly on a crowded highway or anything. Even Trooper Davis admitted he'd been well below the speed limit.

Normally, mean-minded judicial pettiness sends me right up the wall; that frigid January day it sent me right over to the election board where I filed for Harrison Hobart's seat.

I really wished it could have been Perry Byrd's.

2

I Just Came Home To Count The Memories

The County Democratic Coalition was holding a candidates' forum at West Colleton Senior High, a sprawling two-story 'educational plant' built by integration back in 1969.

It took fifteen years and the threat of cutting off federal funds to make the county finally admit that separate wasn't equal. All those shabby old black schools had to be closed because no white tax-paying parents would stand for sending their children there. I shake my head sometimes to hear people fume about the evils of bussing and the benefits of neighborhood schools. You didn't hear any of that kind of talk back when I was in seventh grade and it was black kids being bussed miles past white schools.

We arrived a little before six, and the early May sun was still high in the clear blue sky. It streamed in through floor-to-ceiling cafeteria windows and further brightened tables already cheerful with red-checked biodegradable paper tablecloths. Clusters of red, white, and blue balloons were tethered at each table, and red-white-and-blue crepe-paper bunting draped the head table. Very colorful. Very patriotic.

Lest anyone forget why we were there though, a partisan mural hung on the wall behind the head table. An art teacher here at West Colleton had painted a lifesize donkey kicking the butt of an elephant whose eyeglasses looked suspiciously like those worn by North Carolina's senior senator.

Supper was the usual pork barbecue, cole slaw, hush puppies, and sweet iced tea. I'd graduated from West Colleton, and Knotts had farmed around here since the late 1700s, so the crowd was friendly. Lots of hugs and howdies. For moral support, I sat at a table with John Claude Lee and Reid Stephenson, my two partners; Sherry Cobb, our legal secretary; and their significant others, which in Reid's case seemed to change with the moon. A couple of my brothers and their families were there, too.

Not Daddy though.

He wasn't real thrilled when I went to law school and he's sat on his hands ever since I announced for judge. Being the only daughter after a string of sons, I was supposed to wear frilly dresses and patent leather Mary Janes till I grew up and married somebody who'd worship at the foot of my pedestal the rest of my natural life. He swears he isn't chauvinistic; but truth is, he doesn't approve of ladies messing with politics. (Daddy's like Jesse Helms that way. Neither one of them's ever met a woman. All females are *ladies* unless they're trashy and immoral, in which case they've got other labels.)

I try to take into account that he's an old man now, someone from another era. He says that's disrespectful. People say I'm natured more like him than Mother, another reason I stayed in town with Aunt Zell and Uncle Ash after Mother died. Keeps us from snarling at each other. This way I can stay polite and respectful.

Most of the time.

The evening followed predictable lines once they got rid of the feedback squeal in the sound system: a welcome by the president of the Democratic Women, an invocation by the minister of Cotton Grove Presbyterian, then some brief remarks by our US House incumbent. It's a safe seat. Down at the grass roots level, there're still a lot of farmers, and ninety percent of Colleton County farmers are yellow dog Democrats when it comes to local politics.

We faced the flag for the pledge of allegiance, then sang 'God Bless America,' which usually evokes muddled memories. Grade school assemblies get mixed in with cozy feelings from when '*thru the night with the light from above*' was the blissful security of the hall light that shone through a crack over my bedroom door until I fell asleep.

All incumbents stood to be applauded, including Perry Byrd and Harrison Hobart, then the chairman of the Colleton County Democratic Party gave a seven-minute pitch for Harvey Gantt, who was running against Jesse Helms for US Senate and who sent regrets that he couldn't be with us that night. After that came the parade of candidates to the microphone at the front of the cafeteria. State hopefuls got five minutes, county three.

Sheriff Bowman Poole only took two minutes. He gazed out over the two hundred or so party faithful with that genial expression that never quite masks the watchful alertness of a shepherd collie and said he sure did appreciate their continuing support, he'd try not to let 'em down. Bo plays the role of laid-back good ol' boy as well as anybody, but he runs a modern department. His officers have to keep themselves updated with regular classes at the community college, and he takes advantage of all the special techniques seminars that the SBI runs in Raleigh. Long as he wants to stay sheriff, Bo Poole'll keep getting elected, and people gave him a good hand when he stepped away from the mike.

District judges come down near the end of the slate of candidates even though our judicial district comprises a three-county area. (On the ballot, we come after the sheriff but before clerk of the court, register of deeds, coroner, and county surveyor.) We can't make campaign promises or take stands on particular issues. All we can do is state our background and expertise and promise to uphold the laws of this great land.

Running against me in the primary were three males. One, Luther Parker, was a tall gangling attorney from the next county who looked vaguely like a black Abe Lincoln without the beard. The other two were white, a fat attorney from Widdington and an earnest young assistant DA from Black Creek with a wonderful bass speaking voice that almost made you forget it had nothing to say. Harrison Hobart had let it be known – unofficially, of course – that he favored the ADA, 'a man who thinks like me 'bout where the law ought to be going.'

It was unlikely that any of us would win a clear majority in the primary. I figured the two whites would probably cancel each other out, and then if all my relatives voted for me and if Parker pulled a big percentage of black votes, it'd probably come down to a runoff between him and me. At that point it'd turn into a real horse race. Far as I know, the only Colleton County woman ever elected to county-wide office has been Miss Callie Yelverton, our register of deeds, and she sort of inherited the job from her daddy, who first got himself elected about 1932.

Just because Democrats don't pay as much attention to color and gender as Republicans doesn't mean they don't take both into account when they step inside the voting booth.

I'm white, but I'm female.

He's male, but he's black.

I'm single with some dirty linen I'd hate to have washed in public.

He's a family man with a spotless reputation.

Actual qualifications would count for damn little, but then they never do in any other election, so why should judgeships be any different?

After five verses of 'Democrats Are on the Move,' a unity song set to the tune of 'Old MacDonald Had a Farm,' the evening broke up in a burst of enthusiastic optimism. November was a long way off.

My two white opponents tried to work the room, but most of the blacks were clustered around Luther Parker or Gantt's representative; and, as I said before, I *had* graduated from West Colleton High so I was on home ground among folks who acted tickled to see me running for judge.

I was passed from one familiar bear hug to another, scolded for not coming home more often, told I was getting prettier every day and asked when I was going to quit breaking hearts and settle down.

Some things will never change. Not in eighteen million years.

I gave a mental shrug, said the things they wanted to hear, and hugged everyone back till I suddenly fetched up in the arms of a tall, good-looking man with silver flecks in his thick black hair.

Jed Whitehead.

'Little Debbie,' he grinned, the laugh lines falling into easy crinkles around his eyes and lips. He never lets me forget when I was a chubby teenager who used to pig out on those cream-filled cupcakes Dinah Jean kept in their refrigerator for when I baby-sat for them. 'I wanted to tell you how much I liked your talk yesterday, but you got away too quick.'

Yesterday I'd given a speech to the Civitans and it'd gone well. Especially the question and answer session.

'I had to get back to court,' I said.

True.

I disentangled myself and smiled politely as someone else claimed my attention. 'Sorry I missed you.'

Lie.

I'd seen Jed in the audience and I'd also seen him purposefully working his way over to me, which was why I cut out a little more abruptly than was strictly necessary.

Here in the cafeteria, the party was winding down. There was barely enough fading daylight to see by as people began

32

to wander out to their cars. I did the courtesies with the organizers and party officials and moved toward the doorway myself, where my brother Seth stood talking with some neighbors. He put out his arm and gave my shoulder a squeeze as he drew me to his side. 'You did good, honey,' he said.

Suddenly feeling tired, I leaned against his comfortable bulk. Seth's five brothers up from me, but we've always been close.

'Hey, congratulations, Jed,' he said.

I hadn't realized that Jed was right behind me.

'Know you're real proud of her,' said Seth's wife, Minnie, beaming at him.

'Oh, I am, I am,' Jed agreed.

I finally remembered what they were talking about. 'Hard to believe Gayle's old enough to be winning college scholarships,' I said.

'Tempus sure keeps on fugiting,' someone observed. 'Seems like it was just Christmas and now I've already cut my grass three times.'

'We've got bluebirds nesting in three boxes,' Minnie offered, but the men were off on crops, allotments, and the prospects of rain before the weekend, so she and I spent a few minutes talking strategy. Minnie's always been active in the Colleton County Democratic Women and was my closest thing to a campaign manager.

Sherry and her boyfriend passed by in the deepening twilight. 'We'll be at the car when you're ready to go,' she told me.

I promised to visit Seth and Minnie real soon and started

to follow Sherry across the crowded parking lot when Jed fell into step with me.

'Let me drive you back to Dobbs,' he said. 'I need to talk to you.'

I frowned.

'About Gayle,' he said. 'She's got a crazy bee in her bonnet and you're just the person to smash it for me.'

For Gayle was a different story. I told Sherry that I had a ride home and to go on without me. Seeing Jed waiting over by his car, she winked at me. Probably thinking Jed and I ought to get back together.

Not that we ever really were together.

I couldn't say what it was that kept it from happening. God knows I'd had a heavy enough crush on him when I was a kid and he'd been one of that gang of teenage boys that dropped by the farm every weekend to tussle with my brothers over whatever ball was in season.

I was a teenager myself, though still much too young for him, when his first wife was killed; but the gap had narrowed by the time he and Dinah Jean were divorced a year or so ago. We'd had a mild flurry of dates – dinners, movies, a couple of dances at the American Legion Hut – but I'd let them dwindle out to nothing.

'*There is a tide* . . . ,' said Shakespeare. If so, it must have crested years earlier because being with Jed never quite loosed the floodgates of adult passion. He certainly made all the right moves. There'd even been some heavy breathing after one of Reid's parties, but that turned out to be the full moon and three of Reid's Orange Blossom Specials. Sunlight and black coffee soon lowered my pulse rate. I told myself it'd been a case of forbidden fruit, and to test my hypothesis, I let a week pass, then met him for a movie; two weeks, then a concert to show there were no hard feelings. After that, I told Aunt Zell and Sherry to make excuses if he called. He only called once more.

Nobody ever had to draw Jed a diagram.

But I kept a soft spot for Gayle. I was the first sitter Janie had trusted outside her own family, and I'd continued to sit for Gayle after Dinah Jean and Jed were married. There hadn't been much real contact in the last few years though, until Jed and I began seeing each other. I think Gayle wanted me to be stepmother number two, but when it was clear that wasn't going to happen, she gradually stopped finding excuses to phone.

Actually, I still felt a little guilty about that.

'So what kind of bee's bugging Gayle?' I asked, when we were in the car and buckling up.

Jed clicked my seat belt into place and switched on the ignition. It was finally full dark and headlights from other cars swept the school parking lot as he pulled out onto the highway and turned the car toward Dobbs.

'She wants to hire a private detective to find out who killed Janie,' he said.

'What?'

'Right.' His handsome face was illuminated by the pale green lights of the dashboard and a worried frown crumpled his eyebrows.

Eighteen years ago, when Gayle was less than three months old, she and Janie had disappeared one rainy gray afternoon in May. It was three days before some field hands heard a baby crying in the loft of an old abandoned gristmill. Gayle was dehydrated and raw bottomed from going all that time with no milk or water and no change of diapers, but an overnight stay in the hospital for observation showed no lasting injuries. Janie's body was lying on the cold stone floor, her limbs straightened, her hands by her side. She'd been hit over the head and there was a bullet hole behind her right ear.

Jed's hands clenched the steering wheel. 'She says she has to know once and for all who killed her mother, so she can finally put it behind her.'

'But what exactly *is* there to put behind her?' I asked as cars flashed past us in the opposite lane. 'She wasn't even crawling, for God's sake. There's no way she could remember Janie or a thing that happened then.'

'Tell me about it.' He flicked the high beams impatiently as an oncoming car with badly set high beams nearly blinded us. Half the time, these back roads drivers never dim their lights unless you remind them three or four times.

'When she turned sixteen, she said she didn't want a new car; she wanted me to pay a psychiatrist to hypnotize her and try to regress her back to when it happened.'

'You didn't do it, did you?' I knew Gayle had a little red Toyota that couldn't be more than two years old.

'Eight hundred dollars it cost me,' he answered wryly as two more headlights flashed by in the darkness. 'On top of her car.'

Well, he'd always been foolish over Gayle from the minute she was born.

36

'What happened?'

'He got her back to that time she was so sick with a strep throat. You remember?'

I was impressed. 'She couldn't have been much more than what? Eighteen months?'

'Sixteen months and still in her crib,' he confirmed. 'But that was as far as he could get her.'

'You going to let her hire the detective?'

'It's not a matter of letting,' he said. 'Now that she's turned eighteen, she has the trust fund Janie's dad set up when she was born.'

'But that's for college—' I started to protest, and then I remembered. 'Oh. The scholarship.'

'Yeah.'

We rode in silence for several minutes through the mild spring evening. Stars were bright pinpoints that faded as we approached the outer limits of Dobbs, and soon we were passing tobacco warehouses, the cinder block factory, and several fast-food places illuminated by neon and streetlights.

Like many small towns across eastern North Carolina, Dobbs is having its troubles keeping downtown vital. Strip malls dot the four lanes leading in and out of town and there's a huge outlets mall nearby on I-95. Everybody's just holding their breath, hoping that the last major department store on Main Street won't move out. So far we've kept ahead of store closings by bulldozing the abandoned buildings and turning the sites into convenient little parking lots made almost parklike with benches set under shady crepe myrtles. But most people think that if it weren't for its being the county seat of government, downtown would be one vast parking lot around the churches and the courthouse.

'Would you talk to her?' Jed asked as he turned off Main Street. 'You've always been Gayle's role model. She'll listen to you.'

The storefronts gave way to large brick, stone, and wooden houses set among masses of flowering azaleas. Like all the residential streets of Dobbs, ours was lined with huge mature oaks and maples that nearly met overhead. At the end of the street was Aunt Zell and Uncle Ash's whitewashed brick.

Role model?

Did he know how old that made me feel?

Jed drove through the opening in the white brick wall and pulled up at the far end of the long low veranda, in front of the door that led directly to my rooms.

'I think I have a clear hour tomorrow afternoon,' I sighed. 'Tell her to call Sherry and set it up.'

3

Do You Know What It's Like
To Be Lonesome?

Lee, Stephenson and Knott, Attorneys at Law, occupies a neat wood-frame story-and-a-half that was built right after the Civil War across the street and half a block down from the courthouse. The county did an architectural survey a few years back and our place is described as a 'charming example of tasteful vernacular,' a phrase I take to mean that some local builder had heard about Victorian styles but didn't have a millwright who could turn out yards of rococo gingerbread trim without a pattern to go by. John Claude's wife, Julia, keeps wanting to paint the narrow clapboards pale green and pick out the moldings and porch trim in white, but so far we've headed her off and kept it plain white with black shutters.

John Claude's grandfather, Robert Claudius Lee (no relation to Robert E.), was born there and so was Robert's brother, my maternal grandmother's father – which, if you're trying to work it out on your fingers, makes John Claude my second cousin once removed. Although I'm related to both my partners, they're no blood kin to each other.

The historical society put a plaque on the front porch, but the only thing historically authentic about the house is its outside. Lees and Stephensons have been practicing law here since the twenties, when John Claude's father and Reid's grandfather (my great-grandfather) set up the partnership, and the inside's no longer a monument to nineteenth-century sensibilities. Most of the woodwork's original, but when the ceilings were dropped in the seventies to allow for new wiring and modern plumbing and lighting, they didn't try to save the crumbly old plaster decorations.

The central staircase was relocated to make a reception area for Sherry Cobb's predecessor.

(Reid's mother and Julia had a tiff over who was going to get the walnut banisters. Julia won. Julia's what people here call a right strong-minded lady. If she'd been born five years later, she'd probably have gone to State and majored in architecture or design. Instead, they sent her to a girls' school – and I use the term deliberately – for a 'Father Knows Best' insurance policy: a degree in elementary education, 'so she'll always have teaching to fall back on, just in case.' Just in case her husband ran off with another woman or turned out to be too shiftless to support a family. Half my grade school teachers were women whose husbands had fulfilled their fathers' direst premonitions. It did not make for happy classrooms. Fortunately, Julia's children were the only ones who ever had to cower from her.)

As our current senior partner, John Claude has his daddy's old office, the double parlor on the front left. I have Brixton

Senior's original office on the front right, and Reid has what used to be the dining room behind me. It's the same office *his* daddy had. Brix Junior keeps his license current, but the month Reid came into the firm was the month he quit practicing law and moved to Southern Pines to start practicing his golf swings.

(My daddy isn't a lawyer, of course, but Brix Junior and John Claude never held that against me – especially since he's generated a lot of the firm's business over the last fifty years.)

Upstairs, two small bedrooms were opened to make a single large one, with a modern bath and roomy storage cupboards under the eaves. In theory, the bedroom's for putting up out-of-town expert witnesses if we need to, but when Dotty kicked him out of the house and filed for divorce, Reid crashed there for so long John Claude and I were ready to start charging him rent. He still uses it at least once a month for what he thinks are sub rosa assignations – as if anything half a block from the courthouse could be sub rosa, but men in rut have a way of rationalizing what they want to be true.

So far we've kept the carpenters out of our personal offices, but Julia redid half the downstairs about four years ago. She ripped out partitions and turned the old kitchen into a computerized work area for the three clerks who help Sherry. The sunporch across the back acquired a tiny modern galley that can disappear behind louvered doors when we use the big sunny room for official conferences. There's a long deal table that looks official enough, but Julia also brought in some comfortable chintz chairs and ottomans that were too

41

good to throw away the last time she remodeled their house. All in all, the old sunporch has devolved into a pleasant place to lounge over a cup of coffee after court and catch up on the *News and Observer*.

That's what I was doing when Gayle Whitehead arrived promptly at 3:30, carrying a flat white cardboard box. Instead of putting her in my office and telling me she was there, Sherry brought her straight back to the sunporch. Sherry's not all that much older than Gayle, but she kept clucking around like somebody's mama hostessing a tea party.

'Can I get you anything?' she asked. 'There's drinks and ice tea in the icebox.'

'That's okay,' Gayle said politely as she took a chair opposite mine. She held the white box on her lap – it was about the size of a shirt box – and centered her purple purse on top of it.

'What about something to eat? We've got Nabs and stuff.'

'No, thank you.'

Gayle's spine was a straight line that remained three inches from the chair's cushioned back. Aunt Zell's always trying to get me to sit like that. I think my grandmother Stephenson must have had a thing about a lady's back never touching the back of chairs because Mother used to tell me to sit up, too.

Who had nagged Gayle? Dinah Jean?

I knew I had a soft spot in my heart for Gayle, but looking at her sitting there so poised and mature, a young woman now and no longer a child, I wondered how I could have been the role model Jed claimed. It'd been years since we'd had more than passing conversation at church or ball games or run-ins around the county. She was six and I was in my first year of law school the last time I baby-sat her. It's true that we'd been thrown together again when I was seeing Jed last spring, but we'd both been too self-conscious about the circumstances to do anything except chatter about surface stuff.

Sherry's hovering was making her even more uptight.

'Let's go back to my office,' I said, and Gayle rose from the chair with the quickness of a coiled spring.

We walked up the hall, Sherry leading the way, and I was struck afresh by how fully grown Gayle suddenly seemed to be. She was small-boned and dark-haired just like I remembered Janie being, only Janie's hair had been long and straight and, except for an occasional beehive, she'd worn it flowing over her shoulders like everybody else in the early seventies. Gayle's was french braided, but where stray tendrils escaped, they were curly like Jed's hair. A white knitted top and short purple skirt set off her cute little figure without being obvious about it.

Even after we were in my office with the door closed on Sherry's curious face, Gayle still seemed stiff. Daddy always said I could talk the ears off a mule, but it was several minutes before I got a smile out of her and she relaxed enough to set the box on the floor beside her and actually settle into the green velvet wingback in front of my desk.

I congratulated her on the Beaufort Scholarship. 'Your dad's mighty proud of you winning.'

Her smile turned wry. 'I don't know about that. I don't think he's happy with what I want to do with the trust fund Grampa Poole left me.'

'Well, you can't really blame him, can you? It's been

eighteen years, and after all this time, what's a private detective going to dig up that the police and SBI haven't already found?'

'Maybe nothing,' she said calmly. 'All I know is that I can't go off to college with all this stuff hanging on me.'

'All what stuff?' I asked.

The placid adult surface wavered and I was suddenly face-to-face with the seething adolescent below.

'You saw how Sherry was out there? That's the way it's been my whole stupid life. As soon as anybody hears my name, it's like there's a neon sign hanging around my neck.' Her small hands sketched a flashing signboard – '*THE JANIE WHITEHEAD MURDER!*' – and her voice dripped scorn as she mimicked, *'Oh my God, it's that poor little thang that nearly parched to death when somebody shot her mother and left them both to die at Ridley's Mill.'*

She took a deep breath and tried to pull the surface back into place. It didn't quite work. 'So they fuss over me and they sweet-talk and part of it's that they're just so, so sorry for me and the other part's that they're dying to know what it's like to have a murdered mother and not know who did it.'

'What *is* it like?' I asked.

She started to glare, then realized I wasn't being cute. Despair replaced her anger.

'I don't know. It's like – like having a loose hair tickling on the back of your neck,' she said bleakly. 'You keep brushing at your collar, but you never quite get it and just about the time you forget about it, there it is worrying you again. I just want it *gone*!'

I shook my head. 'Sorry, honey, but I don't see how some strange detective's going to—'

'Not some stranger,' she interrupted. '*You*, Deb'rah.'

Before I could start shaking my head, she plunged on. 'I've been thinking about it and thinking about it and Dad's about to freak because I've been looking in all the phone books and the nearest private detectives are in Raleigh and you're right. Nobody's going to tell a stranger anything Sheriff Poole hasn't already heard, probably; but you could do it, Deb'rah, I *know* you could. Soon as Dad came home last night and said he wanted me to talk to you, it was like the answer to everything. That's the only reason I came today. You know everybody and everybody knows you and they'd trust you and—'

'Now wait a minute,' I protested. 'I'm a lawyer, not a detective.'

'Oh, *please*!'

Gayle's eyes beseeched with such intensity that for a brief instant of déjà vu, I was a pudgy, lank-haired sixteen again, wondering why I had been stuck with ordinary run-of-the-mill blue eyes when other people got luscious melting brown. I already envied Janie's size eight bell-bottoms, her long black hair, her town-bred sophistication and, most of all, her husband. Now there I was, jealous of even her eyes, damn her!

'Besides,' I added. 'I really, honest to God, don't have time. I've got a campaign to run and the primary's next week.'

'Please,' Gayle repeated earnestly. 'You're going to be campaigning in Cotton Grove, too, aren't you? So you'll be

45

seeing most everybody anyhow, won't you? Besides, judges have to know whether people are telling the truth, don't they? It'll be practice for you.'

Well, I'd already sat in enough courtrooms to know when I wasn't hearing the whole story.

'Who do you think's not told the truth?' I asked.

Her eyes fell and she began twisting the zipper tassel on her purple clutch.

'All my life, everybody's said the killer was some sorry tramp or migrant that's probably been killed himself in New York City or Mexico by now.' She paused and looked me straight in the eye. 'How come you quit seeing Dad?'

A shock of acknowledgment went through me and I could only stare at her, appalled.

'I've never said this to a single soul before.' Her level brown eyes glanced off mine and immediately dropped to her purse again. 'Dad couldn't have been the one who physically carried us out to Ridley's Mill. He was in Raleigh all day. Everybody says so. But he could have hired somebody to do it. I'm not saying I think he *did*, but . . .'

'No, no, *no*,' I told her. 'Of course, he didn't.'

The hopeful look told me she wanted to believe. Well, who wants to think her own daddy's capable of killing? I sure as hell never found it a barrel of laughs.

'*Any*body could have hired someone, but he loved your mother, honey. He really did.' Into my mind unbidden came the thought *each man kills the thing he loves*, and I knew it must have been lying just beneath the surface of consciousness last spring.

'He married Mom – Dinah Jean – eight months later,' Gayle countered.

Dinah Jean was the only mother Gayle had ever known, and they'd seemed as close as any mother and daughter till Dinah Jean let her drinking get totally out of hand a couple of years ago. When the divorce came, I heard Gayle had trouble choosing who to go with. Jed won out, not only because he was her natural parent and she was still underage, but also because Dinah Jean's people had put her someplace out in the mountains to dry out.

'He was a young man,' I reminded Gayle, 'and he had a baby daughter to take care of. In fact, a lot of people said he was thinking more about you than himself when he married her. He never looked twice at another woman while your mother was living and I'm sure he never loved Dinah Jean half as much.'

That was certainly how I'd consoled myself for months after Jed married Dinah Jean: that if he didn't love me, neither did he really love her. A few weeks after Janie's funeral, Jed and Gayle moved in with his parents so his mother could keep Gayle during the day. I still got asked to mind her occasionally; and from where I sat, a sixteen-year-old bundle of raging hormones, consumed with yearning frustration, it was no whirlwind romance. Even on the night before their wedding, when I brought Gayle home early from the rehearsal party, I'd seen none of the sexual tension that once flowed between Jed and Janie. And that wasn't just wishful thinking either. He and Dinah Jean turned into an old married couple almost before the ink was dry on their marriage certificate.

47

It was the first time I'd thought about it from Dinah Jean's viewpoint. No wonder she'd eventually crawled into a bottle and tried to pull the cork in after her.

Nevertheless, it wasn't Dinah Jean's ghost that had stood between Jed and me when he finally got around to noticing that I was grown up.

'*Let the dead past bury its dead,*' I murmured.

'Shakespeare?' asked Gayle.

I couldn't remember the source, but it seemed like good advice and I told her so.

'I've tried that,' she said impatiently. 'It doesn't work. You're just as bad as Gramma and Dad. They keep telling me not to think about it, too.'

She stood abruptly and smoothed the wrinkles from her purple skirt. 'I'm sorry I wasted your time. Do I pay you or Sherry?'

'Sit down,' I said. 'You're really going through with this, aren't you?'

She nodded.

'Even though the man who did this probably *is* long gone to his own reward in New York or California?'

'It was somebody she knew,' said Gayle.

As she perched back on the edge of the chair and began laying out theories, I realized that this was probably the first time she'd ever spoken freely to an adult about Janie's death since becoming an adult herself.

'They never kept it a big secret from me,' she said. 'It was sort of like being adopted. You know the way they start telling babies they're adopted as soon as they bring them home so it never comes as a shock?'

I nodded.

'Well, I always knew that Mother and I were kidnapped and she was killed and it was three days before they found us – but it was almost like a bedtime story. Something with all the edges taken off. I hated the way people oozed over me, but I never really gave it a lot of thought. I mean it was like you don't give a lot of thought to why grass is green or water's wet. It just is, you know? Then the Christmas right before I was sixteen, I was sleeping over at Gramma Pope's and I found this box of newspaper clippings.'

She put the box on my desk and lifted the lid. It was crammed with yellowed news articles jumbled in with no particular order. I saw pictures of Janie and Jed, the mill, even Janie's abandoned car.

'Grampa cut out everything the *Ledger* and the *News and Observer* wrote about it from the day we disappeared till it stopped being news.'

She gave a wobbly little grin that almost broke my heart. 'That's when it quit being a bedtime story, Deborah. Reading it like that put the sharp edges back on, made me start thinking it must have been somebody she knew.'

'Because she gave someone in a raincoat a lift?' I shook my head. 'It didn't have to be someone she knew. Back then it wasn't automatically a foolhardy thing to give a stranger a ride.'

'But if he was a stranger, how'd he know where to leave her car?'

That was one of the many questions that had puzzled everyone else at the time. Weather conditions had been rainy and foggy on the May afternoon that Janie and Gayle disappeared. Her car had been seen in the deserted parking lot beside the old abandoned Dixie Motel. There'd been someone else in the front seat with her, someone wearing a beige or light tan raincoat and thought to be male by the one eyewitness who saw them.

If indeed old Howard Grimes had actually seen them.

There were at least three dark blue Ford sedans in Cotton Grove, including one that belonged to my brother Will; and Howard said he'd taken a good look because rumors were going around town about then that Will's wife, Trish, was having an affair with somebody and he wanted to see who. (Not that the *Ledger* or the *N&O* printed Will or Trish's names. But everyone involved knew who he was talking about.)

'I hadn't heard nothing before about Jed Whitehead's wife having round heels,' he was quoted as saying. 'But the windows were too fogged up for me to see who he was. Saw *her* plain enough though.'

Howard's account had kept the police from getting into it too heavily for the first twenty-four hours. For all they knew, little Janie Whitehead might well have gone off for an extramarital fling. Jed wouldn't be the first husband, the Popes wouldn't be the first parents, to say she'd never do something like that.

But then Janie's sedan was discovered the next morning in the parking lot behind the Whitehead Real Estate Agency. It had not been there the evening before when old Mr Whitehead closed early upon hearing that Janie and Gayle were missing. Street parking was plentiful, so the lot, shared by three other abutting offices, was not one used by the general public.

Access in from Broad Street and out to Railroad was through narrow alleys screened by azaleas and high camellia bushes, not readily apparent and certainly not a place a stranger would stumble into on a dark foggy night.

'That's why you tried to have a hypnotist take you back?'

'It didn't work, though.' Lingering disappointment shadowed her voice. 'I was really hoping maybe I'd remember *her*.'

My own mother died the summer I turned eighteen, and trying to imagine never having known her made it easier to understand why everybody could get sentimental and maudlin about Gayle's semi-orphaned status. Gayle's next words, however, made it clear that something else was going on in her head.

'What was her tragic flaw, Deborah?'

I looked at her blankly. Okay, we all knew Gayle was bright. They don't give out full four-year scholarships to the university just because someone's mother got killed. But was she brains or book learning?

'I took an interdisciplinary honors course last fall,' she said. 'Hamlet, Edward the Eighth, Richard Nixon. We discussed their tragic flaws, and I couldn't help applying it to my mother. Not *who* killed her, but *why*? What was *her* tragic flaw?' She leaned forward. 'Everybody says she was good and sweet and beautiful and that I'm just like her. Well, nobody's that damn sweet and good. I'm not and I bet she wasn't either.'

Brains, then?

There had been a million unanswered questions when Janie Whitehead was killed, but every question was predicated on the belief that innocence and purity had been cruelly slaughtered that chilly May afternoon. Yet, in the months before, lust for Jed Whitehead had made me acutely aware of Janie's flaws and, yes, she had her human share. I had collected them secretly and gloated over them like a miser polishing his coins. God knows I'd been wracked with guilt when I saw her cold stiff body lying in that coffin, her shining black hair spread across the pink satin pillow, her luminous brown eyes closed for all eternity; but remorse and guilt and prayers to God for forgiveness had not washed away the question with which Gayle now struggled.

'They say everybody carries within themselves the seeds of their own destruction,' she said.

'Sounds like another way to blame the victim for the crime,' I hedged starchily, as if I were already a judge.

'She was only twenty-two,' said Gayle, her voice passionate. 'Four years older than I am right now. What if I really am like her?'

'Nobody's going to kill you,' I told her.

Again it was the wrong comment and she waved me off impatiently.

'I've almost quit wondering about who killed her, Deborah. Now I think if I just find out why, that might be enough. People either pat me on the head when I ask what she was like or else they tell me another bedtime story. You knew her and you know everybody in Cotton Grove. And I'm not asking you to do it for nothing either. I've got Grampa Poole's trust fund, and I'll spend every last cent if that's what it takes to find out what she was really like that somebody felt she needed killing.'

* * *

Jed didn't like it when I called to tell him that Gayle was determined to go through with it one way or another. Not one little bit did he like it.

'She's as headstrong as her mother,' he said finally, but his voice got softer. 'Janie always had to have her way, too, didn't she?'

'Just tell me what you want me to do, Jed,' I said impatiently. 'I've got enough on my plate right now. I don't need this. You want me to tell her no, I will.'

He sighed. 'No, I reckon we'll have to do what she wants.' He sighed again. 'Better you than some real detective.'

4

All My Rowdy Friends Have Settled Down

North Carolina houses our State Bureau of Investigation in what used to be a school for the blind on Old Garner Road south of Raleigh. Some of us don't let the agents forget it either.

When I showed up in his office without an appointment just before five that Friday afternoon, Special Agent Terry Wilson leaned back in his swivel chair, put that canary-feathered grin on his big ugly face and drawled, 'Well, looky who's here! You want to hear something funny? Somebody said you was running for judge.'

'Naah. Dogcatcher.' I tried to look serious, but a matching grin spread over my own face. Terry does that to me every time. Even when I used to get furious with him, I couldn't stay furious. He'd cut those hazel eyes at me, the tip of his long nose would twitch and I'd laugh before I could help it.

There was a moment about six years ago when I seriously considered marrying Terry just because life with him could have been so damn much fun. The moment passed, since three things stood between us and the altar at Sweetwater Missionary Baptist: one, he was working narcotics undercover at the time and, as his first two wives had already learned, undercover agents don't make good husbands; two, he'd made it clear that his son, Stanton, would always come first; and three, I'd made it just as clear I wouldn't take second place for anybody or anything – not to Stanton, whom I actually liked, and certainly not to his job.

So we stayed buddies, and though we no longer partied together, we did still go fishing occasionally. In fact, the large-mouth bass mounted on the wall opposite his desk came out of one of my Daddy's lakes. Stanton and I were both in the boat the day Terry pulled it in. Only eight pounds, but he was using ten-pound test, so it'd been a classic battle between man and fish. There'd been other, bigger bass, but that was the day we acknowledged our moment had passed and I sometimes wondered if that was the real reason he'd mounted this particular fish. Of course, at the time, he said it was because its big mouth reminded him of me.

Looking at him now, I suddenly realized it'd been over a year since we'd gone fishing together. His flat brown hair had thinned a little more, his crisp white shirt didn't quite conceal the faint beginning of a paunch, and laugh lines were just a shade deeper around his hooded eyes. He was checking me for changes, too. I wore my sandy blonde hair a little shorter these days, and though I'd taken a few pains with makeup and clothes, time hadn't exactly stood still for me either.

'How far'd you have to chase him for those ugly

suspenders?' I teased even though they matched his maroon tie and actually looked rather sharp against the white cotton.

'He was right behind the good-looking gal you took that raggedy old blouse off of,' Terry grinned, maligning the beautiful turquoise silk shirt that I was wearing with a soft paisley skirt. He propped his feet on the open top drawer of his desk and leaned all the way back in his chair till his long body was lying almost horizontal beneath a large blue-and-gold plaque depicting the great seal of North Carolina. *Esse quam videri* with Liberty and Plenty for all.

I helped myself to the chair in front of his executive-size desk.

Except for one or two papers, the broad top itself was quite tidy for someone in charge of MUST, the SBI's Murder Unsolved Task Force. In fact, the whole office was strangely bare of excess books and papers, as if the real work must surely be done elsewhere, not in this roomy, stripped-down office with spring sunlight blazing through the two tall windows onto the clean white rug. Nothing was piled on the two matching sand-colored file cabinets. A narrow white Parsons table beside Terry's desk held a laptop and a printer and nothing else. The bulletin board over the table was only one layer deep, and there were even a few open spaces between an up-to-date wanted poster and some cryptic memos to himself.

His tackle box was always just that neat. No broken lures, no clutter of leaders, weights, or feathers.

On the opposite wall, the head-high bookcase was empty except for a row of looseleaf notebooks on the bottom shelf

and some framed pictures of Stanton on the top shelf. He'd
be about fifteen now, and of the three of us, he'd changed
most of all, if the pictures were any indication – a young man
all of a sudden and not a little kid anymore.

'Stanton's getting handsomer all the time,' I said, picking
up the wood-framed photograph on his desk. When Terry
started to beam, I added, 'Must take after his mother.'

'Like hell! Everybody says he's me all over again.'

'What's he up to these days?' I asked, truly wanting to
know. I liked Stanton from the beginning. He lived with his
mother, Terry's first wife, and I knew he looked forward to
weekends with Terry, yet he'd never seemed to mind when I
came fishing with them.

'Doing real good. Plays shortstop on the varsity baseball
team. Carrying a good solid B, too,' he bragged.

I put the picture back on his desk. 'Starting to break a few
hearts?'

The tip of his nose twitched. 'Like I told you – he's me all
over again.'

'You wish!'

We talked trash a few minutes more before I broached
Janie Whitehead's murder and explained why I was asking.

'That was before my time,' Terry said, and without sitting
up, he stretched across to snag a slim folder from the rack
neatly aligned with the far edge of his desk. 'I believe Scotty
Underhill worked that case.'

He leafed through the eight or nine sheets in the file folder.
From where I sat, I couldn't make out specific words, but it
looked like a condensed printout of all the unsolved cases
assigned to Terry's MUST team: names, dates, a one- or two-

sentence description of each case and some comment as to any solvability factors.

'When was the last time it was worked?' I asked.

'Seven years ago,' he murmured, still reading.

The MUST force was developed only four years earlier.

'You didn't rework it when you took over?'

'Oh, come on, Deborah,' he said. 'I've got eight men and over two hundred cases. Janie Whitehead's murder was thoroughly worked at the beginning and Scotty went back and poked around some more back in eighty-three. Nada.'

I vaguely remembered a flurry of hushed talk around Cotton Grove in the spring of 1983, but I hadn't paid it much mind, especially since it died down almost as soon as it began. 'And no suspects either time?'

Terry closed the folder and replaced it in the rack. 'Now you know well and good I wouldn't name names if we had any, which, as a matter of fact, we don't. You can ask Scotty yourself if you want.'

He glanced at his watch. 'I'm supposed to meet him at six. Want to come along?'

Miss Molly's Bar and Grill on South Wilmington Street hadn't changed all that much since I was last there with Terry. A few more neon beer brands had been added to the already crowded walls and I saw that Spot had finally found him that old blue guitar he'd been looking for last time we talked about his collection of neon signs. He hadn't taken Little Richard and Elvis off the jukebox, but Randy Travis and Reba McEntire were there now, too.

Spot acted glad to see me.

'The usual,' Terry said as we passed the bar.

'You still drinking gin and tonics?' Spot asked me.

'Yeah, only make it a virgin,' I told him. 'I've got to drive to Makely tonight.'

'Getting old, kid?' Terry needled.

'Getting cautious. All I need's a headline in the Dobbs *Ledger*: "Judicial Candidate Cited for DWI."'

We headed back to the big round table at the rear, which had always been populated by law people. That hadn't changed much either.

I recognized two homicide detectives from the Raleigh PD, a couple of SBI arson investigators, and someone from the attorney general's office, all males if no longer all white. We'd barely reached the table when a familiar whiff of musky perfume overtook me and I felt light fingers on my shoulder.

'Deborah? That you? Well, hey, gal! How you been? *Where* you been? God, it's been *ages*!'

I turned and there was Morgan Slavin, a blur of long blonde hair, long gorgeous legs, and the clearest, brightest blue eyes south of Finland. We hugged and grinned at each other and found chairs while she pulled out a pack of Virginia Slims and lit up, talking all the while.

'You remember Max, don't you? And Simon? And, hey, Jasp! Lacy know you've slipped your chain?'

Last time I saw Morgan she looked like one of those skinny, white trash motorcycle mamas – tight jeans, denim jacket studded with red-white-and-blue glass nailheads, no makeup, hair skinned back under a baseball cap, and flying high. She'd just infiltrated the busiest crack house in the Triangle and was waiting for the warrants and backups to get there before she closed it down.

Big change from the high heels and chic teal suit she wore this evening.

'Busting corporation types now?' I queried as we pulled out adjacent chairs.

'Naw. This is how supervisors dress.' She poked Terry's shoulder. 'Less'n you've got one of them Y chromosomes.'

'Always bragging about double Xs,' Terry grumbled. 'Only reason they promoted you.'

'Hey, that's great,' I said. 'Congratulations.'

'Thank you, thank you,' she said with mock modesty. 'And you're going to be a judge, I hear?'

I held up crossed fingers as Spot arrived with a tray of drinks. Morgan was still drinking scotch on the rocks and the other men had beers, but I lifted my brows at the can of Diet Pepsi and glass of ice cubes that Spot placed in front of Terry.

'Getting old, Terry?' I mocked, squeezing the slice of lime into my tonic water.

'Stanton's got a game tonight.'

'Yeah, sure.' I was going to let him get away with it, but then he remembered I'd heard him order 'the usual' and he raised the can sheepishly.

Across the table, the men were trading war stories.

'Y'all work that Smithfield warehouse last week?' Terry asked.

They nodded and Morgan laughed with delight. 'You hear about that one, Deborah?'

I shook my head and leaned back and waited for it.

SBI agents have to be brave, cheerful, thrifty, loyal, and

all those other Boy Scout virtues, but I sometimes wondered if an SBI director hadn't added 'warped sense of humor' to the job description somewhere along the line.

'Tell her, Max,' said Morgan, acting like a big sister pushing her little brother out to show off.

Max was the agent directly across who'd been coming on to me with those big brown eyes ever since I sat down.

'These two guys got a contract to burn out an old dilapidated tobacco warehouse over in Smithfield, see? Insurance scam. You sure you didn't read about it?'

I shook my head. Smithfield was in Johnston, a county that touched Colleton but wasn't in my judicial district.

'They had the preliminary hearing yesterday, and one of the perpetrators copped a plea and blamed it all on his partner. He just carried the can, he says, and it was his Dumbo partner who sloshed around all that gas. And it was Dumbo that made the Pall Mall fuse. You know what that is, don't you?'

Actually I did, but he was cute and wanted to stretch it out.

'It's a delay device,' he explained, taking his own cigarette from the ashtray and threading the unlit end through a book of matches. 'See, tobacco burns at approximately 350 degrees Fahrenheit. I could burn this cigarette all day long and never set off gas vapors because it takes between 550 and 850 degrees to ignite them. Now this cigarette'll take about ten minutes to burn down to the match heads, giving me time to get back here to Miss Molly's and establish my alibi. The match heads'll ignite at less than 350 degrees and generate enough fire and heat to set the paper on fire. The paper will generate up to 1,000 degrees and that's finally hot enough to ignite the vapors, see?'

I nodded.

'Well, Dumbo does it all – matchbook nailed low to a center post 'cause he *did* know gas vapors are heavier than air, cigarette laced through the matches, only he forgot to light the cigarette till the last minute and what does he do?'

Everyone was grinning in anticipation.

'He flicks his goddamn Bic. I figure ol' Dumbo probably had time to say *Oh* . . . but by the time he got to *shit*, he was standing in front of St Peter, one pitiful crispy critter.'

Through the laughter, Morgan said, 'Pretty good, Max. Almost beats one we had a few years ago. Before your time. He and his old lady'd been fighting half the night and she kicked him out of her trailer at two o'clock in the morning. He was so pissed he went next door and borrowed a match.'

I sipped my virgin GT and smiled lazily at Max. Enough to show him he was appreciated but not enough to move him around the table. I couldn't afford any new entanglements right then.

Morgan misinterpreted and, with misguided generosity, offered me a Wake County sheriff's deputy. 'Tell Deborah 'bout that guy from California yesterday,' she said, gracefully stubbing her cigarette in one of the glass ashtrays.

'That call we got about some suspicious activity out near Fuquay?'

This one was a big, corn-fed blond with an easy aw-shucks-ma'am smile, who didn't have to be asked twice to perform.

'I got out there and found a red GT with California plates. Unattended. Trunk lid up though, and the trunk half filled with that there stuff we call green vegetable matter when we have to take the stand.'

Terry leaned forward to listen. This was evidently a new story to him and he'd worked drugs. Tobacco is North Carolina's biggest legal cash crop, but they say marijuana puts more cash into the state economy than tobacco, and Terry takes it personal.

'Well, I just hung around a few minutes and pretty soon, here comes this joker crashing out of the underbrush with his arms full of more green vegetable matter, freshly cut. He's stripped to the waist. Sweaty. Briar scratches on his chest. Man, he's been working double-time.'

He paused and tipped up his beer glass, then wiped his lips with calm, assured motions.

'He's halfway up the ditch bank before he sees me standing there, my unit nosed right in behind his little GT. He drops his load so quick you'd think all that g.v.m.'s suddenly turned to poison oak. I don't move a muscle or say a word till he gets up level with me. He's scared shitless and just stands there looking.

'Finally I say, "Son, what the hell you think you're doing trespassing on private property?"'

'He doesn't know whether to lie or tell the truth and starts moaning, "Omigawd, omigawd, omigawd."

'"Son," I say, "let me see your driver's license." He hands it over and now he's whining, "Please, officer, I didn't mean nothing. I was driving through – everybody says North Carolina has good weed growing wild – I thought I'd check it out. I swear to God I've never done anything like this before."'

'Sure he hadn't,' said Terry sarcastically.

'Well, now, Terry, that's where you and me might differ. There was something that made me believe maybe he hadn't. And that's exactly what I told him. "Son," I said, "you've got the pure look of truth in your eyes, so I'm gonna let you off easy this time. You empty your trunk and then you get your tail out of the state of North Carolina and don't ever come back, you hear?"

'Well, he dumped all that g.v.m. and was in his car hightailing it back to California before you could spit twice.'

He took another deep swallow of his beer and leaned back in his chair, smiling through those sleepy blue eyes.

Terry frowned. 'You let him go?'

'Well, hell, Terry,' the deputy drawled. 'Far as I know, there ain't no law yet against filling your trunk with fresh-cut ragweed.'

Laughter erupted all around and Terry threw Max's book of matches at him. 'You sorry rascal!'

As the raucous hoots and gotchas turned into general conversation, Morgan waved to a quiet older man across the room. I knew Scotty Underhill by sight, but he'd always been a family man, not one to dawdle long in bars after-hours, so I didn't know him all that well.

According to Terry, his daughters were grown now so he'd started stopping by occasionally. Morgan offered to scoot over and slide in another chair next to hers, but he shook his head and went off to a side booth with Terry. When they'd finished their business a few minutes later, Terry motioned for me to join them.

Underhill started to rise. I appreciate good manners, but

he looked tired, so I said, 'No, don't get up,' and slipped into the booth next to Terry.

'I told Scotty you're looking into the Janie Whitehead case,' said Terry.

'Her daughter's eighteen now,' I explained, 'and wants to know more about what happened to her mother.'

'That baby's eighteen? Good golly Moses.' He sighed, tucked the ends of his blue plaid tie back inside his neat gray jacket and shook his head at the rapid passage of time. 'But yeah, she was a year younger than my youngest daughter, and Delia's sure enough nineteen now.'

'If you have daughters, then you can probably appreciate how Janie Whitehead's daughter must feel, growing up not knowing why her mother was killed,' I coaxed.

'Yeah, sure, but we reworked it about three or four years ago.' He glanced at Terry for confirmation.

'Seven years,' said Terry.

'*Seven*? You sure? God! Where does the time go?' His blue eyes were probably three shades lighter than what he'd started with and his hair almost completely gray. There were also tired lines around his mouth that made him seem older than the fifty he probably was. 'Well, whenever. We tried to come at it fresh, like we'd just got the call that she'd been found in that millhouse. I'll never forget it. That pretty young thing lying on those cold stones. All those blowflies. Could have been so much worse, of course. May and everything. It can get hot. Look at today.'

He took another sip of his ice water. 'The baby was dehydrated, though, and it was a damn good thing she hadn't started crawling yet 'cause there was a Christ almighty big gaping drop where the paddle wheel used to go.'

'Could you account for all Janie's movements that day?'

He leaned back in the booth and regarded me steadily, though it was Terry he spoke to. 'You say she's going to be a judge?'

'Is that a problem?' I asked mildly.

His eyes may have been pale blue but they were the eyes of a weary old spaniel who'd learned to wait instead of chasing after every breeze that bent the grass, and they didn't waver now. 'Not as long as I go by the book.'

Terry started to stir, but I laid my hand on his arm. 'Primary's not till Tuesday,' I pointed out. 'And we're a long way from November.'

Underhill seemed to consider, then shrugged. 'Well, Terry's my boss now. If he says it's okay . . . ?'

'It *is* okay,' said Terry.

'All technicalities anyhow. We didn't find a damn thing the first time through and not a hell of a lot more the second time. So what do you want me to tell you?'

'Everything,' I said, and signaled Spot for another round of drinks. Terry and I switched to coffee; Underhill opted for tomato juice.

It was sensible. It was healthy. We were all going to live to be a hundred.

But sometimes I missed feeling like John J. Malone.

5

Searching For Some Kind
Of Clue

Before Scotty Underhill could finish doctoring his tomato juice with Tabasco and Worcestershire to turn it into something that had the taste, if not the kick, of a Bloody Mary, Terry had gulped his coffee, given my shoulder a brotherly pat, and charged off to make Stanton's ball game.

'I haven't looked at those records in months, so I can't give you chapter and verse,' Scotty warned as he squeezed a slice of lemon into his tomato juice and laid it on the napkin beside his glass. 'Still, when you give it that much time, it's not something you forget either.'

He gave me a tired smile. 'Hell, I even remember you now. You were the baby-sitter, weren't you?'

'Why yes, I'm surprised you remember.'

'We looked at everybody. Even baby-sitters. You thought her husband was groovy, as I recall.'

Unexpected embarrassment washed over me. I felt myself

turning red and was thankful Terry wasn't there to see. 'Who on earth told you that?'

'Does it matter?'

'No. Just sounds funny hearing that an SBI agent paid any attention to a schoolgirl crush.' A crush I thought I'd hidden from the world.

'Schoolgirls have done crazy things. Besides, you weren't some little kid. You'd just turned sixteen, a young woman driving her own car. A white Thunderbird, as I recall.' Almost as an afterthought, he added, 'You were also Kezzie Knott's daughter.'

I let it pass. If he knew that, then he also knew that the only thing my father's ever been convicted of is income tax evasion. He would also know that Daddy served his eighteen months in a federal prison well before I was even born. By the time I was eight, a governor and two senators had pulled the necessary strings to get him an unconditional pardon. Theoretically, that single conviction had been expunged from his record.

In practice, helicopters continued to circle Knott land like buzzards, looking for stills and probably even strips of marijuana tucked in between tobacco rows, though I don't think Daddy's ever messed with pot. He always said he made his money the old-fashioned way, and he may be a scoundrel but he's never been a hypocrite. Nevertheless, the drone of spotter planes was one of my earliest memories, and even Terry has been exasperated enough to complain about them spooking the bass when he's fishing one of Daddy's lakes.

Max waved to me on his way out and his place at the big

round table was taken by two women I vaguely recognized from the attorney general's office. On the jukebox, Tina Turner was belligerently demanding to know what love had to do with it – Spot's jukebox has always been a comfortable five years behind the hits – and the strident beat muffled words, bursts of laughter, and the tinkle of bottles and glasses as Miss Molly's geared up for Friday night. Above the music, Morgan gave me a what's doing? look, and when I gestured that I'd be a little longer, she lit another cigarette and turned back to the conversation at her own table while I got on with mine.

'Who else did you look at?' I asked tightly.

'The husband, his parents, her parents, neighbors, friends, old boyfriends. You name it, we did it.'

He stirred his tomato juice with a straw, sipped, added a sprinkle of pepper and stirred again.

'You probably know as much how she died as I do.'

'I doubt it.'

'Okay, let's see. She disappeared on the first Wednesday in May.' He looked surprised to realize the calendar was back to May again. 'Day before yesterday, eighteen years ago.'

Unlike this year, that May had begun unseasonably cool and rainy, and I remembered there'd been a heavy fog that never completely lifted.

He nodded. 'A morning that kept people indoors with the heat turned back on. No fit weather to take a new baby out in, but there was nobody to stay with her. Not her parents. Not you. You were in school till three-thirty.'

He spoke matter-of-factly, but it gave me a weird feeling

to realize how thoroughly my movements, too, had been documented back then.

Janie's mother and father had driven over to Durham early that morning to attend the funeral of Mrs Poole's cousin, Scotty continued, and her sister was down with some sort of spring virus that made it risky to expose the baby. In fact, it was her sister's illness that took Janie out that day in the first place. Marylee Poole Strickland was room mother for her second-grader, and she'd promised to take cupcakes for a class party immediately after lunch. The cupcakes had been baked and decorated the night before, but when she awoke too sick to take them over, she'd called on Janie.

According to Marylee, everything was absolutely normal when Janie ran in at 11:45 to get the cupcakes, leaving Gayle in the car. At Cotton Grove Elementary, the second-grade teacher didn't know Janie well enough to confirm Marylee's assessment, but she did think that the only thing on Janie's mind was not leaving her baby daughter in the car by herself too long. She'd stayed just long enough to bring in the tray of cupcakes and the quart-size bottles of Pepsi, and to pass along Marylee's apologies, before hurrying from the classroom.

A fifth-grade teacher on the second floor of the school had been standing at the window overlooking the parking lot, trying to judge if the rain had slacked off enough for her to take her class out for a breath of fresh air before their lunch period. She had known Janie since childhood and was able to state quite definitely that she saw the young mother in her chic red vinyl raincoat cut across the schoolyard to her dark blue sedan. Janie had adjusted the blanket around the infant

in the portable crib on the backseat, then driven off alone
back toward the center of town.

The time was exactly 12:17.

'And that was the last time anyone was positive that they'd
seen Janie Poole Whitehead alive,' said Scotty.

'Except for Howard Grimes?' I asked.

He shrugged. 'We could never be sure whether he really
saw her or whether he just wanted us to give him the time of
day.'

'Did you? Give him the time of day, I mean?'

'I told you we listened to whoever'd talk. Trouble is, ol'
Howard quit talking before we got to him.'

I didn't remember it like that and protested. 'He told
anybody who'd listen that it was Janie he'd seen parked with
some man in front of the old Dixie Motel. That it was raining
too hard and the windows were too fogged up for him to
make out who, though.'

'Yeah, I know, and that story went around Cotton Grove
so quick there were people who still thought she'd run off
with another man right up till the minute they found her body,
but I'm telling you straight: when we tried to pin him down
after she was found, he started saying maybe it was somebody
else's wife he'd seen. There were two other young women in
Cotton Grove driving dark blue Ford sedans.'

'Kay Saunders and my ex-sister-in-law,' I said, meeting it
head on.

'Not yet ex,' he corrected.

'Doesn't matter. Trish and Kay were good friends of
Janie's. They used to run around together in high school.

73

Anyhow, Howard said the woman was wearing shiny red, and neither Trish nor Kay owned a mod red slicker, just Janie.'

Scotty's head came up and for the first time I saw a beagle-hunting gleam flicker down in those weary spaniel eyes. 'You sure he described the raincoat?'

'Of course I'm sure.' Yet even as I spoke, I wondered if I'd confused his remarks with the schoolyard description widely repeated by the teachers. Janie had been clothes-proud, and I remembered the day she bought that coat, the day she modeled it for Jed and me. It was a teacher workday, a week before her death, so I was off from school. I'd kept Gayle and Marylee's little boy, too, so the two sisters could go shopping together at Crabtree Valley, Raleigh's biggest and newest mall.

I'd already fed the kids and Jed had just gotten home a few minutes earlier when Marylee and Janie pulled into the driveway, the backseat of the car loaded down with packages. With her dark hair piled up in a bouffant beehive, high-heeled white boots, and that lipstick red vinyl slicker, she matched my unsophisticated idea of Carnaby Street, and I watched, pea green with jealousy, as she sweet-talked Jed out of being mad because she'd spent so much money. 'But, sugar darlin', you don't think I can keep on wearing all those old things from before the baby was born?'

So was that why the red raincoat remained with me for eighteen years? I concentrated and retrieved a sudden mental image of Howard standing in darkness on the sidewalk in front of Jed and Janie's house. Red and blue lights atop the emergency vehicles were refracted by water droplets. People milled about in the misty fog. I was there, some of my brothers, too, and their wives. Will and Trish. Mother was inside with the older women of the community, trying to reassure Mrs Poole and Mrs Whitehead that Janie and Gayle were going to be all right. Blue lights from the wet patrol cars flashed across Howard's broad, self-important face.

'He said he couldn't make out the woman because she was turned toward the man beside her, but her back was pressed against the window and he saw her shiny red coat.'

Scotty twirled his straw between his fingers. It was clear plastic and coated with dull red tomato juice. 'That little detail would have made us take him more seriously. Wonder why he left it out when we talked with him?'

'Did he?'

'This is the first time I've heard it.'

'What about when you reworked the case?'

'We didn't get a chance. We'd just started when he dropped dead.'

I'd been living with Aunt Zell and Uncle Ash in Dobbs by then and had forgotten – if I'd even noticed – that the two things occurred simultaneously. After all, Howard Grimes wasn't someone important to me, and the SBI had kept their heads down so low when they returned to Cotton Grove seven years ago that I'd barely been aware they were there before they were gone again, leaving some uneasy talk that soon faded. Still, for Howard to have died so abruptly?

I stared at Scotty and he gave an ironic grin. 'Yeah, but we had him autopsied and it really was his heart. His doctor said he'd had a bad one for years. Just our luck it picked that week to give out on him. Wish I'd heard about the red raincoat, though. We might have leaned on him a little harder the first go-round instead of thinking he was just the town busybody.'

'He was that, too,' I said and nodded to the waitress who'd come over to refill my coffee cup.

She glanced inquiringly at Scotty's empty glass, but he shook his head. 'I'll have a cup of brewed decaf if you've got it.'

As she snaked her way back through the TGIF crowd gathered noisily around the bar for happy hour, he said, 'Except for Janie's parents, nobody had much of an alibi. You know that?'

'Yes. Gayle brought over a box of newspaper clippings yesterday and I spent last night going over them.'

The beagle look was still there. 'Law school makes a difference, doesn't it?'

It did. I'd found myself studying bland and equivocal statements with a jaundiced eye, wishing whoever'd reported the stories for the county papers had been less solicitous of family feelings and had asked harder questions. The *News and Observer* and the now defunct *Raleigh Times* had both covered Janie's death once she'd been found; but even though her murder had made a brief sensation, they'd merely rehashed what was already known.

Janie and Gayle had vanished on a Wednesday. By Thursday morning, when her car reappeared, some five hundred people were out actively looking for them: rescue squads, a local unit of the National Guard, town and county police, state troopers, and at least four aircraft, including the traffic helicopter from one of the Raleigh TV stations.

'That's when we got into it,' said Scotty. He thanked the

waitress as she set coffee before him, then briefly encapsulated their investigation.

'We coordinated the search but there were a lot of loose cannons rolling through Cotton Grove that week. Later, when we tried to chart everyone's movements from Wednesday noon through Friday midnight, it was like documenting an anthill.'

'And Friday night was when she was actually killed,' I murmured, taking a deep swallow of coffee.

'Friday night was when she actually *died*,' he corrected, shaking out the pink paper packet of artificial sweetener.

'We didn't publicize it, but after the autopsy report came back that she'd been dead considerably less than twenty-four hours by the time we found her, we took a closer look. No marks on her hands or wrists, yet the baby hadn't been fed or changed.'

He waited for me to make the connections.

'She hadn't fought or been tied up, so why hadn't she taken care of Gayle?'

He nodded. 'Page Hudson was still ME back then. He put it in medical terms, but what it boiled down to was that she'd sustained a really bad head wound – probably on Wednesday – that left her unconscious till someone put a bullet in her brain sometime late Friday. There was no need to tie her hands. She would never have moved again on her own. The bullet just speeded things up.'

The bottom abruptly fell out of my stomach. 'Somebody put her out of her misery? Like putting down a horse or an old dog when they get tired of watching it suffer?'

''Bout what it amounts to,' he agreed, crumpling up the

empty packets of sweetener. He stirred his coffee and drank up as I tried to fit the new facts over my old concepts.

We had all heard about Janie's head wound as soon as she was found, but I guess its seriousness hadn't registered. The sensationalism of how she was shot overshadowed a mundane blow on the head. Fanned by one irresponsible newspaper sidebar – 'Cosa Nostra in Colleton County?' – the hottest topic was that Janie had been shot behind the right ear 'execution style,' as if someone had taken out a contract on her life.

'I always assumed she was briefly knocked unconscious and then lived two full days scared out of her mind before she was finally killed.'

'She wasn't molested,' Scotty reminded me.

'Her head wound – did Dr Hudson say what caused it?'

'Nope. The bullet track kinda messed things up too much to say if she took a bad fall or was hit.'

I sat silently as he described in more detail than the papers had carried exactly how Janie had been found. I'd heard most of it, but hearing Scotty's version gave me a different perspective.

After three days with bloodhounds and aerial reconnaissance that produced no results, a call had gone out for everyone to please check any abandoned buildings on their property.

Ridley's Mill fell in that category. It was only three miles from the edge of Cotton Grove as the crow flies, but more like six miles because of the way Old Forty-Eight followed the twists and bends of Possum Creek. Once a small and inefficient gristmill, it had fallen into disrepair back around the thirties when the main millstone broke and electricity proved more reliable than the broad sluggish creek. There were no more Ridleys either, for that matter, and the property had changed hands several times.

Twenty years ago, a Raleigh banker bought it, thinking it might be remodeled into a rustic weekend fishing lodge. He died before he could draw up any plans, and his widow has sat on the estate ever since.

The land's posted, but nobody's ever let a few NO TRESPASSING signs keep them from where they want to go, and the mill's always been used by fishermen, hunters, and teenage kids skipping school. The rutted overgrown lane leading in through the woods from Old Forty-Eight is probably still a lovers' lane. It was back then.

When it became generally known that Janie and Gayle were missing, said Scotty, someone living nearby had driven his pickup through the lane on Thursday afternoon. The man and his older brother had checked the millhouse from top to bottom. Both were on record that the place was empty, nothing out of the ordinary.

Scotty paused. 'Your brothers, I believe?'

'Yes,' I replied. 'Will and Seth. Possum Creek borders our land, too, and all of us have fished from the top of the millhouse at one time or another.'

No point adding that while Will might lie about anything that crossed his mind, Seth never would.

'Will's wife's the one who had a blue sedan, too?'

'My brothers checked Ridley's Mill simply because they knew it was there and they thought somebody ought to take a look,' I said and heard a defensive tone in my own voice.

'Of course,' he said neutrally. 'So you know all about how two black hands were clearing underbrush for Michael Vickery on the opposite bank upstream and heard the baby crying?'

'Where the Pot Shot is now,' I nodded. 'Michael had gone to get drinks or pick up a load of bricks or something and they forded the creek and found Janie and Gayle in the mill loft. Janie still wearing the jeans and – wait a minute. What happened to her raincoat?'

Scotty sat back in the booth while music and people and blue cigarette haze swirled around us, then leaned across the table so that I was the only one who could possibly hear his words above the noise. 'I'm trusting Terry on you, but it doesn't leave this table,' he warned.

'Okay,' I promised.

'No raincoat. The family was too torn up to notice and the news media never picked up on it either – probably because it'd turned off so hot and sunny by then nobody thought about coats. We made sure it really was missing and then we shut up about it because I thought we stood a good chance of finding it if we ever developed a strong enough suspect to get a search warrant.'

'Only you never did.'

'Only we never did,' he echoed grimly. 'Not for lack of trying. We zeroed in on a few right away: the husband, your brothers – because they'd been out to the mill on Thursday, all the old boyfriends, Michael Vickery. You.' He gave a tired smile. 'Even those two blacks that found her. We just couldn't make the times fit. Take Jed Whitehead. He was a salesman with a Raleigh firm back then, out on the road all day Wednesday, but once it was known that his wife was missing, someone was constantly with him. Same with the rest of her family. Any of them could have bopped her over the head and hid her somewhere, but when did they have time to move her car or, for that matter, move her to the millhouse and then go back and shoot her?'

I hadn't realized those were separate times.

'Yeah,' he answered. 'Something about two different kinds of bloodstains. They figured the wound opened up again when she was put in the loft. I forget the details, but forensics determined that she'd bled onto the floorstones for several hours before the shot finished her off instantly. She actually died between five and ten P.M. on Friday evening, according to Dr Hudson.'

'Too bad Michael Vickery hadn't moved into the barn yet,' I sighed.

'Might have been rough on him if he had. As it was, he was lucky he could prove he was in Chapel Hill from noon till nearly midnight on Friday because he was out there by himself all day Wednesday.'

Scotty shrugged. 'It was like that with every man we looked at. Your brothers: both free to come and go without punching time cards or anybody keeping tabs on them. They alibied each other for Wednesday, which we might could question, but your brother Seth helped barbecue chickens all afternoon for a church supper Friday night while your brother Will was umpiring a Little League baseball game.'

'Neither of my brothers had a reason to hurt Janie,' I said hotly.

'So who did?' he asked reasonably.

'Nobody! Anybody. Oh, God, *I* don't know!' An impatient

sweep of my hand upset my empty cup. No one in the place noticed. They were too busy watching three miniskirted secretaries over by the jukebox who were demonstrating some aerobic movements and lip-synching 'Let's Hear It for the Boy' along with Deniece Williams. Morgan was in tight conversation with someone I didn't recognize. 'Didn't you guys turn up *any* motives?'

'Not really.'

'Not really,' I mimicked nastily. 'You told Terry and me you didn't find a hell of a lot more the second time through. What does that mean? Or aren't you going to trust me?'

'We checked out Dinah Jean Raynor when we heard she was going to marry Janie's husband,' he answered slowly. 'Eight months wasn't much of a mourning period. Made us wonder if they'd had anything going before.'

'*Dinah Jean*?' I was scornful. 'He might have dated her in high school, but he'd dropped her long before he started seeing Janie.' I hesitated. Jed had always treated Dinah Jean pleasantly in my presence, the surface between them as placid and unruffled as Possum Creek. But I remembered the yearning on her face at times when he drew away from her or didn't seem to notice her outstretched hand. During the years between their brief high school fling and Janie's death, could Dinah Jean have carried a torch for Jed even bigger than mine?

'She was still in nursing then,' said Scotty. 'Working the four-to-midnights at Rex Hospital. But one thing we did learn when we went over Janie's girlfriends: she and your sister-in-law – sorry, your *ex*-sister-in-law – and Kay Saunders had been really close right up to a couple of months after the baby was born. Then, bang. Overnight, a few weeks before she died, Janie quit seeing them. Quit shopping with them, quit having them over to her house, quit going to theirs.'

Startled, I realized he was right. Janie, Trish, and Kay had graduated from Dobbs High School together and had then married Cotton Grove boys within two years of each other, which brought them back into the same social orbit where two incomes weren't a necessity quite yet. The 'Donna Reed' syndrome lasted a bit longer in the South than elsewhere, and none of the three had held down real jobs back then. All that most young wives like them had to do till the children started arriving was keep the house clean and be there in a frilly apron with supper on the table when their husbands came home from work. The rest of the time they were free to shop, socialize, or volunteer their services to community projects if they chose.

Thinking out loud, I said, 'Well, maybe motherhood slowed her down too much. So far as I know, Kay never had kids, and Trish and Will were divorced before they had any. With her sister there in town, maybe she thought it was time to settle into family life.'

Except that even as I said it, I was remembering that she hadn't really settled. Marylee's kids were both in school and Janie had been out running around with her those last couple of weeks almost as much as with Trish and Kay.

'Well, it probably didn't mean anything,' Scotty said. 'The only reason I gave it a second thought was because there was nothing else. You girls are all alike, though. One day you're best friends, the next day you can't stand the sight of each other.'

I bristled and he started grinning. For a minute his tiredness seemed to dissipate. 'You look just like my oldest daughter. She hates it when I say things like that, even if I'm only kidding.' His grin faded. 'Just the same, that's the explanation Marylee Strickland gave me. What your ex-sister-in-law said, too, as a matter of fact.'

'Did you believe them?' I asked.

'Let's put it this way. I never could verify their movements for that Wednesday afternoon, but I do know that Trish Knott and Kay Saunders spent Friday evening playing cards with some friends over in Makely.'

'*Makely*?' Appalled, I looked at my watch. 'Oh Lord! I'm supposed to be at a meeting in Makely in exactly twelve minutes.'

Babbling my thanks for his time, I grabbed for his bill and he let me take it. 'Two things though, Your Honor – if you learn anything, I expect you to share it.'

I nodded. 'And the other?'

'Just keep in mind that someone's got away with murder once already.'

6

There's Something For Everyone In America

I'd warned Gayle that my campaign was going to come first, a good thing because the next few days were so jammed I hardly had time to shower and change clothes. It was the last weekend before the primary, my last chance to shake new hands in other parts of the district where I was less well-known to voters.

On Saturday morning, I got up early and drove over to Widdington in the next county. My first stop was at a Newcomers Club breakfast followed by a midmorning bake sale for the Widdington High School Marching Band Uniform Fund, where I bought an obscenely rich carrot cake with cream cheese icing that I immediately donated to the Mothers Against Drunk Driving at their lunch meeting in Hilltop, thirty miles further east from Widdington.

'If this is a bribe, I'm easy,' laughed a plump young mother.

While our hostess sliced the moist cake into seventeen

equally fattening pieces, I described the number of drunk-driving cases I'd prosecuted when I'd worked as an assistant in the DA's office.

One smartass Republican-looking mother asked if I hadn't spent the last few years in private practice frequently defending drunk drivers. I took the high ground – 'As long as the United States remains a democracy, even the sorriest hound's entitled to a defense' – and kept the rest of the women on my side by confessing with pretty ruefulness that I'd lost over ninety percent of the DWI cases I'd tried to defend in court. (No point mentioning that most lawyers have an even worse conviction rate. If our DA doesn't think the facts are incontrovertible, he doesn't prosecute. Marginal cases simply don't come to trial all that often, and I'm pretty good at getting pretrial dismissals; but that's not something I like to brag about. Certainly not at a MADD meeting.)

'Win or lose,' I told them truthfully, 'any time a client of Lee, Stephenson and Knott is charged with driving while impaired, we require them to sign up for a substance abuse program before we'll accept the case.'

(Okay – yes, it does usually help mitigate a guilty verdict if you can say to the judge that your client's already entered such a program voluntarily, but again that's not something attorneys go around telling MADD groups. Especially if said attorney's running for judge.)

'Of course, when we're appointed to represent indigent defendants, we don't have the option of turning them down if they refuse.' I smiled apologetically at the Republican. 'I'm afraid that goes back to their Sixth Amendment rights again –

the right to counsel, whether or not they take the counsel's advice.'

The luncheon concluded in time for me to put in a quick appearance at the end of a noontime fish fry to benefit the hospital in Hilltop. I got to pull a raffle ticket out of a gallon jar, and the white-haired gentleman who won the VCR donated by the Hilltop Radio Shack fancied himself a roguish charmer. 'I claim the right to kiss the prettiest candidate in the whole damn election!' he said as he came up to collect his prize.

I smiled – God, how candidates have to smile! – proffered my cheek and mentally put a big red asterisk beside his name. He'd be grinning out of the other side of his mouth if he ever showed up in *my* court.

Midafternoon was Joplin's Crossroads. The volunteer fire department there was sponsoring an auction of surplus farm equipment, and my brother Will was auctioneer. Will is three brothers up from me, the oldest of my mother's four, and a bit of a rounder. Everybody likes Will as long as they don't have to pick up behind him and clean up his messes. He's a fine auctioneer though and makes good money on the circuit. The crowds get to laughing at his fast-talking patter and hardly notice how high the bid's gotten. He'd phoned me the week before. 'Long as you're going to be in the neighborhood, you ought to come on by and say hey to everybody. That firehouse is a polling place, and a lot of those men'll vote for you if you smile at 'em pretty.'

So I climbed up onto the flatbed of a two-ton truck that he was using as a platform, flashed as genuine a smile as I could muster, and used his microphone to make a dignified appeal for their votes. Then, while some announcements were made and another consignment of machinery was rolled into place, Will took a break and I asked him if he remembered Howard Grimes.

'That old busybody? Oh, hell, yeah. Why?'

We were sitting on the far side of the flatbed away from the crowd with our legs dangling over the edge. I popped the top on a can of Diet Pepsi someone had brought us and took a sip. 'I was remembering how he said he looked hard at the man in Janie Whitehead's car that afternoon she disappeared because he thought at first she was Trish and he wanted to see who she was cheating on you with, remember?'

'Yeah, I remember,' he said sourly. His and Trish's divorce had not been amicable. They fought over every single thing they'd acquired together – furniture, appliances, and the dogs; but the major sticking point, and one that almost unglued the settlement, was who was going to keep the album of wedding pictures. Even though she understood the psychological significance of the impasse, Mother wound up paying their photographer to duplicate the whole damn thing right down to the album's white taffeta cover just so she wouldn't have to keep listening to Will mouth about it.

'You dated Janie before she married Jed, didn't you?'

He set his Pepsi down between us, pushed his gray poplin hat on the back of his head, and fumbled in the pocket of his windbreaker for a cigarette. 'So?'

'So was Janie cheating, too? Is that why she and Trish quit being friends?'

Will put the cigarette between his lips and cupped his big hands around a Zippo so old and battered that its square corners were rounded off. It was Mother's originally, a souvenir she'd brought home from the Seymour Johnson Airfield after World War II.

The lighter is burly and masculine-looking, made of stainless steel and engraved with the insignia of the Army Air Forces Technical Training School where she'd worked. It always looked so incongruous in her lovely smooth hands with those long pink fingernails, yet she was never without it. When she died and her things were divided, there were the usual two- and three-way battles, and some of those battles went all the way to skinned knuckles and bloody noses; but that beat-up Zippo was the only item all the boys fought over – not just her sons but her stepsons, too. Even the ones that didn't smoke. Yet I was the only one who knew who'd given her the lighter and why she kept it. None of them had ever thought to ask.

Or maybe they had and she just hadn't answered them.

Like Will wasn't answering.

I waited till his cigarette was going good. 'Was she?'

He narrowed his eyes at me as a mild spring breeze blew the cigarette smoke back in his face. 'How come you asking something like that after all these years?'

'Gayle wants me to help her find out why Janie was killed,' I said.

'Should you ought to be doing that while you're running for judge?' he asked.

Before I could answer, we were interrupted by calls for the auction to resume. He poured the rest of his Pepsi on the ground, crushed the can in his hands, then swung himself back upright on the flatbed and picked up the mike again.

Maybe it was my imagination, but it seemed to take him

longer than usual to work back into his patter and get that first laugh. I smiled my way back to my car, shaking hands as I went, but faces and hands were blurred by the sudden memory I had of Will kissing Janie.

For the life of me I couldn't remember whether it was before she married Jed or after.

Back in Dobbs, I showered, changed clothes, and collected Aunt Zell for a Democratic rally down in Black Creek.

Aunt Zell's my mother without the wild streak – one of those good people that help hold the world together. They pick up the pieces, clean up the messes, and try to make sure nobody goes to bed hungry. If that makes her sound trivial, try running the world without women like her in it.

All her babies died before they walked, but that doesn't mean she took me to raise when I moved in on her and Uncle Ash during college. Still, I think I'm a comfort to her. Anyhow, I try to remember to be.

Not a large turnout in Black Creek, but when you're running for a local office, wherever one or two be gathered in your name, that's where you go. The Women's Missionary Union from Harrison Hobart's church was well represented and gave me a warm welcome. I'd like to think it was because they approved of me personally, but I had a feeling it was because Aunt Zell was with me. She's been active in the WMU all her adult life, even holding district office. Everybody respects her, and some of that respect rubs off on me, a distinct asset for a single woman in a society that still gets a bit uneasy when a halfway attractive woman doesn't marry and settle into monogamy by the time she's twenty-five; thirty if she was ever divorced.

I'm thirty-four and no man's ring is on my finger at the moment.

On Sunday, Aunt Zell and I visited all three of the churches I'd grown up in. The morning began with Sunday school at Fresh Hope, then a quick fifteen-mile drive to Bethel Baptist for morning preaching by Barry Blackman, an old high school boyfriend long married now and the father of three. For dinner afterwards, Aunt Zell and I had been invited to the Bryant-Avery family reunion there in the neighborhood.

The spring day was gloriously warm and sunny. Azaleas and dogwoods were almost finished, just scattered blossoms here and there; but wisteria still draped soft purple ribbons up and down the tall trunks of longleaf pines, and wild cherries had already made me re-memorize Housman's 'Loveliest of Trees.'

Aunt Zell and I drove through a lush green landscape perfumed with wild crabapples and Carolina jasmine. Pears were fully leafed, but I could still see some of the limb structure of the huge oaks when we turned into the yard at Kate and Rob Bryant's house.

At least a hundred Bryants and Averys had gathered under the trees behind the old white wooden farmhouse to spread a picnic dinner on one long table made of planks and sawhorses and draped in white sheets.

Rob's a Raleigh attorney. His brother is Dwight Avery Bryant, head of the detective unit at the Colleton County sheriff's department, and their mother, Emily Wallace Bryant, is principal at nearby Zach Taylor High School. She's a catbird: bright orange hair, bossy, talks ninety miles a minute, asks the most astonishingly personal questions, and is a yellow dog Democrat of the first water.

As our nominal hostess, Miss Emily perched her infant step-grandson on her hip – at nine months old, Kate's son Jake was currently the youngest member of the clan – and welcomed everybody, 'especially Bo Poole, who, as y'all know, is running for sheriff again; and Deborah Knott, who's going to make us a mighty fine judge if all y'all get out and vote as you should on Tuesday. Now neither one of them's a Bryant or an Avery, but they *are* Democrats and that makes them kin in my book!'

Barry Blackman asked the blessing, then the younger mothers in their flowery spring dresses moved in on the table to fix plates for their children.

I love family reunions, even when they're somebody else's family. I love listening to the old-timers reminisce about people dead fifty or a hundred years. I love watching flirty teenagers discover a cute third cousin whose voice has changed since the last time they saw him. And I particularly love it when the eight- to ten-year-olds stand in front of the family tree chart and find themselves down on the crowded bottom row, as if all those births and deaths and marriages took place all those long years ago just so the multiple branches could lead inexorably to their own names.

Every family had brought a hamper of favorite food, and every square inch of the communal table was filled with heaping platters: fried chicken and pork chops, chicken pastry, and country ham; hot rolls and biscuits; corn, butterbeans, and tender new garden peas; a dozen different cakes and

desserts, including pecan pie and chocolate seven-layer cake.
Two wooden tubs sat at the end of the long table. One held
sweet iced tea, the other homemade lemonade.

I wanted some of everything.

'Now you've *got* to win,' Dwight Bryant teased when I
went back for a helping of fresh strawberry shortcake
smothered in heavy cream. 'You keep on eating like that and
a judge's loose gray robe's going to be the only thing'll fit
you.'

'Not that anybody's counting or anything,' I said, 'but
didn't I see four of Aunt Zell's angel rolls on your plate?
They may taste like air, but I've watched her make them. A
whole pound of butter, my friend.'

'Yeah, but I've had help,' he said, smiling at a sandy-
haired little kid who grinned back and snitched another roll
from Dwight's plate.

'That's not Cal, is it?' I asked as the child darted off to
watch the horseshoe pitching that had begun down by the
barn. 'Lord, Dwight! He was barely walking the last time I
saw him.'

'Yeah. Every time Jonna lets me have him for the weekend,
I notice how he's grown up just a little bit more.'

There was such painful resignation on his big good-natured
face that his brother Rob handed over his squirming red-
headed stepson and said, 'Here, wrestle with this one for a
minute.'

Baby Jake grabbed the strawberry atop my dessert and,
before anyone could stop him, squashed it in his chubby little
hand. Red juices dribbled over Dwight's chinos and Kate
swooped in with a wet cloth.

'No, no, no!' she scolded, wiping pureed strawberry and whipped cream from her son's tiny fingers. The baby merely laughed at her and patted her face.

'It's okay,' said Dwight. 'Cal was just as bad at this age.' He placed Jake astride his broad knee and began to jiggle it up and down like a bucking horse while Kate and Rob watched with foolishly fond smiles.

Whenever the unabashed happiness and stability of couples like Rob and Kate make me start feeling maybe I've made bad choices somewhere along the way, the Dwights help put things in perspective.

Aunt Zell and I wound up the day at an evening sermon at Sweetwater Missionary Baptist Church, a mile or so from my family homeplace. It's the church I joined when I was twelve years old, brought stumbling down that aisle of humility and repentance by adolescent guilt, a hellfire-and-brimstone preacher, and the lovely yearning strains of the invitational hymn:

> *Just as I am, without one plea,*
> *But that Thy blood was shed for me.*
> *And that Thou bidd'st me come to Thee.*
> *O Lamb of God, I come! I come!*

The preacher knew I was expected that night, but he'd already used *Judges 4:4* as a text when I was there back in February. (Since announcing my candidacy, I'd sat through at least six sermons inspired by 'And Deborah judged Israel at that time.') Tonight's text was *Proverbs 3:3*, 'Let not mercy and truth forsake thee; bind them about thy neck; write them upon the table of thine heart.'

It was the first quiet time I'd had in days, and with the preacher's words twisting in and out of my subconscious, I thought about truth and mercy and of actively judging another human being. As a professional. When it would affect, perhaps even alter forever, the course of their lives.

The practice of law – though never Justice itself – has always been something of a game for me, not unlike playing bridge for a penny a point – stakes high enough to be taken seriously, but not so high that the loss would seriously inconvenience me. Like bridge, it's a partnership in which my client and I defend a bid of innocence against the DA and the state, who hold most of the trump cards. I've always been competitive – too damn competitive for a woman according to most of my brothers, some of whom will no longer play cards when I'm at the table because I hate to lose with a purple passion. (On the other hand, there are those who say I lose much more graciously than I win.)

How would it be, I wondered solemnly, if I were no longer *in* the battle but above it, face-to-face with pure Justice in all its awful majesty, with only the imperfect tools of Law to mitigate the whole force and weight of government upon the petitioner at my bar! *Now comes the plaintiff, complaining of defendant, who alleges and says—*

I thought back to the anger I'd felt over Perry Byrd's blatant racism and how I'd filed for election on what might have looked like a whim. Yet, in the end, it really didn't matter whether my decision to run was based on impulsive whim or reasoned judgment. Sitting that night in Sweetwater

Church amid citizens of Colleton County that I'd known all my life, I made a solemn vow to myself then and there that I'd never misuse the office to indulge my personal biases. If I won, I'd be entrusted with the full power of the State of North Carolina to dissolve marriages, set child support payments, send malefactors to prison and—

'Right,' said the cynical pragmatist who sits jeering at the back of my brain when the preacher in the forefront starts acting too pious. 'We're not talking Supreme Court here, you know. More like Judge Wapner.'

True. Even if I won, district judges are only one step up from magistrates. I'd have original jurisdiction over misdemeanor cases and I could hold probable cause hearings for felony cases; but I'd be limited to judgments of under $10,000 and I couldn't send anyone to jail for more than two years.

'Still,' whispered the pragmatist, 'there'll be power, power no less real for being minor. Just as a sandspur jabbing in your foot can make walking every bit as painful as a broken bone, you can make life difficult for criminals and mean-minded no-goods. And people will stand for you when you enter or leave the courtroom. Other attorneys will have to address you respectfully. DAs will—'

At the piano to the left of the pulpit, the fifteen-year-old pianist rippled flawlessly through a handful of chords, and the youth choir stood and sang:

> *Yield not to temptation, for yielding is sin;*
> *Each vict'ry will help you some other to win . . .*
> *Be thoughtful and earnest, kind-hearted and true.*
> *Look ever to Jesus. He'll carry you through.*

Don't tell *me* God doesn't have a sense of humor.

Abashed, I consciously subdued vainglorious thoughts and tried to put myself into a properly reverential mood.

No one else ever seems to have the same trouble concentrating in church that I do. Aunt Zell's face was smoothly contemplative beside me. Beyond her, my brother Seth and his wife sat in stolid meditation. Across the aisle and two rows nearer the pulpit, the patrician profiles of Dr and Mrs Vickery were inclined attentively to the minister's closing remarks. Even the teenagers in the choir seemed to be taking his words deeply to heart. Of course, I suppose a casual observer might say the same of me. I wasn't actively fidgeting or coughing or turning my head. Only my eyes roamed the church.

They came to rest on the Vickerys again and I idly wondered what they were even doing here at Sweetwater. Evelyn Dancy Vickery's personal wealth was well beyond 'comfortable.' Dr Charles Vickery had been our family GP, but he'd retired before routine lawsuits and astronomical insurance rates ate into a doctor's income, so together they were probably even a few zeroes past 'affluent.' I was under the impression that they usually worshipped at First Baptist of Cotton Grove where 'Almost Persuaded' on a piano had been replaced by organ chorales.

Then I remembered that Dancys had helped found Sweetwater and many of Mrs Vickery's forebears were buried out there in the churchyard.

After Janie died, Jed moved in with his parents so Mrs Whitehead could help with Gayle. Then he went into business with his father, married Dinah Jean Raynor, and bought the

Higgins place on South Third. But when I first used to baby-sit with Gayle, Jed and Janie lived in a modest little house with a backyard that bumped up against the Vickery grounds.

I'd stand at Janie's kitchen window and gaze across to the tall Palladian windows that overlooked a flower garden as exquisite as anything ever seen in a Burpee's seed catalog. Camellias and thick oaks formed a partial screen, yet I glimpsed lighted candelabra when the formal dining room was used or heard music when the dinner party spilled out onto the terrace. I used to daydream about what life in the large brick house must be like.

Although I never wanted for anything growing up, Knotts do tend to keep their money in land. Stephensons, being town-bred, may spread themselves a little more lavishly – Aunt Zell married well, and her house in Dobbs is almost as large as the Vickery house in Cotton Grove – but no one in our immediate family ever aspired to the things the Vickerys aspired to. Mother and Aunt Zell might take some of us shopping in New York once a year, and yes, we always saw a comedy or musical while we were there; but the Vickerys had season tickets to the Met and seemed to think nothing of flying up during the middle of the week to hear a noted tenor or soprano.

My brothers played guitars and banjos by ear and those that wanted more education went to State or Carolina and were then expected to earn their own livings. The three Vickery offspring went to Smith, Vassar, or Yale, and all of them had trust funds to play around with. Which is probably why none of them felt the need to go into medicine or banking, the traditional professions in their family.

The two Vickery daughters lived on opposite sides of the continent. One was in the film industry, something to do with the production side of it, I believe; the other was currently married to an avant-garde composer in Toronto. But Michael had come out of the closet years ago and he still lived out at the Pot Shot.

It was unlikely that any of the senior Vickerys had paid much attention to the doings of the junior Whiteheads at the other end of their garden, but I wondered if Michael had?

'Let us pray,' said the preacher.

7

Changes In Latitudes,
Changes In Attitudes

I was in early on Monday morning and already into my
second cup of coffee by the time Sherry and the clerks arrived
at the office. They were willing to talk about their weekend if
I was interested, but when I mumbled around my jelly doughnut
that I hadn't had a chance to read the newspapers since
Friday, they left me to get on with them.

The biweekly *Dobbs Ledger* is owned by a family with
unabashedly liberal leanings, and Linsey Thomas, its current
editor and publisher, had come out for Luther Parker the
week before, citing the need for more minorities on the bench.
I suppose white women do hold a narrow margin over black
men and Parker would have been my choice, too, if I weren't
running. But I was, and it hurt my feelings not to have my
own hometown paper endorse me. On the other hand, Friday's
letters-to-the-editor columns had carried several letters written
in my support and they'd positioned my ad – *Deborah Knott
for District Court Judge . . . isn't it time?* – very nicely, just

above the fold on the obituary page.

People here usually turn to the deaths before the engagements and weddings, so that's the most read page in the paper. Doesn't matter whether the deceased are stillborns or pushing a hundred. If somebody has a local connection, the *Ledger* will list parents (and sometimes both sets of grandparents) even if they've been dead fifty or sixty years, followed by the names of all immediate survivors, cause of death, and what the deceased did for a living. Each obituary concludes with the name of the funeral home, visiting hours, what church, who's preaching the funeral, and where the body's to be interred. No mistaking one Willie Johnson for another by the time the *Ledger* gets finished.

My picture was small, but I thought it conveyed competence without grimness. I also hoped that the contrast to all those sober suits and short male haircuts in the other ads would add subliminal appeal, remind the electorate that they might need a judge with a woman's tender heart sometime.

John Claude arrived at his regular time and acted surprised to find me there on the sunporch already leafing through the newspapers. Usually he's the first one in after Sherry and, despite pro forma grumbling about Reid and me wandering in at all hours, he prefers it that way. Gives him a chance to drink his coffee in peace. Sherry knows better than to let the clerks disturb him. Not that he'd be rude to them – John Claude is seldom rude to anyone – but pained shadows do cross his thin patrician face; and while Sherry never notices *my* exasperated sighs, she's alert to John Claude's every nuance. Must be fun being a man in a Southern town.

The pained shadows fought with pleasantries as he saw the shambles I'd made of the paper. (Okay, so I notice nuances, too. But I'm older than Sherry. My generation was raised to notice. Doesn't mean I still react with an automatic 'I'm sorry' or 'Let me take care of whatever's bothering your little ol' manly sense of rightness' the way she does.)

Monday morning's big 'local' story was yet another drug deal gone wrong over the weekend, this one down at Fort Bragg: shotguns, three dead, no arrests yet. The *N&O*'s editorial page carried endorsements for most of the major candidates. They did not reach down as far as outlying judgeships, and I'd already moved on to the sports section, where the owner of the Durham Bulls was still shaking his minor league monopoly over Raleigh's dreams of getting its own team.

'I'm finished with the front part, if you want it,' I said, cheerfully handing it over.

'Is that jam?' he fretted as he tried to restore the virgin alignment of each sheet only to be foiled by a sticky smear on the op ed page. A very small smear, I might add, and one I'd wiped away so carefully that any normal person would never have noticed.

'You mean to tell me Julia *still* hasn't finished redoing y'all's breakfast room?' I asked.

'Touché.' He looked contrite. 'Forgive my shortness, Deborah. You're quite right. I shouldn't allow disorder at home to affect relations here.'

I groaned at the mild pun, and my cousin smiled with restored good humor. He saw the feature section of Friday's

Ledger still face up at the end of the table and said, 'That's a nice picture of you.'

Despite fulsome campaign ads on every other page, the paper had used its Focus page for a here's-who's-running look at all the local primary candidates: age, education, background, work experience. There wasn't enough room on the page for everyone's picture, so only the candidates for district court judgeships, clerk of the court, and county commissioners got to have their shining faces published. For the first time it dawned on me that those were also the only three races with serious black candidates – Linsey Thomas's subtle way of alerting blacks and liberals to the potentials for racial balance?

'I was right surprised to see Talbert's letter,' John Claude said as he poured himself a cup of coffee and added a precise tablespoon of half-and-half from the refrigerator.

'What's to be surprised about?' I asked, shifting all the papers over to make room for him at the end of the table. 'G. Hooks writes a letter every year supporting Jesse.'

'Not G. Hooks's letter in yesterday's *News and Observer*. I meant *Gray* Hooks's letter in Friday's *Ledger*.'

'Oh, yeah. That sort of surprised me, too,' I admitted. 'You reckon he and his daddy had another fight or something?'

Grayson Hooks Talbert – everyone called him G. Hooks – is one of the movers and shakers of the state's Republican Party, a man so far to the right that he almost makes Jesse Helms look liberal. Chairman of the board and major stockholder of Talbert International, a pharmaceutical company of global proportions, he also sits on the boards of several major corporations that have profitable ties to government. Talberts always had money, but the Reagan-Bush years have been particularly good to G. Hooks, and his country estate on the Durham side of the Research Triangle now boasts its own private airstrip and two Lear jets.

All that jetting off to open new markets out on the Pacific rim was probably how a relatively moderate Republican had slipped into the lovely old Victorian governor's mansion back here in North Carolina. Not that G. Hooks hadn't contributed heavily to James Hardison's election two years ago. It must have been like sucking lemons though, since the antediluvian Democrat who'd tried to pull an upset was probably closer to him philosophically than Governor Jim Hardison would ever be.

He had two sons: Gray – short for Grayson Hooks Talbert, Junior – and Victor. As near as I could tell, listening to gossip and reading between the fine lines of newsprint, the younger son had emerged from the womb with G. Hooks's single-minded devotion to business. A dutiful ant who ran their New York office while shuttling back and forth to Capitol Hill, Victor Talbert had graduated with a Wharton MBA, married a Harvard Law whiz, and appeared quite happy to stay out of the South.

Gray, on the other hand, started off a happy-go-lucky grasshopper. Flunked out of Carolina, UVA, and the Citadel, smashed up two Porsches and a Jag before he was twenty. Without getting into a heavy nature/nurture debate, you have to wonder about the psychological damage you can do if you name your first son Junior and then don't add Senior to your own name. To give him credit though, G. Hooks hung in and kept trying to find a proper niche for his namesake. After all, Talbert Pharmaceuticals was a huge empire, surely there was some little duchy where the princeling couldn't screw up?

Evidently not.

Nobody knew what the final straw was – a television reporter once told me that G. Hooks had on retainer at that time a full-fledged personal publicist whose sole mission in life was to keep Gray's name out of the papers and his face off the TV screens – but the upshot was the equivalent of being told to go sit in the corner and keep his mouth shut or plan on sweeping floors or begging on street corners the rest of his natural life.

The corner he was sent to happened to be a farmed-out piece of Colleton County dirt that joined my daddy's land at the edge of Cotton Grove Township. G. Hooks had inherited it through his mother's side, then never bothered to do anything with it beyond listing it for a tax loss. (Daddy'd once offered to buy it – Daddy's like the USSR before Glasnost: always looking to put another buffer zone between him and the rest of the world – but G. Hooks had drawn himself up all righteous-like and sent word through his local manager that he didn't deal with bootleggers.)

To everyone's surprise, young Gray turned out to be a real farmer. Oh, there were a couple of rough years at first when he tore up the roads with his silver turbo Carrera. Some of the wild crowd followed him into exile, and there were weeklong brawls out at the farm and messy aftermaths – I represented one of the local women in her paternity suit and got her a decent settlement – but eventually things settled down. Gray settled down, too. Guess he had to. Daddy said that every time the sheriff got called out, G. Hooks would halve his allowance.

(Don't ask me how Daddy knows that. He just does. But then he's always kept tabs on everything that goes on around his part of the county. He may not've ever studied Francis Bacon, but he sure does subscribe to Bacon's tenet that knowledge is power.)

Before Gray Talbert got his act together, he was down to ten dollars a week. A thirty-year-old playboy can't raise much hell on that, so the rowdies quit coming around. Daddy says at that point it was probably a combination of boredom and farm genes kicking in. Whatever, Gray took to messing around in one of the old greenhouses back of the house. Then he signed up for some horticulture classes at Colleton Community College and next thing you know, he's started himself a little nursery business. That was eight years ago, and the single dilapidated greenhouse has expanded into at least a dozen sprawled around under the pines out there. He soon got out of the retail end and just does wholesale. I have the impression that he roots liner shrubs, mostly azaleas and boxwoods, things that don't take a lot of intensive labor.

Like everything else Talberts touch, there must be pretty good money in wholesale shrubbery because he still drives a Porsche, although more sedately these days, in keeping with the low profile he's maintained since buckling down to business. Unlike his father, Gray's never involved himself in politics. If I'd been asked, I'd have said that along with G. Hooks's work ethics, Gray has probably grown into a similarly conservative mindset as he nears forty. That's what made it so surprising that he'd write a letter to the *Ledger* supporting me.

'Maybe he's just being neighborly to Kezzie,' said John Claude. 'Your daddy's been helpful about providing Talbert with people who'll work steady.'

'Maybe he's sweet on you,' said Sherry, who'd come in on the tail end of our conversation. Never mind that Gray Talbert and I have hardly ever even spoken to each other. Sherry's always on the lookout for potential romance.

At which point, there was a click of high heels on the stairway and we caught a flash of honey blonde hair and the rear view of a shapely female form as it sped through the wide reception hall, past Sherry's desk, and out the front door. Then Reid followed, knotting his tie, his jacket slung over one arm.

'Y'all leave me any coffee?' he drawled, enjoying it that none of us had realized he'd spent the night upstairs again.

The pained shadow returned to John Claude's face.

8

The Race Is On

I woke on election day to the smell of hot corn muffins
entwined around fragrant tendrils of sage and fried pork.
Country sausage. That comforting nostalgic blend of aromas
took me straight back home to Mother's kitchen, back to a
time and place where no one worried about calories, much
less cholesterol levels. As I remembered what day it was my
appetite faded, but I still slipped on a robe and followed my
nose down to the kitchen.

Barely six o'clock and Aunt Zell was already fully dressed
to go out. She was one of the poll watchers and had to get
over to the fire station early. A white denim chef's apron
protected her neat blue shirtwaist from splatters as she finished
browning sausage patties in a cast-iron skillet. Corn muffins
studded with blueberries big as marbles had just come from
the oven, and her face was slightly flushed beneath short
white hair neatly waved.

'Smells wonderful,' I said, pouring myself a cup of

coffee, 'but I'm not very hungry.'

Aunt Zell's china blue eyes swept over me appraisingly. 'Not feeling nervous, are you?'

She brought the sausage and muffins over to the breakfast table and took the chair opposite mine. Spring sunlight fell across the table and bounced off the cut crystal sugar bowl in splintered rainbows. The bright rays turned Aunt Zell's hair to pure silver, and when she lifted her glass of orange juice, it glowed like liquid sunshine.

'At least try a little of this sausage meat,' she urged. 'Your daddy sent it over yesterday evening, just special for you.'

I lifted one eyebrow in a skeptical tell-me-another and she smiled. 'Well now, he did say it was for me, but then he went and slipped and said how he knows you like it with a little extra sage and not much red pepper.'

I nibbled the piece she put on my plate and God, it was good!

Hog killing used to be a two-day affair when I was little. I'd drag my footstool up to the kitchen table to watch Mother and Maidie, the black woman who worked for Mother, grind the pork and then mix it up in huge tin dishpans. They'd add salt and spices and then fry up a little 'try' piece till the whole house was redolent of browned meat. The sample would be rolled around on their tongues with a critical thoughtfulness I've only since seen on the faces of serious wine connoisseurs.

'What do you think, Maidie?' Mother would ask.

'I believe a pinch more sage, don't you reckon? And maybe half a dab of black pepper?'

More mixing, more try pieces, until Maidie said, 'That's it right there. We've got it just perfect.'

And it always was because if there's one thing eastern North Carolina has over the rest of the whole damn world, it's the way we know what to do with pork.

Just the same, delicious as it was on my tongue this morning, I wasn't going to be mollified by a couple of sausage patties.

'Five whole months without even a phone call,' I said. 'Not one single word of encouragement.'

'Oh, honey, what do you think this sausage is? Don't you know yet how afraid he is that you're going to wind up getting hurt?'

'I'm not little missy from de big house anymore,' I muttered.

'Saying something doesn't make it so,' she said tartly.

'Meaning?'

'Meaning that even when you're an old white-haired lady and he's been in his grave fifty years, people around here are still going to remember that you're Kezzie Knott's daughter. He recognizes it even if you won't.'

Her own breakfast finished – half a muffin and two bites of sausage – Aunt Zell stood briskly and began to clear the table. Before I could think of a withering retort, the phone rang.

As soon as the first syllables reached her ear she started smiling with pure pleasure. Five years dropped from her pretty face and she signaled for me to go get on an extension. Uncle Ash was calling from South America – he's a buyer for one of the big tobacco companies – and, unlike my own father, who wouldn't pick up the phone and him only fifteen miles away, Uncle Ash had called all that distance to wish me luck. His booming voice was like a warm encouraging hug. 'And don't worry, shug. I sent my absentee ballot in last week by registered mail. Bet I'm the first grain of sand in what's gonna be a real landslide.'

Ever since I woke, I'd been assailed by doubt and misgivings. 'I'll be happy if it's just not a sand bucket,' I said.

'Aw, naw, you're going to do just fine, idn' she, Zell?' he boomed.

'Well of course she is!' my aunt answered smartly. 'And I want your solemn word right this minute, James Ashley Smith, that you'll be home at Thanksgiving so you can see her swearing-in.'

'Already got it on my calendar, Miz Ozella.'

I knew the conversation was about to get mooshy – Aunt Zell and Uncle Ash sometimes act like they were married only four months instead of forty years – so I got off the phone and went up to brush my teeth and find something fitting to wear.

The flowered dress and cherry tunic I'd laid out the night before looked too sweet-sixteenish this morning; and I was rummaging in my closet when Aunt Zell called up that she'd see me later. 'Now don't forget to come vote – early and often!'

I finally settled on a red-and-white houndstooth skirt with a red patent belt, red patent heels, white silk shirt, and navy blue blazer. Bright red lipstick and bright red earrings.

I looked patriotic as hell.

Reid arrived at the office just as I was leaving for court,

took one look at my clothes, and offered to send over to the little theater for an Uncle Sam top hat.

Everybody's a comedian.

The polls opened at 6:30 A.M. and closed at 7:30 P.M. It made for a very long day.

Judge Harrison Hobart managed to keep his feelings reined in as I walked a couple of misdemeanor larceny cases by him. Now that primary day was upon us and he was barred from running again, the old fossil had decided to go out with dignified formality.

Judge Perry Byrd was a different horse altogether.

A horse's ass, to get more specific.

With his broad face more florid than usual, he was sarcastic and snide and nitpicked every motion I made in the routine breaking-and-entering I had to argue before him. As soon as he'd rendered a guilty verdict and I'd given notice of appeal, I got out of his courtroom before I said something we'd both regret.

Most everyone around the courthouse wished me luck and swore that they'd either already voted for me, or surely would before the polls closed. I took it with a grain of salt big as a cow block and drove on over to the fire station.

Lunch hour had filled the polling place with familiar faces, and the usual jokes and glad-handing went on as we waited in line to vote. One of my high school classmates was tending the Republican register. 'I'd wish you luck, Deborah, but you're sitting in the wrong pew.'

'That's okay, Kath,' I smiled. 'Can't everybody sing with the angels.'

We still use paper ballots in Dobbs. One of the party elders handed me this year's sheaf of seven IBM cards and a soft pencil, and I went into an empty curtained booth to mark my choices. Aunt Zell was posted by the machine at the end and she smiled at me encouragingly as I fed in my ballots one at a time, face down.

'I'll be home soon as the polls close,' she promised. 'Folks'll probably start coming in before nine.'

I told her I hoped she hadn't fixed all that fancy food for nothing.

'Family's going to come whether you win or lose,' she said. 'But you're going to *win*! You'll see. Now go have some lunch and quit worrying.'

Following Aunt Zell's advice, I drove through a fast-food lane, ordered a cheeseburger with everything, fries, and a drink, and took them back to the office. Sherry eyed the yellow-and-red bag hungrily when I came through the door.

'The phone hasn't quit ringing all morning,' she said. 'I haven't had a minute to go eat.'

Since most of the calls were well-wishers for me, I guiltily pretended I'd been thoughtful and brought her lunch. 'I couldn't remember if you liked it all the way or not,' I lied, 'but maybe you can scrape off what you don't want.'

My appetite was gone again anyhow.

'Now isn't that nice of you!' said Sherry, flipping on the answering machine before heading for the kitchen. 'And you can just go right on in and work in peace,' she added officiously. 'I won't put through any phone calls unless they're real business.'

Both Reid and John Claude were out, so I had no excuse to idle around the place, and Sherry was right in hinting about the work that needed my attention. There were pleadings to write, depositions to read, motions to draft, but I couldn't concentrate. The afternoon dragged along on little snail feet, and the few calls that got past Sherry were more than welcome.

Eventually, the grandmother clock on my mantelpiece limped its way around to four-thirty and I was ready to pack it in when Reid stuck his handsome face in the door and started humming 'Hail to the Chief!'

'Idiot!' I laughed as my spirits began to rise again.

'So what time do the games begin?' He pushed his way on in, followed by John Claude, who had to carry the firm's mantle of dignity by default.

'Aunt Zell says around nine, but y'all can come on anytime. You, too, Sherry,' I called through the open door. 'Bring that good-looking boyfriend, too, if you want.'

'Does that mean I can bring Fitzi?' asked Reid.

'What the hell's a Fitzi?' I laughed. 'That blonde we didn't see yesterday morning?'

'Hey, you *really* didn't see that particular lady,' Reid warned. 'All the details of her divorce settlement haven't been worked out yet and—'

'Dammit all, Reid!' John Claude was past pained shadows and into outright indignation. 'You promised!'

'Promised what?'

'You know very well what,' our senior partner said icily.

'I promised not to fuck any more of our clients.' Reid's face was that of an innocent child unjustly accused. 'You didn't say I couldn't fuck Ambrose Daughtridge's.'

115

'She's Daughtridge's client?'

'Well, of course. Didn't I give you my word?' He drew himself up and put on an exaggerated drawl. 'A Stephenson never breaks his word. Suh, you have impugned my honoh as a gentleman.'

'A gentleman doesn't use the *f* word in front of a lady,' John Claude said crisply.

I gave Reid my fiercest glare before he could make the obvious rejoinder.

By ten o'clock, Aunt Zell's whole downstairs was jammed with people. From the kitchen to the front veranda, it seemed like Knotts and Stephensons were there in their thousands, and Smiths and Lees in their ten thousands. Not to mention half the neighborhood.

The initial returns were in and just as I'd hoped, the two white men had knocked each other out of the race. Luther Parker and I were the front-runners, predicted to wind up with fifty-three percent of the vote, although our actual finishing positions were too close to call. Sherry had gone over to the courthouse, stationed herself in the lobby outside the board of elections office, and kept calling over with the figures till it was clear that the runoff would be between Luther Parker and me.

I finally managed to get through to him and we congratulated each other and someone on an extension line – whether his or mine I couldn't tell – exclaimed, 'And may the best man win!'

Parker chuckled. 'You might want to rephrase that, Miss Knott.'

The party swung into high gear after that, despite the lack of anything harder than sparkling cider and iced tea. The dining table was loaded with platters of finger food, and there was too much laughing and talking to hear myself think. Minnie was so ecstatic about me passing the first hurdle that she wanted to sit down in the middle of all the hoopla and start mapping out the rest of my campaign.

'Not tonight!' cried Seth and grabbed her hand and danced her out into the wide central hall where fiddles and guitars were tuning up on the staircase.

Further up, near the landing, a bunch of teenagers – cousins, nieces, and nephews – camped on the staircase to watch their elders play. They always start out too cool to join in. Nevertheless, I saw toes tapping and signaled to my brother Haywood's youngest son, eighteen now and a senior at West Colleton High. Stevie turned red, but he eased past his daddy, who was cutting loose on the fiddle, and met me at the bottom of the stairs. Someone had carted out the Persian rug that usually covered the parqueted floor and we two-stepped up and down the hall, following Minnie and Seth. Then Will handed his guitar to Reid and everyone clapped hands as he and Reid's red-haired Fitzi did a cross between an Irish jig and mountain clogging. (A Fitzi, I'd discovered, was a gorgeous third-year law student named Patsy Fitzgerald, who was going to spend the summer clerking for one of the state justices in Raleigh.)

Most of the kids knew a little clogging and soon they were into it too. Minnie and I passed from hand to hand as more dancers crowded into the hall or spun off into the living room. Eventually, Stevie came round again.

Margaret Maron

'So whose heart are you breaking this year?' I asked him as we swung through the dining room for another glass of cider.

'Not me,' he shrugged, suddenly serious.

'Somebody breaking yours?'

'That's what I need to talk to you about,' he said. 'Could we? For just a minute?'

'Sure, honey. What's wrong?'

We took our glasses out onto the side terrace and I sat down on the white brick wall. Stevie leaned against a nearby pillar. The mild night air felt good after the warmth of dancing among crowded bodies. Overhead, the moon was one night from full and shone in the sky like a battered silver platter handed down through the generations: most of the decorations polished flat now, but a precious heirloom all the same. I'd shed my jacket and changed earlier into a more festive skirt, but I still wore my red patent heels and they glistened in the moonlight. I tapped my heels together lightly, experimentally, and looked up to see Stevie watching.

He grinned. 'Does it feel like Oz?'

'Not yet. Ask me again after the runoff next month.'

'You'll win,' he said loyally. 'Aunt Minnie says you have poll appeal and Dad says she knows politics.'

'Yes,' I agreed, 'but that's not what you wanted to talk about, was it?'

'What's going on with Gayle Whitehead?'

'What makes you think anything's going on?' I countered.

He gave me a patient look. 'She *said* there was. She said she doesn't want to talk about it, but if I really wanted to know, you'd tell me.'

118

'Stevie—'

'Is this the famous attorney-client confidentiality you always hear about on those lawyer shows?' he asked.

I leaned back on my hands. 'If you're still planning to go to law school, you'd better quit thinking it's like a Paramount sound stage. I didn't know you and Gayle were going together.'

'We're just starting,' he said. 'We've been good friends for years, but lately – I don't know. It's like now that high school's coming to an end, we've suddenly realized it's maybe something more than just a friendship.'

Before I could say something wise and auntlike, he grinned. 'Yeah, we know all about nostalgia and fear of the future. We also know we've got at least four years of college before we can do anything about it. All the same, right now . . .'

Ah, the sweet right now!

'Anyhow, she really did say you could tell me,' he finished earnestly.

I believed him, so I did.

When I concluded, he was quiet. All the kids had grown up knowing that Gayle's mother had been murdered, but now that he cared for her, I guess it was the first time the edges had been taken off for him.

He gave me such a pure look of '*Here am I, Lord, send me,*' that I jumped up and hugged him hard. 'Thanks for offering, honey. If there're any dragons you can slay, I *will* ask you, I promise.'

The party was winding down as we came back inside. 'Ah, there's our candidate,' beamed Miss Sallie Anderson. 'Come right here and let me hug you good night, honey, before I take these poor old bones home to bed.'

More neighbors followed, but there were plenty of friends and kinfolk left as Will and Haywood picked up their instruments and began to play a final and familiar tune. Seth carried the verse in his clear baritone and I went and stood beside him to sing alto. One of my earliest memories was harmonizing with Seth, me just a baby and him nearly grown. The others stood and listened till the chorus; then everyone linked arms and swayed together, and all our voices blended in a sweetness too beautiful to bear:

> *Will the circle be unbroken*
> *By and by, Lord, by and by?*
> *There's a better home a-waiting,*
> *In the sky, Lord, in the sky.*

Corny as that old song is, it always brings tears to my eyes. My mother dead, Seth and Haywood's mother dead, our daddy too proud to come celebrate tonight – our circle sure was gapped.

Even so, enough of it remained.

9

Now That We're Alone

My one scheduled court case next day had been postponed, but it didn't help as much as I'd hoped for catching up on office chores. Every time I'd start to dictate a letter or abstract a deposition, the phone would ring. I'd finished about a half a percentage point ahead of Luther Parker – exactly sixty-two votes ahead, to be exact – and everybody who hadn't come by the house last night seemed minded to call in their congratulations.

'I'll say you're busy if you want me to,' Sherry offered. Wednesday mornings were usually slow for her, too, because that's when John Claude normally attended court in Widdington and Reid headed for Makely.

'No, I'll talk to them.' As long as people felt like they had a personal stake in my election, every conversation could mean one more vote in June.

Most well-wishers were disposed of quickly, but Minnie kept me on the line forty-five minutes discussing how best to utilize our less than thirty days till the runoff election. Even the defeated ADA from Black Creek called to say – at pompous length – that I could count on his support both now and in November. No word from Perry Byrd's fat protégé. He'd struck me as a closet Republican though, so I doubted if he'd be supporting Luther Parker either.

I kept going straight through lunch and by midafternoon had just about had it with telephones. When Sherry buzzed that Gayle Whitehead was there, I immediately pushed aside the papers and had her sent in.

'This is probably a bad time,' Gayle apologized.

'Your timing's perfect. You don't know what a relief it is to actually see who I'm talking to.' I waved her over to a chair and caught a whiff of fragrance. I almost never wear perfume and it makes me sensitive to everybody else's. This was something light that reminded me of my mother's spring gardens. Wisteria? Narcissus? I was caught offstep by an underlying hint of tobacco. A lot of high school kids still think it's cool to smoke; evidently that included Gayle.

'I'm sorry you didn't flat-out win yesterday.' She wore jeans and sneakers today and her hair was caught up in a loose ponytail by a yellow plastic clip that matched her yellow shirt. 'I voted for you.'

'Hey, your first time voting, wasn't it?' Incredible to realize that little baby Gayle could now help pick judges and presidents, negotiate contracts and marry or join the army without parental consent.

'You really *are* all growed up, aren't you?' I teased.

'Yeah.' Dimples flashed in her cheeks. 'Still not old enough to buy beer though.'

'Do you want to?' Despite what I see in the courtroom, I'm always curious about what turns people on.

'Not really. It's the principle of the thing. Kids buy pot or white light' – her voice faltered, and in that split second, I knew she was wondering whether to take her foot out of her mouth and apologize and maybe make it worse, or pretend there was nothing personally embarrassing to me about bootleg whiskey – 'ning all over the county, but when it comes to something as harmless as a Bud Lite for anybody under twenty-one, forget it.'

It would have been a perfectly smooth recovery if she could have kept from flushing.

I'd had more practice at pretending not to notice things. 'So what brings you over to Dobbs today? I'm afraid I don't have anything new to tell you yet.'

'Oh, I didn't think you would,' she said, though she was too transparent to hide a slight disappointment. 'Dad made me promise I wouldn't do anything stupid by myself and I know you're busy and all, but I was wondering if—' She hesitated. 'I've never been out to Ridley's Mill.'

I was surprised. 'Never?'

She shook her head and her ponytail swayed with each movement.

The phone rang for the ten-thousandth time, and all at once, getting out of the office suddenly sounded like a great idea. 'But we'll have to run by the house first and let me change clothes,' I told her.

My strappy green sandals and linen skirt weren't up to hiking through brambles and poison oak.

* * *

The sun was still high and hot in the western sky when we reached Cotton Grove. Gayle left her car at the Tastee-Freez and we got us a Mountain Dew with lots of ice to drink as we drove on through town together.

New Forty-Eight – new in the fifties before I was born – crossed back over Possum Creek on a wide four-lane bridge and headed due south to Makely; but I automatically took Old Forty-Eight, a narrow, two-lane blacktop that followed the bends and crooks of the creek past birches and tulip poplars and weeping willows on one side of the road and broad fields of young green tobacco on the other. Once I could have driven this road with my eyes closed, just put my T-bird on automatic pilot and let it find its way back to the farm exactly like my grandfather's mules always carried him home no matter how blind drunk he was.

'And if he'd stuck to mules, he'd still be alive to this very day,' Daddy always said, even though the last time I heard him say it my grandfather would have been pushing a hundred and five. Knotts are long-lived but I never heard of any that made it much past ninety-five.

What actually killed my grandfather was when he passed out at the wheel of his T-model truck, the way he used to pass out at the reins, and crashed into the creek.

That's one version.

Another's that he had a load of whiskey in the back and was trying to outrun revenuers when they shot out his lights.

In both versions, so much whiskey went into Possum Creek that night that the bullfrogs started croaking out 'Sweet Adeline' in four-part harmony and catfish were staggering up on the banks to cheer them on.

I tried to find an objective version in the *Ledger* once, but that was back when the editor's wife was writing the death notices and they say she was a good-hearted person who hated it when her husband printed facts that shamed an innocent family. Miss Annie's flowery language didn't always make it clear whether a person died in bed or with a noose around his neck, but 'untimely tragedy' usually meant an unexpected death that wasn't going to have legal repercussions – anything from a mule hoof in the head to a husband coming home unexpectedly.

In my grandfather's case, mention was made of the bereft widow, of grieving progeny with 'no father's hand to guide them,' and of a fifteen-year-old son suddenly 'o'er-burdened with manhood's somber responsibilities by fate's stern necessity.'

They don't write obituaries like that any more.

Or give out many tombstones like the ornate monument Daddy reared to his father's memory a few years later when he had the money.

Nowadays, they stick you out in a field with flat brass nameplates that won't hinder the tractor mowers. Instead of marble urns, you get little flip-up brass vases, so that on decoration days a modern graveyard looks like a child's drawing of a treeless cow pasture with tufts of plastic flowers stuck in all over. Personally, I want to lie beneath huge magnolias or under live oaks draped in mournful Spanish moss. And if I can't have a ten-foot obsidian shaft with gold lettering, or a lifesize weeping angel, I say the hell with it. Just cremate me and scatter my ashes over the Colleton County courthouse where I can be an irritating cinder in Judge Perry Byrd's eye.

The Whiteheads tried to talk Jed out of it, but he got a double stone for Janie. Gleaming white marble, three feet high. Her side has her name and dates and a broken lily to signify that she'd been cut down in the bloom of life. His has a stem of bleeding hearts, his birthdate, and then a dash.

He probably really did think he'd spend the rest of his life grieving for her. Wonder how Dinah Jean felt attending sunrise services every Easter morning, watching Jed and Gayle put flowers on the grave with that place at Janie's side reserved for Jed?

As if she'd been following along in my mind, Gayle said, 'Did you know they had to take Mom back to the sanatorium?'

I eased off the gas pedal and glanced over at her. All the windows were open and her brown ponytail was streaming in the wind as her coral lips pursed around the straw of her drink. Like me, she had on sunglasses, too, and I couldn't read her eyes.

'What happened?'

'The same old thing. She got to drinking too much again, and then she'd call up and just start crying if it was me answered. If it was Dad, she'd hang up. I tried not to let him know, but . . .' Her hand sketched futility. 'Anyhow, the Raynors took her back up there day before yesterday.'

'Rough on you, honey.'

'Not really. I mean, I hate what she's doing to herself and I just wish I could help somehow. I thought if I went up to see her. Maybe talk with her doctors? But Gran says I ought to wait awhile. Give her a couple of weeks to dry out.'

'Probably a good idea,' I murmured. My hair swirled over

my sunglasses and I propped an elbow on the window edge
to keep it pushed back while steering with the fingers of my
right hand. Except for an occasional tractor, there was almost
no traffic on the road.

Gayle finished her drink, then drew a pack of cigarettes
from her purse. 'You mind if I smoke?'

'I grew up on a tobacco farm, remember?' Part of my
income still came from an allotment I'd inherited from Mother.
All the same, schizoid and hypocritical or not, it disappointed
me a bit to see her light up with such graceful familiarity.

'I just don't understand how Dad can be so cold about it,'
Gayle said, exhaling pensively. 'The way he's cut her off
completely and won't see her and doesn't want to talk about
her. I know he gives her alimony, but he acts like he never –
that they never – I mean she was his *wife*! Not a hired
housekeeper or something. And the Raynors don't know how
to help her. They say they watch her like a hawk, but she
keeps getting liquor from somewh—'

Again she caught herself.

'Listen, Gayle,' I said. 'I'd appreciate it if you'd quit
acting like I've never heard of white liquor, okay?'

She tugged at her seat belt and twisted around to half face
me. 'You don't mind talking about it?'

I tapped my horn and pulled around a slow-moving farm
truck loaded down with hundred-pound bags of fertilizer.
'What's to talk?'

When I didn't answer, her hand gently touched my blue-
jeaned knee.

'Deb'rah? I'm sorry. I guess it must be for you like it is for
me when people slip and talk about murders and shootings

and then remember it's more than just words.'

I was suddenly seized by a perverse curiosity. 'What *do* people say about my father?'

She fiddled with her cigarette and didn't answer.

'Do they still say he's the biggest bootlegger in eastern North Carolina? Go ahead. I really want to know. It won't hurt my feelings.'

'Really?'

'Really.'

'I've heard he *used* to have men working stills for him all over the county,' she began carefully. 'I also heard they even did a television program on him one time?'

'He was mentioned,' I admitted. 'The program was supposed to be about Southern politics.'

The filming of that documentary accidentally coincided with right after Daddy got his conviction expunged, and they used his circumstances as yet another illustration of the power wielded by one of our senators back then. Mother probably let me stay up to watch it with the rest of the family so I'd be prepared, but I was only eight years old, for God's sake. Even though I felt the tension in the living room as the program unfolded, the segment about Daddy must have been full of speculations and innuendoes that went right over my head because I know I kissed him good night and went to bed happy that his picture had been on television and still thinking he sat on God's right footstool.

I didn't know a thing about those eighteen months in Atlanta till I got on the school bus next morning and was greeted by silent stares. Tax evasion, federal penitentiaries, expungements – none of those terms had meaning for me. I'm not sure I fully understood what bootlegging even was, only that it was something shameful and criminal and suddenly connected to us. I still remember the bewilderment I felt, then the scalding embarrassment when later that day in the girls' bathroom, my best friend walked away from me and two of the other girls started chanting, '*Your* daddy's been in ja-il! Your daddy's been in ja-il!'

I jumped them both and the teacher had to come in and break it up, but not before one girl went flying against the sink and cut her jeering lip. Fighting normally got everybody involved five smacks on the palm with the teacher's ruler, and though this was my first school fight, I expected the usual punishment. Instead, we only had to put our heads on our desks for the rest of recess. No note went home to my parents and the injured girl's mother did not call mine, though she had always screamed when anybody touched her precious daughter.

I think that's the day I realized Daddy did have a dark power that everyone else recognized.

As for the jeering of the other kids, that lasted barely a day. The little twins (three inches taller but fifteen years younger than the 'big twins') were in eighth grade then and Will was a senior. Not that I ever went running to any of my brothers to fight my battles, but they always seemed to hear about it pretty quick and nobody messed with me without risking black eyes or bloody noses.

A slab-sided hound started across the road and I braked sharply. 'Fool dog!'

It slunk back into the ditch weeds.

'What else do folks say?'

'Mostly they always talk about what a good man Mr Kezzie is and how if anybody ever needs anything, they can always go to him.' Gayle leaned over and carefully stubbed out her cigarette in my ashtray. 'Just last week he was sitting with some men in the store near Amy Blalock's, and her mother and Mrs Medlin were talking about the air conditioner giving out at the parsonage. They didn't even know he was listening till he stood up and reached in his pocket, pulled out three hundred-dollar bills, and told her to put it in the collection plate toward a new unit. Some of the rough kids at school joke about getting some white lightning as good as Kezzie Knott used to make, but honest, nobody thinks your daddy's actually messing with it any more. I mean, he's really *old* now, isn't he?'

'Almost eighty-two,' I agreed. Never mind that he moved and looked like a vigorous sixty and could still straight-arm an axe.

What she'd said came close to echoing what I heard from Reid last time I asked. After all, Daddy'd served his time before I was even born. And he'd kept so closely to his own land after Mother died that people were starting to think of him as part of the county's colorful and rapidly disappearing past.

Or so Reid said.

I just hoped it'd stay that way till after the election, but Aunt Zell's words yesterday morning had made me uneasy. Everybody 'knew' that Daddy's first wife had kept his secret books, just as everybody 'knew' he'd kept that part of his life from touching my mother and – by extension – me. So far it hadn't been an election issue. Probably because when cancer took Mother and Daddy moved back to the farm, I'd stayed in Dobbs with Aunt Zell and Uncle Ash whenever I came home from college.

The road curved again. I made a left turn into a rutted drive, then rolled to a stop, blocked by a heavy steel cable that had been stretched tautly across the lane to Ridley's Mill. I would have ignored the NO TRESPASSING sign, but the underbrush was too thick and the terrain too rough to drive my car around the barrier.

'Is it a long walk to the mill?' asked Gayle, peering down the lane that soon dissolved behind a leafy green barrier. Judging by its overgrown condition, no one had driven down there since winter.

I threw the car in reverse. 'Less than a quarter of a mile, but I've got a better idea.'

It was only a short distance to where Old Forty-Eight crossed Possum Creek at the north corner of Knott land and then bordered our farm on the east side of the creek. About a half-mile on, I turned left into a rutted clay-and-gravel road that cut over to New Forty-Eight.

'Where're we going?' Gayle said as we bucketed along, red clouds of dust boiling up behind us.

'Over to the Pot Shot.' I had to lift my voice to be heard above the rattles of the rough road. 'If Michael Vickery's there, we'll get him to tell about the day you and your mother were found.'

10

I Go Crazy

At New Forty-Eight I made another left and headed back north toward Cotton Grove. A few minutes later, we were turning in at a ye olde quainte-type sign that pronounced this the entrance to the Pot Shot Pottery, open to the public only on weekends or by appointment.

This wasn't the weekend, but neither were there any cables stretched across this lane, so I drove through a double line of high rose hedges for at least a quarter of a mile till the lane opened into a wide level farmyard graced by weeping willows that swept down a broad grassy bank to Possum Creek. Except for that one vista, the rest of the view was obscured by hedge roses, breath-of-spring bushes, mock oranges, and crepe myrtles.

Off to the right and still on the last level area before the land begins to slope away stood a large wooden barn built of weathered gray boards. Yellow roses climbed as high as the second-floor windows on one side and twined up over a trellised doorway in the front. Once the barn had sat in a meadow at the edge of cotton fields. Now the fields were grown up in Queen Anne's lace and brown-eyed Susans, and wild cherries, oaks, sweet gums, and poplars had reclaimed the meadow.

Michael Vickery had converted the barn loft into living quarters the spring Janie died. The ground floor was used as a workshop with a huge kiln out back, and the old wood smokehouse, now a display shop for retail sales, had been salvaged from someone else's farm halfway across the county.

A CLOSED sign hung on the door, but Michael's gray Ford pickup and Denn McCloy's maroon Volvo were both parked in front of the shop, along with two Japanese imports that probably belonged to their help.

As I pulled into a space next to the truck, a medium-sized dog trotted over, jumped up into the bed of the pickup, and gazed at us with friendly alertness. She was a black-and-tawny brindle, a Lab crossed with Doberman maybe, with a little touch of setter somewhere down the line. Her thin tail whipped the air as she welcomed us. I tapped my horn, countrywise, to signal visitors, and eventually Michael waved from the barn door that he'd be right with us.

Michael Vickery must have been a sore trial to his parents.

To his parents? Hell, he must have been a sore trial to himself.

Down here where males are men and females are supposed to be their comfort and pleasure, it had to've been hard coming to terms with who and what he was. God knows he tried to play the role assigned to him by birth and sex because God also knows (indeed His spokesmen still thunder that message from every evangelical pulpit) that this state's never been all that tolerant of open homosexuality.

Colleton County's no longer as provincial as it used to be. The Triangle's gay community is too large and too deliberately visible for us to pretend it only exists in California or New York (or even Chapel Hill, long considered Sodom and Gomorrah South by most of the state's conservatives). Oprah, Phil, and Dr Ruth are on every television screen, so we even know that one doesn't willfully choose to be a homosexual. That doesn't mean that we don't feel enormous sympathy for a neighbor if that neighbor's child comes out of the closet, and it doesn't mean there's not a lifted eyebrow or salacious derision behind the same neighbor's back.

Nevertheless, Michael Vickery and Denn McCloy are welcome almost everywhere any other men of their socioeconomic class care to go. They might have trouble putting money down at a cockfight back of redneck tavern, but so would my cousin Reid. They go to church, eat at local barbecue houses, and seem to take part in any of the community activities that interest them. Michael's on call with the volunteer fire department, for instance, and Denn designs costumes and builds sets for the Possum Creek Players, the county's little theater group.

Back in the fall of 1972 though, even money and family prominence hadn't provided the grudging tolerance now given. There'd been midnight drive-bys with drunken yells, hurled bottles, and some poorly aimed shotgun blasts. A couple of better-placed shots from Michael's Winchester bought him back a little respect, and the night-riding pretty much stopped after Daddy let it be known up at the crossroads store that he didn't appreciate that kind of ruckus in his neighborhood.

Michael was in his midforties now. He'd studied art at Yale, tried painting in Paris and sculpting in New York, and finally came on back home to Cotton Grove. Maybe he got tired of wandering in alien corn. Not that he's ever struck me as a professional Southerner. Or an overly effete artist either. When he first came home to stay, it soon got around that he was going to dig clay out of the banks of Possum Creek and make ceramic statues. No one actually accused him of planning to make mud pies and him a grown man, although there was some shoulder shrugging about it being a strange way for a Dancy to make a living.

'His sisters must of got his share of the family balls,' I heard Daddy tell Mother, but that didn't stop me from mooning over him briefly that spring when Gayle was first born and I'd stop by to help Janie.

He was – still is – very handsome, with muscular arms and dazzling smile, and he seemed as macho as any guy in town back then. Certainly nobody I knew had the least idea that he was gay. I guess he was still fighting it because I know he was dating Pat Wiggins – sleeping with her, some people said – right up till he sent for Denn McCloy. Folks assumed he was fixing up an apartment over the barn so he could come and go without his mother knowing who he was coming and going with, she being so proper and puritanical.

The back of the Vickerys' grounds edged Jed and Janie's backyard, and whenever I saw Michael outside sketching, I'd grab the laundry basket and go hang out diapers. The end of the clothesline was only a few feet from the edge of their property and I could casually work my way down till I was within easy speaking distance. He was always friendly, but I could tell he thought I was just a lump, so I went back to giving Jed my full adoration.

'God, that's such a waste,' Gayle sighed as Michael walked across the barnyard towards us. 'How can such a good-looking hunk like that be queer?'

I had to smile, remembering my own astonishment when he first came out of the closet. Michael Vickery really does look like the answer to a maiden's prayers: tall and trimly muscled, with strongly handsome features, piercing blue eyes, wavy brown hair that's starting to go gray at the temples, and an air of reserve just begging to be shattered. Slouchy walk, tight end – he's got it all.

Denn McCloy on the other hand, hit the place like a fireball eighteen years ago. He may not have flamed, but he sure did smolder. He's toned down a lot over the years, but back then he'd gotten off the plane with bushy hair and wearing a vest and bell-bottoms (white suede) over a pirate's shirt (pink polyester) left unbuttoned to show a gold St Christopher's medal swinging on his chest (thin and hairless). Three generations removed from County Cork, straight from Hempstead, Long Island, via the alternative clubs and would-be theaters of the East Village, he even talked in stereotypical italics, like a bad imitation of Tiny Tim. Except

137

for Tiny Tim (and he was on television), Cotton Grove had never seen anybody like Dennis McCloy close up unless he was standing under a spotlight with an electric guitar in his hand. He must have been Mrs Vickery's personal nightmare from hell, but she held her head high and said not a word against him.

Neither Mother nor Aunt Zell particularly liked Mrs Vickery – 'Evelyn *Dancy* Vickery,' Mother always called her, with that little ironic quirk her eyebrows took whenever she was secretly amused.

The Dancys had lived in Cotton Grove since the Revolution. Up until the postwar boom, they'd owned its only bank. Yet somehow, except for Dr Vickery, who'd married in from Tennessee, they weren't really *of* Cotton Grove. It was almost like there was a one-way glass wall – a teller's window, Mother claimed – between them and the rest of the town. They could pass among us, but no one ever got real close to them. In times of community stress, Dancys would do all the proper things, pull out their checkbook and shoulder their fair share of the load, but Mother had noticed that they never seemed to hug or reach out to another human with a warm impulsive hand. She thought all the Dancys overly proud and much too cold natured.

'They never let anybody or any *thing* touch them,' she said.

Normally I accepted her evaluations, but that winter there were so many snickers and ribald speculations going around about what Michael Vickery and his 'New York fairy' were doing out at the old barn that it seemed to me pride might not be altogether bad if it could help such a sternly moralistic woman as Evelyn Dancy Vickery rise above what had to've been a personal Gethsemane. Everybody knew how much she adored Michael and how proud she'd been of his artistic achievements.

She might could've glossed over it if he'd stayed with his original fine-art pretensions – by the seventies, most of Colleton County understood that real artists had different standards of behavior – but no sooner had Michael emerged from the closet than he abruptly lowered his sights and started churning out commercial pottery. With a pragmatic eye for what would sell at craft fairs and decorative art shows, he developed stunning blue-green glazes for pots and jugs and tableware that seemed country naïve and city smart at the same time.

These days he and Denn employed three full-time assistant potters at the kiln and a part-time sales clerk for the shop where they test-marketed new items and sold their culls and seconds on weekends. A department store in Atlanta took all the first-quality stuff they made. Even without Michael's Dancy trust fund, Pot Shot Pottery seemed to be bringing in a very comfortable living.

Gayle and I got out of the car as Michael, trailed by Denn McCloy, came up to us with a friendly if slightly puzzled smile. This was probably only the fourth or fifth time I'd ever dropped by and each previous visit had been to see Denn about a costume or some stage business.

Like many attorneys, I have a large streak of ham in me and I'd even taken the prosecutor's role in *The Night of January 16th* a couple of years back. Playacting was too time-consuming for me to indulge in it often, but I loved it. Part of the fun was Denn, of course. He may never have starred on Broadway or even on Off Broadway, but he was New York, and he brought with him an aura of bitchy backstage glamor and outrageousness that made our amateur theater feel connected to a worldlier tradition.

Today, both were in jeans (Denn's still black leather, of course), lumber boots, and blue chambray work shirts, but whereas Michael's shirt strained over well-developed biceps, Denn's hung loosely on his small wiry frame.

'Congratulations,' said Michael. 'Do I have to call you "Judge" now? I hear you won.'

'Not by enough. It'll be a runoff with Parker in June. Appreciate your vote, though. Yours, too, Denn,' I said, extending my hand to his for the ritual kiss he always gave his female friends. 'Y'all both know Gayle Whitehead, don't you?'

I wasn't actually sure they did since she was so much younger. Michael nodded, but Denn openly stared. The tailgate of the pickup was down and he hoisted himself up to sit cross-legged while the setter nuzzled his ear. The years had not been particularly kind to his gamin looks. Whereas Michael had grown ever more handsome as he entered his midforties, I thought that Denn was beginning to look wizened and already fifty. His hair had been a tangle of long black curls the first time I saw him. Now it was nearly white and cropped to a quarter-inch stubble, which he usually covered with a flat black leather cap that matched his jeans. His skin had a grayish tinge and his dimples had deepened into wrinkles that creased his cheeks from eye sockets to jawline.

He pushed the dog away, adjusted the small gold earring that she had disturbed, and said, 'Whitehead? Are you the baby that—?'

His head jerked toward the creek.

'Yes,' said Gayle. 'In fact, that's why we're here.'

She'd pushed her sunglasses up into her hair and her warm brown eyes gazed up at Michael Vickery. 'I'm trying to find out how it all happened and Deborah said maybe you'd tell me about the day you—'

'No!' snapped Denn. 'He doesn't like to talk about it. It was too awful.'

Michael cut him off with a sharp gesture. 'That's okay.'

Their eyes locked with such tension that I suddenly realized they must have been fighting before we came.

'It's okay,' he repeated in a quieter tone.

Denn stared off into the distance, his wrinkled face like a stony mantle over the lava boiling up beneath. 'You *hate* it when people ask.'

'This is different,' said Michael. 'She has the right.'

Denn flicked his shoulder impatiently. 'It's morbid.'

'Not to me, Mr McCloy,' Gayle said.

'It's okay,' Michael said again as the dog jumped down from the truck and began sniffing my hand.

I ruffled her silky ears and her wagging tail announced a friend for life.

'Gayle's trying to put it all in perspective,' I explained, as much to Denn as to Michael. 'We were going to the mill, but the lane's been blocked off, so I thought we could cross over from here if you don't mind.'

'Not at all,' said Michael, and Denn gave him an angry look.

'Did you know my mother?' Gayle asked diffidently. She was still child enough to be intimidated by Denn's displeasure.

'Not very well,' Michael replied. 'She was from Dobbs and I was out of the country when she and your father moved to the house back of my parents. I probably returned around the time you were born, so I didn't see much of her. From what I remember though, you're very like her.'

'You were one of the men that found us, weren't you?'

'Not really.' Michael glanced at Denn; then, as if suddenly coming to a decision, he said, 'You see, I had a couple of boys working out here that day and—'

'Holy shit! Do you *hear* yourself!' Denn exploded in rage, springing down from the tailgate. '*Boys?* You're reverting all the way back to type, aren't you, Massa Michael?'

Even after all these years, his accent was more Long Island than Southern.

'Stop it, Denn.' Michael's fist clenched and unclenched and the ice in his voice chilled the warm May air. 'You're embarrassing our visitors.'

'Well ex*scuu-uu-uuse* me!' said Denn in a deliberately swishy Steve Martin takeoff. 'No ice cream for me tonight, girls.'

He started off toward the barn, then turned back in an abrupt change of tone that sounded conciliatory to me. 'We still didn't decide on which slip for the next rack.'

'Use whichever one you like,' Michael said coldly. 'I'm

going to walk these ladies over to the mill.'

Out of a corner of my eye as we passed through an opening in the fence, I saw Denn flip him the bird before slamming the barn door with a bang.

11

It's Been One Of
Those Days

'If there were homosexual marriages,' observed Michael as
we hiked down the slope to where Possum Creek sparkled in
the late afternoon sunlight, 'gays could then get legal divorces
and there would be a clean ritualistic break when things go
wrong.'

'You haven't seen as many messy divorces as I have,' I
told him dryly.

We paused instinctively when we reached the bank and
watched the slow-moving water ripple over rocks in the
shallow creek bed. The dog, Lily, splashed out ahead of us
and looked back to see if we were going to throw her a stick.

Gayle had pulled her sunglasses back down over her eyes.
'Even when divorces aren't messy, they can be sad,' she said,
and I knew she was thinking of Dinah Jean and Jed.

'In any event, my apologies for that scene.'

For a moment as we stood on the creek bank gazing down
into the water, I thought Michael was about to add something

more and looked at him inquiringly, but Dancy reserve pulled him back behind that glass wall. Once more he became an urbane guide.

'Were you told that the first couple of days after you and your mother disappeared, the National Guard and everybody else were out looking for you?' he asked Gayle.

She nodded and brushed at a dog fly circling her head.

'By the fourth day though, they were starting to slack off. People began to think you'd never be found because they'd looked in all the logical places. Including the mill.'

'You searched it?' I asked.

'Not I. I would have that Thursday afternoon on my way out to the barn, but a couple of your brothers were here before me. Didn't you know?'

I did, but I hadn't realized he did.

'Just as I started to turn in, I met them driving out. Seth and – I get them all mixed up. Which is the one that's an auctioneer?'

'Will,' I said. Was I being sensitive or was he talking about my brothers as if they were a litter of dogs? Just as numerous and just as indistinguishable?

'They said they'd checked it out and I saw no reason to do it again.'

Something snotty in his tone reminded me of Scotty Underhill's insinuations, and I was again on the defensive when I said, 'They searched both floors. The mill was empty.'

He nodded after a split second, then continued his narrative for Gayle. 'By Saturday morning, there just didn't seem anywhere else to look. The weather'd been too wet outside, and I'd had to be in Chapel Hill all day Friday. But it faired off on Saturday, and I'd hired two guys to clear off the underbrush along the bank here while I was stacking bricks for my first kiln on the other side of the barn.'

More pesky dog flies had appeared and, as we talked, Michael pulled out his pocketknife to cut us some leafy twigs so we could brush them away from our heads.

Suddenly, from back up on the crest of the slope, we heard a car engine crank up with a loud racing of the motor, then a screech of brakes and a glimpse of the rear of the maroon Volvo as it shot out of its parking spot and almost slammed into the weeping willow beside the rail fence. There was another angry clash of gears before it dug out of the farmyard in a great cloud of dust.

A muscle jumped in Michael's clenched jaw, but his voice was steady as he went on describing to Gayle that long-ago May morning – how the two workmen had followed the sound of her crying down along this very path. I lagged behind a moment, noticing that from this angle down below, the rose stakes nailed to the fence up there made an odd pattern against the sky.

Then, brushing at flies, I caught up with the others, and we retraced those workmen's steps till we were opposite the abandoned gristmill. The creek was even lower this afternoon than it'd been back then, and we were able to cross on big flat rocks near the old dam without getting our shoes wet.

Lily beat us across and was waiting to shake water from her brindle coat all over our legs.

'One of them stayed here, the other hiked out and met me at the road as I was returning with their snacks.' Michael pushed the dog aside and it ran off up the bank. 'The phone hadn't been hooked up yet, so we had to drive back to the store. I called the sheriff myself and then drove on around and through the lane to wait for them.'

The mill yard was badly overgrown now. Pokeweeds were head high and beginning to put out flower stems. Poison ivy grew even more lushly. The trees around the stone walls were wrapped in vines as thick and hairy as a man's arm, with rampant green leaves. Beneath the leaves were clouds of greenish-white blossoms. It seemed incongruous that anything so noxious could smell so sweet, but the air was permeated with a cloying fragrance I couldn't quite trust.

The heavy wooden door had long since fallen off its hinges and we entered uneasily.

'As soon as I switched off my truck I heard your cries,' said Michael. 'The sheriff had told me not to disturb anything, but I couldn't just stand down here and listen. Besides, those two boys had already been up.'

The lower chamber felt pleasantly cool after the hot afternoon sun outside. Even better, we could discard our twig fly brushes. An end wall had half broken away and more vines had grown up through the opening where the paddle wheel had once turned. Sunlight off the water reflected light onto the stone stairwell.

'We came up these steps,' said Michael, 'and I warned them to keep their hands in their pockets so we wouldn't leave any extra fingerprints.'

The upper level was almost completely open to the elements now. Only a small section of the roof remained. Michael gestured to a spot near a sheet of fallen tin roofing. 'Your mother was there. When we found her, she was on her back with her arms by her side.'

'The papers said it was like she'd been laid out for burial,' Gayle said in a small voice.

'Yes.'

There must have been bloodstains once, but eighteen years of sun and rain had scrubbed the stones clean.

Michael gestured to a spot further from the stairs. 'You were over here, buckled into one of those portable plastic baskets that sit up on a metal frame. It was pink, like your blanket.'

Gayle pushed her sunglasses up as if the tinted lenses were keeping her from seeing what Michael seemed to be seeing all over again. Her eyes glistened as he described the scene.

'The sheriff said leave everything, but your voice was hoarse. Not like a baby at all. I unbuckled you and carried you downstairs and tried to get you to stop crying. You were so tiny . . .'

He took a deep breath, and Gayle put out her small hand and touched his arm.

Even then the Dancy in him, if that's what it was, couldn't let him sustain her touch. Not that he flinched dramatically or anything – I doubt if Gayle even noticed – but he shrugged self-deprecatingly and walked away from her hand, over to the edge of the floor where the dilapidated wooden paddle wheel had almost completely rotted away.

'She must have been so frightened,' said Gayle, looking around the ruins.

'No,' I said. At least I could add that much. 'She never knew she was here, honey.'

I repeated what Scotty Underhill had told me about Janie's
head wound, though not his theory that she'd been put down
like a sick and dying animal.

'As far as your mother was concerned, it was all
over immediately. Her brain was so damaged that she
can't have known a thing after the moment she was first
injured.'

From across the wide loft, Michael said, 'So even if she
hadn't been shot, she would have died?'

'Not necessarily. And maybe not very soon. Modern
medicine, and all that,' I reminded him. 'But she would have
been a vegetable.'

Gayle flinched at the thought.

'Yes,' Michael agreed. 'There are some things worse
than—'

Ka-pingg!

Suddenly the wall above his head seemed to explode,
sending sharp chips of stone flying every which way. A split
second later we heard the actual crack of a rifle.

Michael's hand flew up to his face and came away bloody
just as a second bullet hit the tin roof with an explosive
clatter.

Instinctively, we all ducked down behind what was left of
the wall.

'Hey! Hold your fire!' roared Michael. 'There're people
here! *Hey!*'

Silence.

After a few minutes, we stood up warily. I expected to
hear shouts of apology through the thick trees, but none
came.

'Goddamn poachers!' Michael growled.

He mopped at the cut on his cheek with his handkerchief and his face was pale beneath his tan. It was just a scratch from where one of the stone chips had hit and the bleeding wasn't serious, but the nearness of the bullets had shaken all three of us.

'You could have been killed,' Gayle said.

It was bad enough that someone should be out hunting this time of year. 'Someone that careless with where his bullets go needs to be reported,' I said, more shaken than I wanted to admit.

'Nothing's in season now, is it?' Michael asked, still dabbing at his face.

'Nothing I know of. Which is probably why they're halfway back to the highway by now. I'll bet they think you're the game warden.'

Sure enough, from far in the distance, we heard someone crashing away from us through the underbrush towards Old Forty-Eight. Michael whistled for the dog, but she didn't respond.

The mood was as shattered as the mortar and stone where the bullet had struck. Gayle had seen all there was to see anyway, and Michael seemed to have nothing else to add, but I hesitated after they started for the steps.

'Michael?'

'Yes?'

'Was there anything else of Janie's when you got here?'

'What do you mean?' He looked blank. 'Like a purse or car keys or something?'

'Or a scarf or sweater or a baby bottle?' I'd promised

Scotty Underhill I wouldn't mention Janie's red vinyl slicker to anyone.

Michael shook his head. 'Nothing.'

'It was in the paper,' said Gayle. 'My empty bottle and extra diapers were in a diaper bag with her purse on the backseat of the car when they found it parked at Grandaddy's on Thursday morning. Her keys were still in the ignition.'

There wasn't much conversation on the way back across Possum Creek. As we went up the slope to Michael's place, I said, 'The way you've nailed those posts and crossbars up for the roses, they look almost like crosses.'

'Yes.'

His quiet concurrence effectively silenced me. I never know quite what to say when I'm confronted with unexpected religiosity.

'No place should be unexpected,' my internal preacher scolded. *'Is God not everywhere?'*

Fortunately my awkwardness was short-lived. Lily finally caught up with us, panting heavily in the warm afternoon. As Gayle and I crossed the barnyard, she thanked him for taking the time to come with us.

'I appreciate you telling me what you remembered,' she said.

'Not at all,' he murmured.

I'd taken out my keys and stood with them next to his pickup, trying to put my finger on what was different.

Then I realized that Denn's Volvo wasn't the only thing gone.

'Wasn't there a rifle on that rack before?' I asked, gesturing toward the pickup's rear window.

He stared me straight in the eye. 'No.'

I stared right back. 'I think there was.'

He was back behind his plate glass wall.

'Maybe you *do* need a divorce lawyer,' I said gravely. I glanced at the Pot Shot sign over the shop door and his eyes followed. 'Unless that was an advertisement?'

He stayed behind the glass wall, but an ironic smile flickered through. 'We don't need business that badly.'

Gayle's eyes were big as saucers as we drove away. 'You think Mr McCloy shot at us?'

I shrugged. 'Michael Vickery thinks so. And I'm no Sherlock Holmes, but that dog *didn't* bark.'

12

All My Friends Are Gonna
Be Strangers

Dwight Bryant was waiting for me in his official Colleton County Sheriff's Department cruiser when I drove into my parking spot beside the office next morning.

'Come ride and I'll buy you a cup of coffee,' he said. 'We need to have a little talk.'

'There's a whole pot of coffee waiting inside. I'll buy *you* a cup,' I said, trying to think what I'd done now. 'How long's this little talk going to take?'

'Depends. Half-hour?'

'Okay. Just let me tell Sherry.'

I went on into the office, dumped my briefcase on my desk, told Sherry I was going to take a quick ride with Dwight Bryant ('What've you done now?' she asked), and carried two foam cups of black coffee out to the cruiser.

Dwight's a few years older than me, and from the time he was a kid, he's hung out with my brothers so much that he tries to boss me around just like them. Has just about as much luck, too, but none of them quit trying.

Bunch of slow learners.

Dwight's also an ex-basketball player who's muscled out over the years and he filled up his whole side of the patrol car. With his sandy hair and craggy face, I had to admit he looked pretty sharp in his summer tans. The head of a detective unit usually wears regular clothes, but that doesn't stop Dwight from putting on his uniform at least once a month to cruise around the county checking things out. Probably a carryover from his years in the military. He was with Army Intelligence in DC when his marriage to Jonna went bust and he came on back home.

As soon as I was properly buckled in, we rolled out of Dobbs heading west. Dwight turned down his radio till the calls and codes were barely audible, and breathed in the coffee's fragrant aroma.

'Y'all have the best coffee of any law firm in the county.'

'Thank Julia Lee for that. She picks it up at some fancy store in Cameron Village.'

'This tastes like it's got something else in it.'

'Hazelnuts,' I said sweetly. 'And I just can't tell you how glad I am to make time in my schedule to have this fascinating discussion about coffee. You might want to come by for our vanilla creme blend sometime. Next week, Julia's promised to get us a chocolate almond that—'

'Okay, okay,' he laughed. 'What's this about somebody taking a potshot at you yesterday?'

'How'd you hear about that so quick?'

'I'm a police officer. I'm supposed to hear things quickly, remember?'

156

'Well, this time you heard wrong. I wasn't the target. If it wasn't hunters, then it was probably meant to scare Michael Vickery. He and Denn McCloy seem to be having problems.'

'You're positive you weren't the target? Now that you're poking into Janie Whitehead's death, it might be that someone's trying to scare *you*.'

'That would be a stupid thing to do.' I sipped my coffee. 'Hey, you're not worried about me, are you?'

'Janie's killer could be somebody you know,' he said sternly, 'somebody who's nervous that you might poke too close.'

'It'd be dumb to say that's silly,' I conceded. 'But honestly, Dwight, doesn't a migrant worker passing through make the most sense? Or that Janie took pity on someone hitchhiking in the rain and for some reason, what was supposed to be a lift turned violent? Obviously he didn't mean to kill her since he didn't take her money or molest her.'

(Dwight was stationed in Germany when Janie was murdered, and I wasn't sure if he knew about the red slicker.)

'First he whacked her on the head and then two days later shot her? That's not your average migrant behavior, Deb'rah. I've been to enough Saturday night brawls – hell, you've seen enough of the players in Monday morning court to know the difference.'

'Okay, okay. But even if the killer was somebody local, the SBI's already worked it twice. If they couldn't find any loose strings to pull on back then, there's no reason to think I could come up with anything new. Mainly I'm just going through the motions because Jed thinks it'll keep Gayle from bringing in some stranger.'

Dwight turned north at the next crossroads, which would head us back toward Dobbs. He finished off his coffee and set the cup in a holder between us. 'Just think about this a minute: if the killer's someone Janie knew, it might make him more nervous to have you out poking around than if it *was* a stranger.'

I heard concern in his voice. 'Hey, you really are worried about me, aren't you?'

'Not me.' As the road teed into North Twelfth Street, he gave me a mocking smile. 'You're not *my* little baby girl to worry about.'

'Oh, *shit*!'

I might have known though. Stupid of me to think I could take a stroll through woods less than a mile from my homeplace as the crow flies (or a blabbermouth walks) and not have Daddy know. 'Look, would you please make it clear to him that it really was Denn McCloy out there banging away at Michael?'

'If you say so.'

He turned up the radio to catch a code directed at someone patrolling a few miles south. Nothing urgent. We rode in silence till he coasted to a stop in front of my office door.

'How serious do you think Sheriff Poole and I ought to take what happened?' he asked as I reached for the door handle.

I shrugged. ''Bout like you'd take any domestic disturbance. Michael's not one to talk about his feelings and Denn's only too willing to talk about his. I've heard Michael goes over to Durham more than he used to, though. Without Denn.'

'Yeah. If they were straight, you'd say it's the seven-year-itch.'

'*You* might,' I jibed, opening the door. 'Everybody else these days calls it male menopause.'

'Just the same,' he said through the lowered window, 'I think I'll ride out there and have a little talk with McCloy. And listen, Deb'rah – if they're going to keep shooting at each other, would you please try to stay out from between 'em? You get hurt and your daddy's not going to be very happy with us.'

He drove away, leaving me to wonder if 'us' was Bo Poole's whole sheriff's department or just Dwight and the boys.

The only time I ever saw Daddy take a switch to the little twins was when I was twelve and they brought me home with a broken arm. It didn't matter that I'd pestered them to death to let me swing out over the creek on their rope swing. I remember being furious that he whipped them and then even more furious with them because they acted like they deserved it. Even at twelve I knew that such protection somehow diminished me.

Mother was usually my ally, but that time she made me wear dresses till the cast was off.

Tracy Johnson was calling one of my cases just as I slid into court.

I was supposed to defend a couple of indigent Haitians who'd been netted in the raid of a crack house in a trailer park off I-95. They spoke almost no English; my college French wasn't idiomatic enough to get through to them, so we'd had to wait for an interpreter to come out from Raleigh before I could get the whole story.

According to them, they'd been hitchhiking back from New York and had heard that they could find a friendly place to flop at that particular trailer. They claimed to have been sleeping the sleep of innocence when DEA agents knocked on the door with a search warrant. Their 'host' seemed to have temporarily vanished; and when the trailer was searched a half-kilo of cocaine and three grams of crack were found in a bedroom at the opposite end from the room they'd been given. Since they were the only ones there, they took the fall. And they'd been lodged in the county jail for two weeks, refusing to give their names or plead until the interpreter could get there.

Even though Harrison Hobart was hearing the case, I didn't bother asking for a jury trial. All I had to do was put everyone on the witness stand and let them tell their stories. DEA admitted he had nothing to link the drugs to these two other than their being in the trailer that night.

The two youths were quite personable once the linguist translated everything for them. Charming even. Of course it was quite clear to everyone in the courtroom that they were a couple of mules plying the north-south trade route that links Miami to New York. Tons of hard drugs pass up and down I-95, thankfully only a small percentage falls off the trucks here, though of course we're no more immune than any other area. But as I pointed out to the court, there wasn't a smidgen of evidence upon which to hold these particular two.

To his regret, Hobart had to agree.

The charming young men shook hands all around and

promised to send money from Haiti to repay the interpreter and me for our trouble.

The interpreter and I agreed we wouldn't hold our breath.

Between getting the facts translated and then fitting the actual hearing in around other cases, it was after four before I was free to leave the courthouse. As I came down the steps, I was overtaken by a tight-lipped Luther Parker.

'I thought this was to be a civilized campaign, Miss Knott,' he said coldly.

'Come again?'

He handed me a sheet of paper. 'I suppose you've never seen this.'

It looked like my personal letterhead and was headed 'An Open Letter to Concerned Voters of Judicial District 11-C.' It wasn't quite as blatant as *He's a nigger, I'm white, vote for me*, but it was the next thing to it, and it carried my signature at the bottom.

For a moment I thought I was going to throw up.

'You can't believe for a minute that I'd—'

'It's your stationery, Miss Knott, and your signature, isn't it?' he asked, his thin black face looming over me in outraged suspicion.

'Would you please cut out that "Miss Knott"? Okay, yes, this looks like my letterhead, but anybody with a copier could . . .' I examined the sheet more closely. 'Look here, Luther. This is a flat-out cut-and-paste job, a real sloppy one at that. They used the campaign letter I sent out in March and put their own mess over mine. See the cut lines here and here?'

'But then it *would* look like that, wouldn't it?' he asked.

I could see his point. If this were the sort of campaigning I'd stoop to, I'd naturally want to be able to deny it. Therefore I'd do it so crudely that it would look as if someone had doctored my original letter without my knowledge. That way, I wouldn't be blamed for sleazy politics, yet I'd have gotten the message out.

'Where did you get this?' I asked.

'They were stacked on top of every *News and Observer* box in Makely this morning,' he answered grimly.

'Oh, Lord,' I groaned. 'Let's see. When does the *Makely Weekly* go to press?'

'Noon on Thursdays.' He glanced at his watch. 'Four and a half hours ago.'

'Luther, I swear to God I know nothing about this. My sister-in-law's helping with my campaign. Let me talk to her and then, if that's what you want, I'll meet you at the *Ledger* first thing tomorrow and we'll get Linsey Thomas to run a disclaimer, okay?'

Neither of us was very happy with this solution, but we couldn't think of anything else to do.

At least Luther was back to calling me Deborah before we parted.

When I returned to the office, Sherry had put the dustcover over her computer and was ready to leave.

'Minnie's been trying to get you for the last hour,' she said, handing me a sheaf of message slips.

'I'll bet.'

'Mr John Claude and Reid—'

'Ah, Deborah,' said John Claude from the doorway of his

office. 'May Reid and I see you for a few minutes?'

Sherry discreetly left and I crossed the hall to John Claude's office. He and Reid both had angry expressions on their faces and copies of the same trash Luther had shown me in their hands.

'This is quite unconscionable,' said John Claude.

'Really stinks,' Reid agreed.

'Now wait a minute,' I said. 'You don't think I knew anything about this, do you?'

'Of course not!' John Claude snapped.

Reid handed me a gin and tonic, the gin poured with a stingy hand, the way I take it these days when I drink at all.

'John Claude thinks it's Hector Woodlief's people.'

Hector Woodlief had run unopposed on the Republican ticket in Tuesday's primary, even though the only way he could realistically expect to win in November was if the Democratic candidate was dead or under indictment for something major.

'I take it Hector Woodlief doesn't get your vote?' I asked Reid.

'Seems more likely this came from some of Luther Parker's people.'

'*What?*'

'Foolishness,' muttered John Claude.

'No, it's not!' Reid argued. 'Think about it, Deborah. This kind of crap hurts you a lot more than it hurts him. Gets the race thing right out in the open with you as the bigoted villain.'

I thought about it and then shook my head. 'No. It just doesn't compute. If Parker's that Machiavellian, wouldn't he

163

do it closer to the election for maximum impact?'

'I didn't say Parker himself; I said his people.'

'No,' I said again. 'I just spoke to Luther on the courthouse steps not ten minutes ago and he accused me of writing this. He's a good attorney, but I've never seen him try out for any of the Possum Creek Players' productions. He really and truly thought I – or somebody belonging to me anyhow – did this.'

John Claude was distressed. 'Oh, surely not.'

'I think I convinced him.' I took a deep swallow of my drink and sat down on the blue leather couch to leaf through my messages. Most were from Minnie. 'I'll talk to Minnie tonight and I told Luther I'd meet him in Linsey Thomas's office tomorrow morning so we can issue a joint statement.'

John Claude shook his head pessimistically. 'Reid's right, I'm afraid. This does have the potential to harm you more than it harms Parker.'

Supper with Minnie and Seth brought us to pretty much the same conclusion.

I'd driven over to the modern farmhouse they'd built on the northwest side of the Grimes place – still called that even though Daddy'd bought it at auction back in the early sixties when North Carolina's short-staple cotton took a double blow from polyesters and boll weevils. Farm acreage was going dirt cheap then, but even if it'd been high, Daddy still would have bid it in since it bounded his own land. He'd deeded it to Seth for a wedding present and Seth seemed to be doing pretty good with tobacco, sweet potatoes, and soy beans.

Minnie's in her midforties, old enough to be accepting of people and their shortcomings, yet wise to how they enjoy scandalous gossip. She was seriously disturbed over the potential damage the scurrilous flyer could do and had sent the kids off for pizza over in Cotton Grove so we could talk without the distraction of TV or stereos.

'I just wish you didn't have to give it more publicity with a *Ledger* story,' she said.

'I don't see that I have much choice,' I said as Seth poured steaming cups of coffee all around after supper.

'No,' Minnie sighed. 'But right now, not that many people know about it. I called around the whole district. Makely's the only place they were distributed.'

We went over it and over it from every angle, then worked on my statement until my nieces and nephews came home.

As I drove through Cotton Grove on my way home to Dobbs, I passed by the neat house on the edge of town that my brother Will had once shared with Trish. It was still early, barely dark good; and through the thick trees, I saw that a light was on in Trish's living room.

I braked with such abruptness that the pickup behind almost rear-ended me. Well, what the hell, I thought. Talking with Trish about Janie Whitehead would at least make a change from worrying about my campaign.

13

Daytime Friends And
Nighttime Lovers

Will's ex-wife is a vice president in charge of customer service at my bank in Dobbs, so I've run into her frequently over the years. We're friendly enough, but I hadn't been in her house since Mother died.

Mother was what everyone called a 'good woman' (as distinct from 'a good ol' gal') even though I realized right before she died that a narrow streak of wildness lay just beneath her surface serenity. Most of the time she kept it repressed, but when it got out of hand . . . well, that little streak of wildness was what took her off to Goldsboro during World War II and what later made her want to marry a widowed bootlegger with a houseful of motherless boys after the war.

Nine times out of ten, a good woman does exactly what her family and society expect of her.

That tenth time? Better stand back out of her way.

She'll burn down her world just for the hell of it, or risk

everything she's worked a lifetime for on pure-out whimsy.

A similar streak in Trish is probably why Mother liked her and stayed friends even after the divorce. Not that she didn't do everything in her power to talk my brother out of marrying Trish.

'I thought you liked her,' Will said plaintively when he first started talking engagement rings.

'Liking has nothing to do with it,' said Mother. 'I just don't believe you two are suited.'

'Who's not?' he asked. 'Me for her or her for me?'

Mother just shook her head. She never said another word against the match once it was made, and she never said 'I told you so' when it came unmade after two and a half years.

As I pulled into the driveway behind Trish's conservative white Japanese import, I found myself wondering for the first time in years what actually had gone wrong with their marriage. Will just tightened his mouth and we assumed he'd caught Trish in bed with someone since he was the one that wanted out. There'd been talk of her having round heels, but no one specific had ever been named.

Even after the divorce, when she could have been a little less discreet, there'd been no stories of some man's car parked all night in her driveway. True, she and Kay Saunders had spent a lot of weekends down at the beach that year, and everybody knows what kind of messing around two women off the leash can do, especially at the beach; but Kay was going through a rough time with Fred. He'd always cheated on Kay; that summer he quit trying to hide it.

Divorce can be a contagious virus and we half expected

that Fred and Kay's marriage might go bust too, but somehow they kept it going. Last I heard, they were still together, living in Maryland somewhere.

The front drape moved a finger's width, then Trish opened the door.

'Well, I'll be darned! Deborah? Come on in!' She stood back to let me pass.

Time had been nice to her. She had to be early forties, yet her reddish-blonde hair fell softly around a smooth face, her breasts were still firm inside a cotton peasant blouse, her legs as magnificent as ever in cut-off jeans. She was barefooted, and I smelled the open bottle of nail polish on the coffee table just as I noticed that seven of her toes sported glistening pink polish.

On the couch sat another woman, in white slacks, tailored apricot silk shirt, and gold-tooled thongs. Short dark hair, green eyes, probably in her late thirties. Her triangular catlike features were softened by the few extra pounds she carried.

'You and Margie know each other, don't you?' asked Trish, and when I shook my head, she introduced us. 'Deborah Knott, Margie McGranahan. Margie works in our Makely branch. Deborah's my ex's sister.'

'Oh, yes,' said the woman with a smile. 'You're running for judge. Congratulations on your win Tuesday.'

'Thanks,' I said, taking a chair opposite. 'I like your sandals.'

Other women notice jewelry. I always notice shoes.

'These old things?' She stretched out a shapely foot and I saw that her toenails had been freshly painted in the same

169

pink shade as Trish's. 'I got these on sale at the end of last summer. At the Bigg Shopp, of all places.'

She capped the nail polish and slid it across the coffee table to Trish, then began gathering up her purse, car keys, and a folder of papers.

'Did I interrupt?' I asked, noticing the opened bottle of wine and nearly empty glasses.

'No, no,' Trish reassured me. 'Margie was just leaving. We did all we were going to do tonight.'

'My husband had to work late,' Margie explained, 'so this was a good time for us to talk and catch up on some bank mess, but I really do need to get on home. When do you want to let's try and finish this, Trish? Monday night?'

Trish had drifted over to the front door and opened it. 'How about I give you a call when I see how things are working out?'

'Fine. Nice meeting you, Deborah,' said Margie. 'And good luck in the runoff.'

She glanced out the open door and hesitated. 'I'm afraid you've got me blocked in.'

'Oh, is that your car?' I was surprised. 'I thought it was Trish's.'

'No, mine's in the garage,' said Trish.

'But isn't it the same model?'

'Yes, isn't that a funny coincidence? I reckon you *were* confused.'

As I backed my car out of the driveway so Margie McGranahan could leave, I had a vague sense of déjà vu, yet no matter how I grabbed for that tag end of subconsciousness, the whole memory wouldn't come.

Margie tapped her horn in thanks and sped off toward Makely as I pulled back into the drive.

Since Cotton Grove's town limits were less than a thousand feet away, streetlights were few and far between out here. The trees had matured amazingly since I last stood in Trish's yard. Coupled with the overgrown shrubbery all around, the place was effectively shielded from its neighbors on either side and had an unexpected sense of privacy for a town lot. The moon hadn't yet risen, but Jupiter shone with a steady white fire in the western sky in competition with all the other bright points now pricking through the darkness.

'How about some wine?' asked Trish as I followed her back into the softly lit house.

'No thanks, but I could sure use some iced tea.'

Every refrigerator in the South holds a jug or half-gallon jar of strong sweet tea, and Trish's was no exception.

I trailed her out to the kitchen and sat down at her breakfast table while she poured us both tea and then began stacking the dishwasher with the things she and Margie had dirtied at supper. She'd redone the room completely. Everything was blue-and-white gingham and white ruffles. Very feminine.

'Haven't seen much of you these last few years,' said Trish. 'What've you been up to? Besides work and running for judge, I mean?'

'You mean how's my love life?'

She laughed. 'Well, I was going to work up to that more subtle-like. I heard you were seeing Jed Whitehead again.'

'Who on earth told you that?'

A fork clattered to the blue-tiled floor and she stooped for it gracefully. One side of the loose scooped-neck blouse

171

slipped off her shoulder and she pulled it up absent-mindedly. 'Let me think. It was either Toni Bledsoe or Ina Jean Freeman, I forget which. Whichever it was said she saw you leaving some political dinner or something with Jed. Was she wrong?'

'No, I did ride home with him, but that was to talk about Gayle. I'm not actually seeing him.'

'Why not? I remember what a crush you used to have on him.'

'God! Was it all that obvious back then?' First Scotty Underhill, now Trish.

'Not really.' She finished stacking the plates, closed the dishwasher, and then sat down across the table from me. 'I probably wouldn't have noticed only Janie thought it was so cute.'

'*Cute?*' A brand-new wave of mortification washed over me. 'Oh, Lord! Janie said that?'

Trish looked uncomfortable.

'What else?' I demanded.

'Well,' she said reluctantly, picking invisible crumbs off the blue tablecloth. 'You know how you used to go over and help out before the baby was born? And then all that cheap babysitting after? Janie said that you'd probably work for nothing if Jed could just get himself home early enough to drive you back to the farm every evening.'

I could almost hear Janie's ripple of laughter and for the first time in years I felt lumpish and homely again, the way I always got whenever I compared myself to her.

'I don't know if you remember, but I tried to warn you,' said Trish. 'She could be a real bitch, Janie.'

'Is that why you broke up with her?' I blurted.

Trish frowned. 'Broke up?'

'Why you quit being friends with her. You and Kay Saunders and Janie used to run around a lot together, and then a couple of weeks before she died, it was likes y'all had never met.'

She stood abruptly. 'Look at me! I forgot to turn on the dishwasher.'

As she started to measure detergent and rearrange the load, I went down the hall to the bathroom. It was tacky, still, long as I was there and already snooping, I checked out her medicine cabinet. There was an extra toothbrush, but no condoms, no birth control pills, no shaving lotion or aftershave. Trish's love life must be in even worse shape than mine, I decided.

The dishwasher was chugging and Trish was wiping cabinets and cleaning the sink when I returned to the kitchen.

'You don't have time for another glass of tea, do you?'

'Sure,' I said cheerfully, ignoring the delicate hint to say thanks, but I probably ought to be getting on home. 'So why *did* y'all quit being friends?'

'I don't really remember. It was so long ago.' She poured us both fresh glasses of tea, added several ice cubes and said, 'Let's go to the living room where it's quieter.'

We carried our glasses inside, away from the noisy dishwasher. Trish immediately uncapped the nail polish, propped her foot on the coffee table, and returned to the three toenails that had been left undone. As the smell of acetone filled the room, she started to inquire about some of my farther-flung family, but I interrupted.

'Look, Trish, I didn't ask about you and Kay and Janie just to be nosy. Gayle's asked me to do an informal investigation – find out what was going on in Janie's head back then, see if any of it had to do with why she was killed.'

She finished with her toes. A hair clip was lying on the end table and she gathered her long strawberry-blonde hair up into a loose knot on top of her head. 'Aren't you a little old to be playing Nancy Drew, Girl Detective?'

'It's not much different from what I do now when I take depositions from witnesses before a trial,' I said stiffly.

'But I didn't witness anything to do with her death.'

'How do you know? Maybe y'all's fight triggered something.'

'No.' She shook her head vigorously.

I pounced on her unspoken admission. 'But you *did* have a fight?'

'It wasn't really a fight and I don't want to talk about it.'

'But why?'

She stood up purposefully. 'I was awfully glad to see you here again, Deborah, but right now, I think you ought to go.'

'Okay.' Frustrated and puzzled, I stood too. 'I didn't mean to make you mad, Trish. I don't see why you can't tell me, but if that's the way you feel—'

'I'm sorry,' she said as she moved toward the door, 'but it is.'

'Then how about giving me Kay Saunders's address? Maybe she'll tell me what happened.'

The idea seemed to amuse Trish. 'I doubt it. Anyway, I don't have it. We don't even exchange Christmas cards anymore.'

'Really?' Somehow that surprised me more than anything else that evening. 'But you were so close.'

'Fred didn't approve of me,' she said dryly. 'Good night, Deborah. Come back some time when you're tired of digging up all the dirt about Janie Whitehead.'

Interesting, I thought as I went down the walk to my car. *Digging up all the dirt?* Surely that said there was dirt to be dug.

I put my key in the ignition, but before I turned it, the memory that had nagged at me earlier finally came bobbing like a cork to the surface of my mind: Mother and I had pulled into this same driveway that spring behind what we thought was Trish's blue Ford sedan. A few minutes later, we discovered that Kay was there, too, and the blue Ford in the drive was hers. Trish's was in the garage. I'd had to go out and move our station wagon when Kay was ready to leave.

And Janie had owned an identical blue Ford sedan.

I sat with my hand on the key, struggling to put the pieces together, pieces that had to mean something.

Three young wives, three identical cars.

Now Trish drove a white Japanese import.

So did Mrs Margie McGranahan.

Coincidence?

Suddenly I felt really stupid. It had been there all along. Even my subconscious had recognized it when I slipped in my choice of words earlier. Of course there were no condoms or aftershave in Trish's medicine cabinet. Or birth control pills either, for that matter.

I got back out of my car and knocked on the door again.

Trish opened it warily. 'I thought you were gone.'

I looked at her in a new light. That sensuous body. The sexy blouse that kept sliding off her shoulder. The soft light, wineglasses, and half-painted toenails, only it had been Margie McGranahan who had wielded the open bottle of polish.

'No wonder no one ever saw a man's car parked here all night,' I said. 'Do you limit yourself to married women?'

Trish sighed. 'Maybe you'd better come back in,' she said.

14

I'm That Kind Of Girl

In the end, we opened another bottle of wine and carried it out to the back deck and talked from the time the moon rose, swollen and orange, till it sailed like a flat white dime in the midnight sky.

'Well, of *course* Will wouldn't tell anybody about it,' said Trish as crickets filled the night air with their stridulations. 'Put yourself in his place. How could a man like Will admit he wasn't stud enough to keep his wife from getting it on with another woman?'

'Were you always—'

'AC/DC?' She smiled at my reticence. 'Hard to say. I was certainly sexually aware of boys from the time I was ten, but I always had close girlfriends, too. Kay and I'd known each other since first grade. We double-dated in high school, all that sort of schoolgirl thing – pajama parties, comparing bodies when we started to mature, you remember. But the summer right before our senior year, I spent the weekend at her house while her parents were out of town. We'd bought us a couple of six-packs – Kay could pass for legal drinking age, especially if it was a man at the cash register – and after our dates went home at eleven, just like we'd promised our parents, we sat out on a quilt in her backyard to watch the meteor showers and got a good buzz on. That's how I remember it was August. The meteors.'

There were no meteors in this May sky tonight. Only an occasional plane, blinking red and green lights as it headed toward the Raleigh-Durham Airport.

Trish filled our glasses again and there was rueful amusement in her voice. 'If we hadn't been such nice, obedient daughters, we'd have had the boys out there on the quilt with us and maybe the other would never have happened.

'Anyhow, my new bra was cutting into me and I pulled up my blouse to unhook it and the hooks were too tight so Kay leaned over to help me and then . . . I still don't know quite how it began. Her hand touched my breast as delicately as a flower. Then she kissed the other, so sweetly. So gently. And everything followed as if preordained. It felt like the most natural thing in the world, so much better than the way boys fumbled with my clothes or humped themselves against me when they kissed me good night. It was the first time for both of us and it was heaven. We even had meteors putting on a light show, streaking through the sky!'

She shook her head fondly at the absurdity of it all.

'Of course, next morning, we both had heads the size of basketballs and we couldn't handle what had happened, so we tried to pretend it really hadn't, and we made sure we didn't have any more two-girl sleep overs. Not till we both were married. You remember how Will and Fred were such good friends? Well, about a year before Janie died, Will and I spent a long weekend at the beach with Fred and Kay. The guys had to come back Sunday night to go to work, but Kay and I stayed down there till Monday afternoon. And that time, we did know what we were doing.'

There was a long silence. I watched lightning bugs drift across her deck on the mild night air. Trish's yard backed up on Forty-Eight's right-of-way, and though sounds and lights were muffled or blocked by a thick stand of trees and bushes, we could still hear the sparse weeknight traffic as cars swished back and forth intermittently.

'Where did Janie fit in?' I asked.

'Kay and I used to talk about that.' Trish sipped her wine with a meditative air. 'We finally decided that Janie wanted to play with fire without – not getting burned, exactly – more like not admitting it was even fire. All three of us had been cheerleaders at Dobbs Senior, but it wasn't till after we were married and living here in Cotton Grove that she actually started hanging out with us. I don't think she consciously knew until right at the end that Kay and I had become lovers, but she certainly sensed there was something special between us, a force field or something, and it drove her crazy because it made her feel left out and jealous. She could be so high school at times, that "You like her better than you like me" sort of thing, you know?'

I nodded.

'Take the cars. You ever hear how that started?'

'Not that I remember.'

'It was sort of ironic. Will was auctioning off a fleet of

company cars for some business that had gone bankrupt. I needed a new car about then, so he got Fred to bid on one for me. Well, Fred decided it was such a good deal, he bid on one for Kay. At first we were put out with them for getting us two identical cars, but later we realized that it meant people couldn't drive by our houses and automatically know if we were in there together, maybe spending more time together than most married women did.

'Janie thought we did it on purpose and she got one as near like ours as she could find. The front bumpers were a little different, but you didn't notice it in a casual glance.'

'It's hard to think of somebody as shrewd as Janie being that naïve,' I said.

'Isn't it?' Trish asked dryly. 'Near the end, she was bored with Jed and out of sorts with herself and with her body. We used to give her back rubs and massages while she was pregnant, and she'd talk about wanting to nurse the baby, so she used to rub her nipples with cocoa butter to toughen them up like the book said. It must have been erotic for Janie – she was always finding a reason to take off her top, and she did have nice breasts – but Kay and I weren't interested in a group grope, so it was all pretty platonic as far as we were concerned.'

'But it stopped being platonic a week or so before she died, right?'

'You could say that, yes.'

She filled her glass again, and the bottle gleamed in the moonlight when she held it out to me, but I shook my head.

'I'd better nurse this one if I'm going to drive back to Dobbs,' I said regretfully.

'You could stay over.'

'Thanks, but—'

'The guest room has a lock on the door.'

I laughed and she laughed, too, a slightly tipsy chuckle that seemed to bubble up from a generous heart.

'Where was I?'

'Where it stopped being platonic.'

'Right. After Gayle was born, Janie nursed her about two weeks while her uterus contracted, then decided it was too much of a drag. Now, that's not what she told Jed and the grandparents, but that's what it was. She felt like a cow that got milked every two hours, and she was afraid of her breasts sagging, but mostly it was that if she nursed, then she couldn't dump Gayle on her mother or you whenever she wanted.'

Gayle must have been about three weeks old the first time Janie went out and left her with me the whole afternoon. At sixteen, being left alone with that tiny creature – *Jed's baby!* – had seemed such a privilege, such a demonstration of trust. Now Trish made it clear that Janie would've entrusted Gayle to anybody who could warm a bottle without melting it.

'We'd been shopping and we came back here to try everything on the way we did in those days, see what really fit, what we were going to keep, what we'd probably take back. Janie started bitching again about how hard it was to get back into shape, even though it'd been almost three months. Just look at how her breasts were still swollen and look at that layer of fat around her waist. "Look at this, look at that," till Kay and I started laughing because we knew what she was really doing. Kay said, "Oh, the poor little fatty, fatty, two-by-four," and tickled her in the ribs. That set us off. We got the silly giggles, and soon we were rolling around on the rug in our underwear and we could see that Janie was getting excited, so-o . . .'

Moonlight bathed her soft bare shoulders in silver as she left the details to my imagination.

'We had a dog once that used to start begging every time he saw any of us with a piece of candy,' I said. 'Used to worry the little twins and me to death if we didn't give him any, and of course, he wasn't supposed to have sugar. One day we were sitting on the back porch with a bag of those big nickel red-hots and one of the twins tossed me one, but the dog jumped up and grabbed it in midair and ran off under the house with it. He took one crunch and it burned his mouth so badly that he went flying for his water dish with his tail between his legs and you better believe he never wanted another piece of candy again.'

Trish laughed. 'Yeah, that was Janie, all right. She started calling us dykes and whores till Kay pushed her down on the bed and told her to shut her mouth. "You wanted it," Kay said. "You've been wanting it for months and you still want it, only you're too scared to admit it. Too afraid of what people would say if they knew. Well, nobody outside this room ever has to. But, honeychile, *we* know and so do you!"'

'It must have scared the hell out of her,' I mused, turning the stem of the wineglass in my fingers.

'Just like your dog,' Trish agreed as she emptied the last of the wine into her own glass. 'Went yipping off to hide behind her sister's skirts and pretend she was straight as a man's cock. I bet Jed got some of the best loving that week that he'd had all year.'

It was nearly midnight. Most of the traffic had dwindled away to nothing out on the highway. I stretched out my legs, propped them on the deck railing, and asked, 'Who killed her, Trish?'

'Well, to tell you the truth, honey, I used to wonder if it might not be some married man here in town. If Janie needed to prove to herself that she was straight through and through, she might have come on too strongly to somebody and then – just like with Kay and me – maybe tried to weasel out in the end, only he wouldn't let her.'

Whenever a sentence starts with 'to tell you the truth,' I automatically look for the underlying prevarication. '*Which* married man?'

'Oh, hell, Deb'rah. It could have been a dozen different men.'

'Name me some names.'

She was just tipsy enough to do it. Some of them I didn't recognize, others were no longer in the area, the rest were all respectable, middle-aged-to-elderly pillars of the community now. As I ran their faces through my memory, she drained her wineglass, then added two more names: 'And of course, let us not forget my future ex-husband or Fred Saunders.'

15

Somebody Lied

The *Ledger* may be the county's oldest continuous newspaper, but it's housed in a modern structure, a small boxy cube that's slightly canted on its lot next to a former tobacco warehouse that's now a weekend flea market. The exterior's sheathed in cedar shingles that have been stained a dark greenish gray. There are times, especially in deep summer, when the building almost disappears into its plantings of birch and fir. The illusion is further enhanced by the front sheet of glass that lets people gaze straight into a central garden planted with small deciduous trees so that it's shady in summer yet flooded with sunlight all winter, a neat piece of passive solar planning.

Everybody goes ape over gracious old traditional houses, but I grew up in one and I'm here to tell you they cost a fortune to heat and cool, and they're a bitch to clean. If I ever build a house of my own, I'm going to steal Linsey Thomas's blueprints.

Luther Parker was just getting out of his car when I pulled up in front of the *Ledger* building shortly before eight-thirty. The paper goes to press at eleven on Fridays, and we wanted to make sure Linsey had time to put together an accurate account.

As Luther held the door for me, the receptionist, who doubled as Linsey's secretary, looked at the phone she was holding and then at us with an air of confusion. 'Miss Knott! I was just phoning you. Mr Thomas was hoping—'

She flipped an intercom button. 'Mr Thomas? Miss Knott just walked in.'

Almost immediately, he appeared at the door of his office down at the right corner of the atrium. A tall fit man, midforties with a hairline that had receded all the way past the crown of his head, and proud possessor of the world's ugliest moustache, Linsey Thomas had learned to talk while toddling around the press shop behind his grandmother, and his voice had never toned down to normal levels.

'Deborah!' he shouted, big brown eyes gleaming behind shiny rimless glasses. He gestured for us to hurry on down the hall. 'You must have read my mind. Mr Parker, I'm Linsey Thomas. We met at the Harvey Gantt breakfast last month.'

He thrust out his hand to a disconcerted Luther Parker, who murmured, 'Yes, of course,' evidently unaware that this was one editor who honestly never expected people to remember his name, his megaphone manner of speaking, or his bushy moustache.

He swept us into his office. Half of one wall was a floor-to-ceiling window that looked directly into the heart of the atrium. Unfortunately, its tranquilizing effect was wrecked by the piles of books and papers stacked on every surface, even lining the floor along the baseboards. Before we could find empty chairs, he was waving a crumpled sheet of paper in our faces.

'I want to know whose scrofulous sphincter excreted this scurrilous piece of filth?'

(No one has ever heard Linsey Thomas actually curse, but that certainly doesn't mean his mind is pure and virginal, merely that he learned hundreds of synonyms from the same grandmother who wrote my grandfather's obituary.)

'That's what we came to discuss,' I said as I tipped books out of the nearest chair and sat down. 'I have no idea who sent out that garbage in my name.'

'Huh? What in all the sulfuric flames you talking about?' he boomed. 'I was addressing my remarks to Mr Parker here.'

'Wait a minute.' I reached for the paper he kept waving around. 'This isn't my letterhead.'

'Who said it was?'

Luther Parker was too polite to dump a chair full of books on the floor, but he seemed to have no scruples about reading over my shoulder. Evidently he read faster than I did, because I was only halfway through the first sentence when he began spluttering.

This one was on *his* letterhead and it was almost a duplicate of the one circulated in Makely the day before, only this time, the beast with seven horns that Judicial District 11-C was being warned about was *me*.

If one could believe everything in this open letter, Luther

Parker was an upright, foursquare Christian family man who sang with the angels when he wasn't defending Truth, Justice, and the American Way. Ms Deborah Knott, on the other hand, was an unmarried (a) castrating bitch (b) promiscuous whore, or (c) closet lesbian (pick one), the daughter of the biggest bootlegger in Colleton County history, and a defender of foreign drug dealers from whom she was probably getting a cut of the profits. 'If *Ms* Knott is elected to the bench, it will be speedy trials and speedier acquittals for drunks, junkies, and perverts of all kinds.'

'They were on nearly every *News and Observer* box in Dobbs,' said Linsey in his dulcet, window-rattling tones. 'Not the ones here on Main Street, but all the out-of-the-way places where there's not much nighttime traffic.'

He sat behind his desk and twisted a few hairs of his exuberant moustache while reading the flyer with my letterhead. As soon as he'd finished, he swiveled over and flicked the intercom. 'Hey, Ashley,' he shouted. 'Get me Hector Woodlief, okay?'

I don't know why he bothered with the intercom since his door was still open.

'Hold on there a minute,' Luther objected. 'You don't want to involve Woodlief. Even if he had a hand in it, you sure we want to remind voters there's a Republican alternative?'

'Smart thinking,' Linsey agreed. 'Ashley? Cancel that call.' He swiveled back to us. 'But if it's not Woodlief, who else benefits?'

'Correct me if I'm wrong,' I said tightly, 'but I seem to be the only one with serious damage here and I get it coming *and* going. In one I'm a redneck racist, in the other I'm the devil's mouthpiece for organized crime. Mr Parker's accused of being black. Period.'

He acted like he was fixing to protest, but Linsey was nodding in thoughtful agreement, and after a moment's consideration, Luther nodded, too. 'I'm afraid you're right,' he said.

'You don't sound terribly sorrowful,' I observed. 'And the *Ledger* endorsed you, didn't it? Tell me, Linsey. Am I being set up here?'

Both men acted genuinely shocked that I could even consider such a possibility, but when challenged to produce another person who benefited from those two letters, their one pitiful candidate was Hector Woodlief. Yes, Hector files for some office or other almost every election, but it's just to keep Democrats honest. He's never really campaigned and would hardly begin with this sort of dirty trick.

We briefly discussed our two primary opponents who'd come in third and fourth. Sour grapes?

I didn't think so.

In the end, I reluctantly agreed to a story that downplayed specifics and appealed to voter intelligence and sense of fair play when confronted with obviously phony campaign literature.

Sure.

Back at the office, I called Minnie and told her the depressing news. Her initial outrage and indignation quickly gave way to a practical curiosity as to who was behind the flyers and why.

'Makely Wednesday night, Dobbs last night. Sounds like a one-man job. Wonder where he'll strike tonight? Cotton Grove?'

As I hung up the phone, I heard John Claude talking to Sherry and walked out to show them the latest, but John Claude already had a copy in his hand. I told him of my meeting at the paper and he gave a pointed look at the grandfather clock beneath the stairs.

'The first issues of the *Ledger* should be rolling off the press in about twenty minutes. I suggest we take the rest of the day off. Sherry can turn on our answering machine. Most of the novelty should have worn off by Monday. Have a nice weekend, Deborah.'

16

Back Where I Come From

There were fish fries I should be attending, voters' hands I should be shaking, probably even babies somewhere in the district that I should be kissing, but with those flyers kiting around and the *Ledger* due out in Dobbs any minute, I wanted an afternoon off. I wanted to forget lawyering and campaigning, to just get outdoors and—

As soon as I got that far, I knew exactly how I wanted to spend the next few hours. Soon I was in jeans and sneakers heading west toward Cotton Grove. On the way out of town I stopped at a bait store for some night crawlers. All I needed was a cane pole sticking out my rear window with a red bobber, and I figured I could borrow one of those from my brother Seth. I just wanted to go sit on a pond bank and watch a cork bobble on the surface of flat water.

Halfway there though, I had a sudden thought and pulled in at M.Z. Dupree's Cash Grocery.

It was one of those small crossroads general stores that

sell a little bit of everything: clotheslines, plumbing and electrical supplies, tin buckets, canned meats, bread and milk. There was a hoop of deep orange rat cheese on the counter by the cash register, glass bottles in the drink box, and just three fuel pumps out front: regular, high-test, and kerosene. In cold or rainy weather, there'd be four or five pickups nosed in toward the door. On a beautiful May afternoon like this, however, the place was deserted. All those pickup owners were out on huge green tractors, cleaning grass from their tobacco, corn, or cotton.

'Hey, Mr M.Z., you doing all right?' I said to the owner, an elderly thin man whom I'd never seen dressed in anything but a white long-sleeved cotton shirt and a pair of blue overalls.

'Can't complain. How 'bout you?'

As many times as I'd stopped in at that store, I was never quite sure if he remembered from one time to the next who I was, even though one of my campaign handbills with my picture on it was thumbtacked beside his door.

'I can't complain either,' I said, setting a package of cheese Nabs and an ice-cold Pepsi on the counter. Lunch.

'Wouldn't do us no good if we did grumble, would it?' He smiled. 'Now's this gonna be all for you today, young lady?'

'I need ten dollars' worth of high-test, and you reckon I could use your phone, please?'

'Ain't long-distance, is it?'

'No, sir.'

'Well then, you just help yourself,' he said; and while he went out to fill my gas tank, I made a quick call to ask if Dr Vickery would let me visit on such short notice.

The maid returned to say that Dr Vickery would expect me with pleasure.

When I was a child, Dr Vickery had his office behind the drugstore, so I'd never been in this fancy house built by his wife's father. It was all Persian rugs and Queen Anne furniture and smelled of lemon oil and beeswax as the maid led me down the central hall, through a formal parlor replete with grand piano and gilt-framed oil paintings of big tree-filled landscapes, then out onto a lovely brick terrace. At one end a trellis arched on Grecian columns above some wicker chairs and tables and shaded them with the same climbing yellow roses I'd seen out at Michael Vickery's barn. The maid deposited me there as Mrs Vickery stood up from her ministrations to a stunning iris border.

Dr Vickery immediately came around the corner with a pair of pruning clippers.

They were of equal height. As a child, though, I'd always thought of Mrs Vickery as much taller. Probably because she'd been what folks used to call a fine figure of a woman: big boned and stoutly built with strong, well-fleshed arms and legs. These days she was still tall, but flesh had dwindled from her frame until now her good Dancy bones were starkly revealed. Now it was Dr Vickery who looked taller and more vigorously full of life's juices.

Mrs Vickery wore a large straw hat, a trapezoidal garment of blue linen that was a designer version of Aunt Zell's gardening duster, and white canvas gloves, which she did not remove as she greeted me and offered refreshment. When I refused, she nodded briskly and said, 'As your business is with my husband, I'm sure you'll forgive me if I continue weeding? Chickweed's about to take this bed.'

'Certainly,' I murmured, though I could see almost nothing out of place among those regal stalks of blue, yellow, and royal purple.

Nevertheless, she shifted a green vinyl-covered kneeling pad a few feet over and knelt down to extirpate invisible sprouts. Her glass wall was less obvious than her son's, but unmistakable all the same.

'Are you sure you won't take a glass of tea?' asked Dr Vickery as he joined me under the trellised roses. He brushed fallen yellow petals from his chair with his own canvas gloves, then laid the gloves on the glass-topped table where an earthenware pitcher sat beside a matching ice bucket. Both were glazed with Michael Vickery's trademark green. Dr Vickery filled a tumbler with ice cubes, poured the ubiquitous amber tea over it, and held it out to me, but I smelled something much stronger than tea on his breath.

'No, thank you,' I smiled.

As had my brothers, I'd flourished like a green bay tree all the days of my childhood, so my memories of doctor visits were limited to periodical booster shots and the odd sprain or broken bone. He'd been an aloof, no-nonsense doctor who treated his patients' offspring because there was no pediatrician in town, not because he was 'so good with children,' and I felt no warm folksy glow at seeing him again now that I was grown. He'd sold his practice at least fifteen years ago, but he was still trim and dapper. Like Michael, he'd aged well and remained a handsome man, despite the wrinkles in his face and the liver spots on his bony hands. There was a jaded glint in those pale blue eyes that peered out at me from beneath the rim of an old sun-faded canvas boating hat.

Suddenly I had a clear memory of someone's disapproving voice: *'There was that good woman a-prayin' in the garden with Michael and the girls while that fornicator was upstairs a-packin' his bag to go to the beach with his newest girlfriend.'* A white voice, but uneducated. One of Daddy's tobacco-barning crew who'd once helped the Vickery maids here with some of the heavy cleaning? I couldn't put a face to the voice, but it seemed as if I'd known forever that Dr Vickery had never been overly faithful.

Perhaps that's why I wasn't surprised when Trish put his name on her list the night before.

Still, with Mrs Evelyn Dancy Vickery kneeling in her iris border less than twenty feet away, I could hardly ask him if Janie had thrown herself at him.

'How may I help you, Miss Deborah?' His tone was playfully gallant as he skirted the problem of how to address someone he'd treated as a child, someone who might be a professional yet had never become a Vickery equal.

I plunged right in and explained how Gayle had commissioned me to look into her mother's last few weeks of life. 'You were her doctor, weren't you?'

'Oh my, no. Does her daughter have that mistaken opinion?'

'I just assumed since she lived next door—'

'Ah, I see. A natural mistake.' He held the full glass of tea in lightly clasped hands. Moisture beaded up on his glass and dripped on the bricks beside his shoes.

'No, Janie Whitehead came from Dobbs, and I'm almost certain she continued with her family doctor there. Dr Brewer,

I believe. Dead now, of course, I did occasionally treat Jed Whitehead, and I was the first to examine the baby when they found her since her own pediatrician was in Raleigh. Shocking condition!'

He shook his head in wonder. 'Amazing, the resilience of the human infant. I scratch my arm and it takes ten days to heal. Scratch an infant and you'd be hard put to find the mark twenty-four hours later.'

He took a deep drink and set the glass on the table.

'But you did see the Whiteheads occasionally?' I persisted. 'Besides Jed, I mean. Their yard did touch yours.'

The lush spring greenery at the back of their grounds completely blocked any view beyond, but I knew that poky little rental house was still there.

'No, I can't say I did,' Dr Vickery answered promptly.

Mrs Vickery's weeding had brought her within earshot again.

'What about you, Evelyn?' he asked. 'Did you have occasion to speak to Janie Whitehead in a neighborly fashion?'

'Only to ask that she discourage her baby-sitters from annoying Michael,' she answered coolly.

She didn't look up from her task. If your radar's working, you don't have to see flames to know when you've scored a direct hit.

Dr Vickery appeared unaware of her intent. 'Annoying Michael?' he queried.

'That was the spring he painted the picture over the mantel in the breakfast room. My tulips.'

'Ah, yes. Your tulips. But how was he annoyed?'

'Don't be dense, Charles. Don't you recall how he hated

to have us speak to him when he was concentrating on his art?'

'But surely a young man in the springtime will excuse in a young woman what's inexcusable in his parents?'

She rocked back on her heels and glared at him, and I wondered if he'd somehow managed to delude himself about Michael? Then I saw by the bland smile on his cruel lips that he wasn't the one who yearned to be deluded.

I never liked *Who's Afraid of Virginia Woolf?* and I broke the tension by asking, 'What about Howard Grimes?'

'Who?' He turned his handsome head to me courteously and Mrs Vickery went back to her weeding.

'The man who saw someone in the car with Janie the day she disappeared.' Without going into details, I told him how I'd reviewed the circumstances of Janie's murder with the SBI. 'The agent said you were his doctor at the time of his death seven years ago. I thought you'd retired much earlier.'

'I continued to see a selected few of my patients who didn't want to change,' he said. 'Howard Grimes was one of them.'

'And he really did have a serious heart condition?'

'Like many a man in Colleton County, Howard Grimes thought he could eat all the salt-cured ham, fried chicken, or hot buttered biscuits he could cram in his mouth, so yes, ma'am, he did have a serious heart condition. Long as he took his pills and watched his diet, he was just fine. Trouble with men like Howard, they can't help digging their graves with their own teeth.'

He patted his own flat stomach complacently.

'Well, different men have different appetites, don't they?' I said sweetly.

It didn't faze him. 'Some appetites are healthier than others, Miss Deborah,' he smiled. 'Everything in moderation.'

Mrs Vickery stood abruptly and picked up her kneeling pad. 'If you will excuse me, Miss Knott?'

There were two bright spots of color in her cheeks, and even though she'd been snide about my futile attempt to flirt with Michael, I still had to admire her self-control. Been me, I'd have smashed the pitcher over the bastard's head.

Without waiting for my ritual reply, she marched straight-backed down the terrace and through a set of french doors at the far end.

'Three kids, three fucks,' he murmured after her, so softly that I wasn't sure I was meant to hear. Then he turned to me with his heartless smile. 'Now, you sure I can't pour you a glass of tea, Miss Deborah?'

After that, it was a relief to get out to Seth and Minnie's, where I found them together in the den, amiably bickering over the fertilizer figures they were inputting on their computerized farm records.

'Oh, good,' Minnie greeted me. 'I tried to call you back, but I just kept getting y'all's answering machine.'

'John Claude thought we might as well close early before the paper came out and wait for things to calm down over the weekend. 'Course, if there's going to be a new batch of those goddamned flyers every morning—'

'That's what I wanted to talk to you about,' Minnie beamed. 'Your brother's come up with an absolutely brilliant idea.'

Seth swiveled around from his computer screen, leaned back in the leather chair, and said, 'I don't know how brilliant it is, but it seems to me since it's Friday night and all the kids are going to be cruising around anyhow, we might as well tell 'em to keep their eyes open.'

'I've already been on the phone to Haywood and Jack,' said Minnie, 'and I left a message on Herman's machine. We can have some of the children watching every *N&O* box in this end of the county.'

I went over and hugged Seth's neck. 'Minnie's right,' I told him. 'You *are* brilliant.'

'Any brighter and I'd glow in the dark,' he agreed. 'Now if you'll give me five more minutes with my wife on these figures, I'll get out of y'all's way and—'

'I didn't come to talk politics this time,' I said. 'I thought I'd do some fishing.'

'What a good idea!' said Minnie. 'Get your mind off troubling things for a while.'

'You're not gonna catch much this time of day,' Seth warned, 'but all the fishing stuff's out under the shelter. You just help yourself to anything you need.'

There's a decent lane down to the pond I planned to fish, and I could have driven, but I'd had enough of cars, too. I found a bucket, one of Minnie's old straw hats, and a couple of cane poles already rigged with sinkers, corks, and small fish hooks. Then I set off past rows of vegetables – their garden peas were hanging heavy and I made a mental note to pick a mess to take back to Dobbs with me – across a field of young tobacco, to a path through the woods that brought me out at the head of a long pond a few hundred feet on the other side of Seth's line.

It had been dug as a water hole back when the big twins were heavily into 4-H projects and thought they wanted to start a herd of beef cattle. Then Seth and Jack fooled around with catfish for a while, and I seem to remember the little twins talking about raising eels for Asian markets. When all those projects petered out, Daddy drained the pond and restocked with bream, crappies, and bass.

Except for a clump of willows, he kept the banks mowed clean of underbrush, but trees grew right up to the mowing strip and were mirrored in the still water. I sat down with my back against a willow trunk and let peacefulness wash over me. Tractors rumbled in distant fields somewhere beyond the trees and a nearby mockingbird was singing his territory. Otherwise there was only a low steady hum of insects, lizards skittering over dry leaves, towhees scratching for bugs – the country equivalent of elevator music.

It'd been too damn long since I'd gotten off by myself like this, and I blanked my mind of everything except sky, trees, and water. Seth was right. It was still too middle-way the day to expect fish to bite. Further down the bank stood a sweet gum with a bare dead limb that stretched out toward the water. A kingfisher perched at the very end and was silhouetted against the fluffy white clouds.

Up in the sky, a red-tailed hawk spiraled lazily on thermal updrafts. *Yea, he did fly upon the wings of the wind . . .*

I fitted my back more comfortably against the willow trunk and thought maybe I'd just rest there a while, listening to birdsong and crickets . . . rest till the kingfisher's dive signaled fish activity below the surface of the pond . . . till . . .

The sun was edging toward the treetops when I awoke to the smell of cigarette smoke and opened my eyes without otherwise moving.

Heavy brogans. Long skinny legs. Faded chinos that had been washed so many times they were soft as handkerchief linen and more white than khaki colored.

A feeling of well-being suffused me as I looked up, up, up into eyes as blue as cornflowers. Stretching like a sleepy child, I forgot that we weren't talking to each other.

'Hey, Daddy,' I yawned.

'Hey, shug.' Any wariness that might have been there a moment earlier was now gone. He flicked his cigarette away, squatted on the grassy bank beside me, and looked out over the pond. 'Catching much?'

I pushed myself upright and hugged him so hard that his white straw planter's hat almost went into the pond.

'Here now, what's this all about?' he said, but he didn't offer to pull away.

'I was hoping you'd bait my hook,' I grinned. 'Icky crawly worms.'

He laughed, pushed his hat back on the crown of his head, reached for a pole, and said the same thing he always said when I was a little girl. 'Gonna fish with me, you're gonna bait your own hook.'

I took a night crawler from the bait box and passed half of it over to him, then put the rest on my own hook and threw out the line.

No sooner had the line touched water than something

201

immediately grabbed the worm and pulled my red plastic bobber down into the brown depths. The cane pole bent nearly double, and I quickly flicked the tip to set the hook and began easing back on the pole. It fought but I kept the pressure steady and soon a chunky wriggling shape broke through the surface. I flipped him up on the bank, and a moment later, I was removing my hook from the mouth of a thrashing half-pound crappie.

Before I could get him in the bucket, Daddy had a slightly bigger one ready to join him.

'Hungry little boogers aren't they?' he said as three, four, and five elbowed one other aside to be next in our bucket.

'That's all I feel like cleaning,' I said. 'You want any?'

'Nah. Maidie's making me chicken pastry.'

'Oh?' Chicken pastry was one of my favorite suppers.

'With chopped broccoli salad.'

Another of my favorites. Minnie or Seth was probably on the phone before I left their yard.

'You asking me to stay to supper?'

'Just saying there's plenty.'

'You always did have a pretty way with words,' I teased.

With one accord, we pushed our bobs down the line so that our hooks would be set too shallow to attract the big fish. Then we baited up with a generous hand. Dozens of little fish swarmed up as soon as the worms hit the water, and our bobbers dipped and bounced till the hooks were picked clean.

We kept it up till all the bait was gone and shadows began to lengthen over the water. The air was golden all around. I felt utterly at peace.

'Shug?'

'Hmm?'

'Who wrote them ugly letters?'

'I don't know, Daddy.'

'Well, who do you think?'

I shrugged. 'I don't think. It doesn't make any sense.'

'Then how 'bout I throw you a big pig pickin'?'

I twisted around to stare at him. He'd been angry when he heard I'd filed for judge and had tried to get me to withdraw. We'd both said ugly things.

'I still don't see why you need to be a judge,' he said, 'but if that's what you want—'

I could feel myself stiffening up. 'You're going to buy it for me?'

'I just don't want to be the cost of you losing it,' he said, more humbly than I'd ever heard him speak.

Into the silence came raucous screams. The red-tailed hawk had drifted down almost to the treetops and three crows had banded together to fly at him and hector his passage.

'I pure-out hate a crow,' said Daddy. 'A hawk'll maybe take a biddy or two in the spring, but a crow'll get your corn all summer long and strip your pecan trees in the fall. Look at 'em chasing after that hawk, too much a coward 'cept when they can gang up on him.'

His fierce blue eyes followed the birds. Eighty-two years old, yet he still knew what it was like to live as a hawk and feel the sharp beaks of cowards on your back.

'How 'bout I stay for supper?' I said.

17

Didn't Expect It To Go
Down This Way

Saturday morning found me braced for the worst. Those first
two flyers were distributed God knows how widely, the *Ledger*
had been out since Friday noon with its story, and my whole
family had its collective hackles up.

So what happened?

Not one damn thing.

Every time we start thinking we're the center of the universe,
the universe turns around and says with a slightly distracted
air, 'I'm sorry. What'd you say your name was again?'

Oh, a few friends called to ask what was going on, but for
the most part, silence. A runoff contest between two local
judicial candidates is small potatoes compared to the one
shaping up between Harvey Gantt, the black former mayor of
Charlotte out in the western part of the state, and Mike
Easley, a white district attorney from Southport down at the
coast.

At least there'd been no more flyers.

Haywood's Stevie had organized his cousins into teams and they'd cruised Cotton Grove and Black Creek until nearly two A.M. armed with notepads to jot down license plates or comments on suspicious cars, sneaky-acting users of *News and Observer* boxes, or anything clse that scemed worth noting.

'And nobody saw anything?' I asked when he reported in that morning.

Stevie laughed. 'Well, I wouldn't exactly say that. It *was* Friday night. Funny what you can see when you really start looking.'

'Keep it clean,' I told him and went off to work a senior citizens' lunch in Widdington, then an Arts Council meeting in Cotton Grove where I had to field only three mostly friendly questions about the flyers.

After the meeting, I was approached by someone with a vaguely familiar face, a bustling sort of woman who's on the Possum Creek Players board of directors. She trotted over with a flourish of silver bangles on both wrists and an arty paisley scarf so carelessly draped over the shoulder of her flounced dress that she had to keep clutching at it. 'I'm Sylvia Dayley, Miss Knott. You probably don't remember me from our production of *Who Killed the Darling Mrs?*, but I hope you won't mind if I ask you?'

She was another of those who end every other sentence on an upward inflection.

I waited warily. 'Yes?'

'Since you're a friend of Denn McCloy? When you saw him last night, did he say anything about Michael and him maybe going somewhere for the weekend?'

She misread my blank look. 'I've been clerking out at the Pot Shot on the weekends – Saturday mornings, ten till two; Sunday afternoons, one to five? It's only eight hours and I mostly do it as a favor for the boys. So hard for them to find reliable help. I have a key, of course, but Michael and Denn always let me know when they're going to be gone so I'll feed Lily if they leave her home, only this time they didn't say a word to me and I'm not sure what to do with the money?'

She finally ran out of breath and her bracelets jingled as she rearranged her scarf.

'I'm sorry,' I said. 'You must have misunderstood something. I didn't see Denn last night.'

'But Cathy said Denn called you yesterday afternoon to meet him at the theater last night?'

'Cathy King? One of their potters?'

Sylvia Dayley nodded so vigorously that her scarf slid all the way down her arm until one end trailed on the floor. 'I called her when I got in and that's what she said.'

I shook my head. 'He may've left a message on our answering machine, but we closed early yesterday and I didn't get it. Sorry.'

She hitched up her scarf and looked perturbed. 'I hate to just leave the money at the shop. Not that it's all that much, but still . . . And what if they don't come back till Monday? Sundays are such a big day, you know? And what about Lily?'

I edged away from her as she jingled indecisively and was immediately claimed by an elderly poet and a would-be playwright who wanted to debate the Mapplethorpe photos and the First Amendment.

* * *

Wondering who else might not have realized that we'd closed early yesterday, I put in a call to the office and punched in the code that would cause our answering machine to play back. Sure enough, amid some non-urgent routine messages was Denn McCloy's: 'This is for Deborah Knott. Please ask her to meet me at the Possum Creek Players Theatre tonight at nine. I have something very special to give her.'

Like what, Denn? I asked him mentally as I looked up the number at the Pot Shot. *Another round of rifle fire?*

There was no answer. After five rings, *their* answering machine switched on. I left a message that I was returning Denn's call and that I'd be back home by eleven. All across America, it's machines talking to machines.

Dwight probably laid the fear of God and the law on Denn yesterday. Maybe he wanted to apologize in person. Unless—?

I suddenly remembered the luscious dark red velvet cloak he'd created for *The Further Adventures of Red Riding Hood.* The young woman who played Red was awful, but the costumes were great. In fact, I wanted Denn to sell me the cloak, but it was such a useful and versatile costume that he didn't want to let it go. He'd promised though that if he ever changed his mind, I was to have first dibs, and we had a running joke about it.

Now wouldn't that make a nice apology, I thought, turning my car south on Forty-Eight toward Makely. Too bad I'd missed him.

I was scheduled to speak at a Parents Without Partners dinner meeting at Makely that evening – they wanted legal advice about guardianships and trusts; I wanted their votes –

but I had an extra hour to kill. Impulsively, I made a three-point turn right there on the highway and headed back through Cotton Grove.

It wasn't that I expected Denn to still be sitting in the parking lot at the theater twenty-four hours later. On the other hand, if he and Michael had made up and then decided on the spur of the moment to go away for the weekend, an extravagant gesture was well within the realm of possibility. I could see him putting the cloak in a plastic garment bag and hanging it under the back arch with a large sign: MEA CULPA, DEBORAH, or something equally and dramatically penitent.

It was odd about couples, the dynamics of staying together or growing apart. Minnie and Seth got more like each other every year, whereas you had to wonder why the Vickerys hadn't flown apart years ago. Pride? Lying in the bed you'd made? And Denn and Michael. Now *there* was an odd couple for you. Michael so cold and so conventional, if you didn't count stringing his fences with precise crosses. And Denn so theatrical and impulsive – he'd sure given me a whole new slant on the term *hair-trigger temper* – but capable of a warm generosity I'd never seen with Michael. No wonder their union was in trouble.

'At least they're all still honoring whatever vows they made,' said the preacher starchily.

The pragmatist held his tongue.

The Possum Creek Players Theatre began life as a one-room schoolhouse in the center of town a hundred years ago. The one room grew to three before it was abandoned for a new brick school in the twenties. A pentecostal congregation immediately bought the building and moved it to the banks of Possum Creek about five miles north of Cotton Grove. In the fifties, shortly after the church elders had taken out a new mortgage to remodel the structure, long-simmering animosities over scriptural interpretations suddenly came to a boil and emotions ran so high that the church split right down the middle. The wealthier members pulled out and built a new church at a crossroads south of Cotton Grove. The rest of the flock, unable to meet the mortgage payments, soon drifted off to other churches, and the bank foreclosed.

After that, the building sat empty for several years. The property kept changing hands. Different enterprises tried and failed out there, but nothing seemed to work until the Possum Creek Players organized and eventually raised enough money to take it over on a fairly sound financial footing. Raleigh was near enough to furnish better-than-average amateur actors; and Raleigh provided a dependable paying audience as well, once the theater had built a reputation for campy musical comedy, farce, and melodrama.

A gravel road wound in from the highway, through a stand of pine trees and azaleas out to the old white clapboard building on the banks of the creek. With the sun at my back, I drove into the sprawling dirt parking lot where a neat square sign announced that *Bouncing Betty's Betrothal* would open the first of June. As I thought, the parking lot was empty, but I drove around back. There, a covered archway sheltered a set of double doors used to move sets and furniture in and out of the building.

To my surprise, Denn's Volvo was pulled up to the far edge of the concrete loading zone. The theater's double doors were in shadow, but I could see that one of them stood slightly ajar.

I tapped my horn.

Nothing.

I switched off my motor and stepped out of air-conditioned coolness onto sun-parched grass. Warm air flowed around my bare arms almost like the red velvet cloak itself.

The sun was down below the pines now, and silence wrapped the shadowed creek bank. I walked across the concrete pad and pushed the door wider.

'Denn? Michael?' I called. 'Anybody here?'

All at once it struck me what a dumb thing it was to be walking into an isolated building out here in the middle of nowhere. Probably deserted, but maybe not. Not with Denn's car parked only ten feet away.

'And let us not forget who's shown himself to be just a little too damn free in the way he handles a rifle,' said the pragmatist.

'She who fears and runs away lives to fear another day,' the preacher agreed nervously.

I backed away from the door, feeling slightly foolish. On the other hand, I do keep a loaded .38 locked in the trunk of my car and this seemed like as good a time as any to get it out.

The concrete loading zone was only eight or nine inches off ground level, but when I turned, I found myself looking straight down into the front seat of Denn's car. An instant jolt of pure adrenalin jerked me backwards. I was propelled by such a strong and instinctive survival response that I had no time to reason. I could only react in primitive, headlong,

211

terrified flight across the strip of open ground between the two cars. I dived into mine and dug out of there so fast that gravel spun out in all directions, and I hunched as low as I could, expecting to feel a shotgun blast between my shoulder blades at any second.

Like the blast that'd taken out the driver's side of the Volvo windshield and blown away Denn McCloy's whole face.

18

Make The World Go Away

'I'm fine,' I said for the third time.

'You sure?' asked Dwight Bryant.

As head of the detective division, he had all his people moving in the directions he wanted them to go, and now he could make time to come over to the car and get my whole story. I was parked at the edge of the grass behind the theater with my front door open and one foot on the ground, and he leaned his big muscular body against the car as we talked so he could keep an eye on proceedings.

Although there was still plenty of daylight, portable floods had been rigged to light the interior of Denn's Volvo while they took photographs from every angle before they moved him.

So far, everything had been done by the book. I might have disturbed the crime scene by driving in and out, but after I'd gotten to a phone and called the sheriff's department, the first deputy to respond had blocked off the theater's drive out by the paved road. All emergency vehicles had come in by driving straight across the grass to the edge of the back parking lot, while one member of Dwight's team took a close look at the drive and parking lot. I doubted if she'd find anything. Gravel doesn't mark, we hadn't had rain in more than a week, and this sandy soil becomes too dry and powdery to hold tracks after two or three days of hot sun.

Dwight wanted to know how I'd discovered the body, and I told him about Sylvia Dayley and the message Denn'd left on the firm's answering machine.

'You thought he'd wait that long?' Dwight asked skeptically.

'Not him,' I said. 'Whatever it was he wanted to give me.'

A velvet cloak seemed such a petty object in the face of Denn's death that I wasn't going to mention it if I could help it. Before Dwight thought to ask, I said, 'He didn't happen to hint what it was when you talked to him on Thursday, did he?'

'Nope.'

'What *did* he say? About shooting at Michael on Wednesday, I mean?'

Dwight gave a wry grin. 'Swore he didn't do it; promised he wouldn't ever do it again.' He shifted his weight against my car, and I swayed with the motion of the shocks. 'Makes me wonder where Michael Vickery is right now.'

'You think Michael—?'

'Well, you're the one who talked about menopausal males,' he said.

The radio crackled on the county's emergency rescue truck and I was suddenly reminded of where I was supposed to be.

Dwight said I was welcome to ask one of the patrolmen to tell the dispatcher to get word to the Makely Parents Without Partners that I wouldn't be coming.

As I got out of the car, Jack Jamison, a tubby young deputy called, 'Hey, Major Bryant – see you over here a minute?'

It was more than a minute, and whatever it was that Jamison was pointing out to Dwight inside the Volvo, it sure seemed to set off a whole new flurry of activity. The patrolman I'd collared had barely finished giving the dispatcher my message than I heard Dwight putting out an APB on Michael Vickery's gray Ford pickup.

The sun finally melted into the pine trees. Not much daylight left as reaction set in. I began to feel as tired as if I'd barned tobacco all day and so utterly saddened by Denn's violent death. He was nearly fifteen years older than me and he and Michael had done little socializing in Cotton Grove, so we may not have been close friends, but we were friends, and I mourned the loss of his colorful personality. I could almost smile to remember how much fun he'd made *The Night of January 16th*, some of his outrageous comments about my fellow cast members during costume fittings. Bitchy, witty, and surprisingly insightful. The Possum Creek Players would have a hard time replacing him.

All this went through my mind as Dwight gave a physical description of the pickup's probable driver, and I must have been even more tired than I realized because I sat there stupidly for a moment wondering why on earth Dwight was putting Denn's description on an APB.

The rescue people were lifting the limp form from the car.

I went over and tried to focus on the body, without letting myself really look at the head again.

We sure do see what we expect to see, don't we? Earlier, I'd assumed that the man in Denn's car, sitting where Denn was supposed to be sitting, waiting where Denn had said he'd be waiting, was indeed Denn.

Wrong.

Now I saw quite clearly that it was Michael Vickery who'd had his face blown away.

It made the eleven o'clock news on all our local channels and the front pages of several Sunday papers around eastern North Carolina.

Scion of a prominent local family, police seeking his missing male companion, body discovered by an equally prominent candidate for a seat on the bench – all the notice that I'd avoided earlier I was now getting in spades.

The television stories concentrated on Michael and Denn, but the newspapers had time and space to include me since by now it was clear that Michael had died around nine o'clock on Friday night, the time and place Denn McCloy expected to meet me. The sheriff's department wouldn't speculate either on or off the record about why Michael Vickery was there instead or why a meeting I didn't keep should have led to murder.

Nice of Dwight not to speculate out loud, but it didn't stop the media.

In addition to my usual academic and career achievements, I was described as the 'only daughter of Keziah Knott, at one time alleged to be North Carolina's largest bootlegger.' One or two hinted that I was – till now anyhow – the only white sheep of an infamous family, while others picked up on those phony campaign flyers and left the impression that Michael's murder had something to do with my position on sex, race, drugs, untaxed whiskey, and God knows what else.

Although they were very careful to print or broadcast nothing actionable, the open-ended quagmire of personalities, crime, unanswered questions, and suggestive innuendos kept the reading and viewing public tuned in. I had the gloomy feeling that I was watching my seat on any bench trickle right on down the drain.

Monday came and went with no sign of Denn McCloy or the gray Ford pickup.

Mrs Vickery had collapsed upon hearing the news of Michael's death and was said to have spent two days under heavy sedation, devastated and unable to accept Michael's death. It was the first time in anyone's memory that she'd given in so completely to normal grief. There were whispers of a suicide watch, but nobody believed it. Dr Vickery refused to talk to the media, but his son's employees out at the Pot Shot Pottery wouldn't shut up.

One of them in particular, Cathy King, suffered from what Uncle Ash calls congenital tongue deformity: one that's tied in the middle and flaps at both ends.

'I really can't say,' she told any reporter who wandered in, then immediately started running her mouth.

The only good thing – as far as Denn McCloy was concerned – was that Michael wasn't the only one she'd told that Denn was meeting me at the Possum Creek Theatre.

She'd mentioned it in a crowded 7-Eleven store where she'd stopped to pick up a jug of milk and had speculated on it at choir practice that evening. Choir practice let out at eight-thirty so, theoretically anyhow, half of Cotton Grove could have known by eight-forty-five.

What didn't help Denn was the way Cathy described in colorful detail the times she'd heard the two men snap at each other in the last few months as their longtime relationship deteriorated and fell apart. Evidently I wasn't so far off target with my flip remarks about male menopause. When Michael hit forty, he'd begun to stray over into the gay hangouts around the Triangle. At first, Denn ignored Michael's wandering eye; lately though, there'd been bitter and acrimonious scenes.

'This past year's just been *wild*!' said Cathy.

Her two co-workers were less dramatic but grudgingly agreed with her assessment of a growing rift between the two men. They also agreed that it must have been Denn who fired the rifle on Wednesday. Cathy saw him take Michael's rifle from the truck and throw it in the Volvo. She said Denn even admitted that he'd gone out in the woods and fired a couple of rounds at a pine tree, but he certainly hadn't been aiming at Michael. 'If I ever take a gun to Michael, I won't miss,' he was said to have threatened.

'Actually,' said Cathy King, 'I got the feeling he meant to scare Gayle Whitehead.'

Which insured, of course, that Monday's paper carried a complete rehash of Janie Whitehead's death.

Gayle immediately went to earth at her grandmother Whitehead's house.

'I don't want to talk to any reporters,' she said when I called to see how she was, 'but you know, Deborah, this may not be such a bad thing. Not Michael Vickery getting killed – that part's so terrible! I still can't believe we were just talking to him and now he's dead – but if it gets people remembering about my mother . . . You reckon maybe he *did* know something more than he ever told? Something he told Denn and Denn was maybe going to tell you?'

'If that's the case, why would Denn kill him?' I asked, trying to assess the situation logically. 'If it was incriminating, you'd think Michael would have tried to stop Denn, not the other way around. It doesn't make sense.'

'You'll figure it out,' Gayle said promptly.

Oh yeah? With a campaign to salvage?

'Look, honey,' I began, but she interrupted with a wail of protest.

'You *can't* stop now, Deborah. Everything's so stirred up, somebody's bound to let something slip if you just ask the right questions. *Please?*'

Sighing, I agreed at least to listen if anyone should stop me in the street and want to unburden a secret.

Back in the real world, reading the morning papers began to cut into work time at Lee, Stephenson and Knott. Clients can make the news, attorneys aren't supposed to; yet my name was in print so many times that the pained expression seemed to have settled permanently on John Claude's fine thin features.

On Tuesday Reid brought a couple of interesting tidbits to our morning coffee.

Ambrose Daughtridge had been Michael and Denn's

attorney, and he'd let slip that Michael had begun looking into the legal ramifications of untangling their financial assets. Indeed, Michael had made an appointment for yesterday afternoon to rewrite his will.

'They had a joint checking account,' said Reid, 'but the Pot Shot itself and all the real property belonged to Michael. Or rather to Mrs Vickery. It was Dancy land that she inherited.'

'Michael never had title?' John Claude was horrified. He would never have let a client put capital improvements into property that another family member could sell out from under him, even if that family member was the client's mother.

Reid grinned. 'It wasn't quite that bad. Mrs Vickery gave him a ninety-nine-year lease – one of those nominal fifty-dollars-a-year things – so he couldn't be forced off.'

'Oh?' said John Claude, who sniffed the makings of a pretty little legal problem, one that any attorney would enjoy arguing, especially if—?

'Yep,' said Reid. 'Ambrose told me that Michael Vickery and Denn McCloy had mutually beneficial wills.'

'Ah,' said John Claude.

'So if Michael had lived to keep his appointment with Ambrose yesterday, Denn might have wound up with nothing,' I mused. 'Instead, he now gets everything, including a ninety-nine-year lease on Dancy property.'

'Not if *I'd* handled the wording on the lease,' said John Claude.

Unspoken was the knowledge that Ambrose Daughtridge relied rather heavily on the one-size-fits-all standard forms found in form books. Would he have remembered (or even known at the time) that Michael Vickery was more likely to have 'heirs and/or successors and assigns' than 'heirs of his body'?

'It's all academic. Murderers don't inherit from their victims,' John Claude reminded us as Sherry brought in the morning mail and began sorting it at the end of the long table so she wouldn't miss anything.

'Guilty till proven innocent?' I said.

The little alert bell over the front door tinkled and Sherry went out to greet old Mrs Cunningham, who comes in every month to fiddle with the codicils in her will.

After she left, I interviewed a couple of women. One of our sparkplug clerks had married abruptly and moved to New Hampshire, and we'd filled in with enough temporaries to have seen it was going to take two to replace the one we'd lost. Our clerks have to be efficient enough for John Claude and me, homely or married enough so that Reid won't try to bed them, and biddable enough to take orders from Sherry. I was beginning to think such creatures didn't exist, but a new crop of paralegals was due to graduate soon from Colleton Tech. Maybe we'd get lucky.

When I returned from a very late lunch, Sherry said, 'Dwight Bryant's in your office. I think it's something official.'

'Really?'

He was standing by my desk when I got there.

'Do you mind?' I said.

'What?'

'Well, how would you like it,' I fumed, 'if I came in your office and started nosing through *your* papers?'

'Hey, I wasn't looking at papers,' he protested. 'I just

didn't remember seeing that picture of Miz Sue and Mr Kezzie.'

I'd left the photograph propped against my pencil holder and he took it over to the window for a closer look in better light. It was only a snapshot that I'd taken with the camera they'd given me for my ninth birthday. Mother was sitting on the swing on our front porch, Daddy was propped against a nearby post, hat in his hand, hand on his hip. Both of them smiled into the camera, but the way her slender body was half-turned towards him, the way his lean height curved toward her, you could tell that they'd been talking when I came along and called, 'Say cheese!'

It was only a snapshot I hadn't valued back then. Now I saw that I'd captured the electricity that had always flowed between them.

'Daddy gave it to me Friday night,' I said as he handed it back.

Dwight picked up the ten-by-thirteen manila envelope he'd laid on the edge of my desk and took a chair. 'Yeah, I heard y'all made up.'

Normally, I'd have taken exception to his words, but he looked too bone weary to banter. Instead I let it go with a mild, 'We made a start anyhow. What've you got there?'

He opened the flap and slipped out two flat plastic bags, each of which contained a single sheet of paper. It only took a glance to see that these had to be the original pasteups of those two flyers on mine and Luther Parker's letterheads. Both were smudged with what I could only assume to be graphite fingerprint powder.

'Where'd you get those?' I asked.

222

'We got a search warrant for the Pot Shot and the barn. Did a quick and dirty Saturday night to make sure McCloy wasn't out there, then went back a little more thoroughly yesterday. Interesting. Most of his clothes and personal things seem to be missing, but these were hidden under a pile of papers in McCloy's desk. They had their own copier in that little office behind the sales shop. Same kind of paper. His fingerprints were all over these two sheets. He's the one who put them together, no doubt about it.'

I was floored. '*Denn?* He's about as political as Julia Lee's poodle, for God's sake. Why would he do something like that?'

'That's what I wanted to ask you.' He cocked his big sandy-haired head at me. 'To make you stop poking into Janie Whitehead's death?'

'He never even met Janie,' I protested.

'No, but Michael had.'

'Barely. Even if they knew each other well, so what? Michael had no reason to kill Janie.'

'That we know of.' Dwight pushed himself to his feet. 'If I know you, you're going to keep on poking around. You hear anything I ought to know about—'

'Yeah, yeah,' I said.

He grinned at the exasperated tone of my voice, and for about half a minute, I almost had the feeling he was going to reach out and tousle my hair, as if I were a little girl again and he the lanky teenager who was always over to play ball or hang out with my brothers. Our eyes met, locked, and inexplicably, we were both suddenly trapped by a startled awareness that turned our casual ease into clumsy confusion.

* * *

Dwight left – fled? – without any of the usual brotherly admonitions.

Well, well, well, I thought.

But before I could explore that interesting line of speculation, the phone rang.

'Deborah Knott,' I answered automatically.

'Deborah, you've gotta help me,' rasped a male voice.

'Who—?'

'It's me, Denn McCloy.'

19

Too Gone, For Too Long

For two solid weeks, we'd had nothing but sunshine. Now, when fair weather would have been welcome, one soggy cloud after another had rolled across the Triangle since lunchtime, cooling everything down.

Including me.

I'd still been pretty hot under the collar when Denn McCloy first called and not just because of where the thermometer stood either. Where the hell did he get off, I asked him, papering the district with lies about me and then calling up begging for help?

'I'll explain all that,' he promised. 'Just say you'll help me. Daughtridge won't get off his fat butt.'

'You called Ambrose?'

'He says to give myself up and then we'll talk.' Panic edged his voice. 'Michael's dead and he'll throw me to the wolves. He's always despised me. All these years and he still—'

'Look, Denn, if you didn't do it—'

'You, too?' Hysterical howls blasted my ear. 'Oh, God! I'll kill myself. I swear I will!'

I tried to calm him, but he'd worked himself up till nothing I could say about the wisdom of Ambrose's advice seemed to penetrate. I was still pissed at him. On the other hand, if he wasn't Michael's killer, then maybe he was entitled to the grief and panic that flooded through the telephone wires.

'It's not a matter of what I think, Denn. It's what you can prove.'

'Then help me prove it. Please, Deborah? I need a lawyer who believes in me. At least come and talk to me. Please?'

Against my better judgment, I finally agreed to meet him at Pullen Park, a venerable Raleigh landmark a mile or so west of the Capitol.

When I hung up the phone, the sun was shining brightly, so I'd driven out of Dobbs with nothing warmer on my arms than the thin beige cardigan that matched my tailored beige slacks. Even before I reached Garner, I'd passed through two heavy downpours and the temperature had dropped considerably.

Definitely not my idea of merry-go-round weather.

The latest cloudburst had dwindled into a fine mist as I drove into the nearly empty parking lot beside Pullen Park, and when I got out to lock my car, I shivered in the damp chill.

No umbrella, of course. Reid borrowed it back in March and still had it.

I followed the sound of an old-fashioned calliope past banks of rain-drenched roses and day lilies, past hydrangeas

226

so heavy with water that their blue flower heads bent to the ground, till I came to a round wooden structure bounded by wire netting and a waist-high plank wall.

Raleigh's carousel is a true jewel, a beautifully restored turn-of-the-century Dentzel. Purists think it ought to be in a museum and are horrified that the city keeps letting children clamber around on the fanciful menagerie, kicking their heels against those enameled flanks to spur them on year after year. Personally, I applaud the city's thinking: the animals are much happier out here than they'd ever be in a museum.

But how like Denn to choose a place like this for a rendezvous. He knew perfectly well he should turn himself in to Sheriff Bo Poole and try to hire himself a Perry Mason. Instead, he wanted to do the carousel scene from *Strangers on a Train*. With all this rain turning on and off like somebody fixing a water spigot, I had the feeling it was going to be more Larry, Curly, and Moe than Farley Granger and Robert Walker.

Oh well, at least it wasn't the observation deck of the Empire State Building. (Yes, I'm a video junkie.)

Actually, if the day had continued as hot and sunny as it began, the park might have made a good place to meet, crowded as it usually was with kids of all ages. Here in the rain, though, there were only a half-dozen children waiting to ride, one accompanied by what looked like a part-time father, the others divided between two young mothers and an older woman.

Obeying Denn's now-ridiculous instructions, I bought a ticket and watched the beautifully tooled, overhead iron cranks raise and lower the animals as the whole wonderful contraption moved round and round with a measured grace almost lost in our computerized world. Back then, people were less fastidious about hiding the gears and crankshafts of their machinery. In fact, it must have been solid and comforting to see, proof and promise that man could solve almost every problem with sturdy engineering.

The loopy swirling music of the restored Wurlitzer band organ made me think of Teddy Roosevelt, trolley cars, and white eyelet dresses tied with pink and blue sashes.

The round wooden platform slowed to a stop and I went straight to the very same animal that had been my favorite as a child: a proud gray cat with a green saddle blanket and a goldfish in his mouth. Back then it was the only animal I trusted to go up and down in proper merry-go-round fashion.

Farm kids don't get taken to city parks all that often and I was almost too big for the carousel before I finally figured out how to tell in advance whether the steed I'd chosen would prance or remain frozen in place. Till then, if my cat was already taken and I was forced to choose another animal, it was all pure chance. I would sit apprehensively in the alien wooden saddle till the music started, waiting to see if I'd been lucky. Dismayed resignation if my tiger or reindeer kept its feet on the ground, but, oh, the sheer bliss if it slowly surged upward as the menagerie gained momentum!

The first ride came to an end and I bought a second ticket. The muscular young man who manually shifted the mechanical gears in the center acted like he thought I'd come straight over to the cat near him because I wanted to flirt. Since it was a slow day, he gave us a longer ride. The children and the two mothers were delighted, the father and grandmother exchanged disapproving frowns. I didn't feel like explaining about childhood trust and checked my watch wondering where Denn was.

'Don't look like he's coming,' said the operator as the second ride finally ended.

I just smiled enigmatically and walked off into the mist like Lauren Bacall, past the fish-feeding station, over the bridge, under the willows, around the lake, and back past the swimming pool – all deserted except for the ducks that paddled along in case I had a loaf of bread with me. If Denn McCloy was anywhere in the park, I couldn't see him.

A gray Ford pickup had materialized near one of the service areas, but before I got my hopes up, I saw that it sported one of those silver-gray permanent licenses issued to state-owned vehicles.

The skies turned dirty gray again, the mist became distinct drops. The hell with it, I thought. It was bad enough I hadn't called Dwight the minute I hung up from talking with Denn, why should I stand out here and get drenched to the bone playing out his games?

I rounded the full-sized 1940s-style caboose parked beside the miniature train track and was heading for my car when I heard, 'Psst! Deborah!'

'Denn?'

'Shh!'

I looked up and saw him gesturing dramatically from one of the caboose windows. Damned if it wasn't going to be *Strangers on a Train* after all.

The interior of the old red caboose was painted a shiny gray enamel. Big iron boxes were bolted to the wall and floor to form wide benches. I wondered if these were old-time bunks and wished that one of the lockers still held a rough wool train blanket.

Denn looked warm in corduroy trousers, plaid wool shirt, and a quilted vest. Since his normal wear was black leather, I guessed this getup was his idea of a disguise. He even wore a John Deere cap to hide his short white buzz cut and, without his usual earring, looked almost like a little old farmer come to town to sell watermelons.

Keyed up though he was, he noticed my damp and chilled condition and said, 'I've got an extra jacket on the truck. Want me to get it?'

'If it's not too far away.'

He pointed to the gray pickup sitting in plain sight.

'You *stole* a state license plate?' I said.

'Borrowed. And I've got to give it back by five o'clock.'

It was three-thirty.

I watched as he splashed over to the truck, slipped aside the tarp that covered the bed, and pulled out a black plastic garment bag, which he brought back to the caboose. Inside were several shirts, a couple of tweedy slacks, and a Durham Bulls warm-up jacket.

It felt wonderful around my shoulders. I settled back on one of the iron benches and said, 'Okay, talk.'

'How about some coffee, kiddo?' he asked. 'I bet they have some at the concession stand.'

'C'mon, Denn. You promised if I came without telling Dwight—'

He slumped down on the opposite bench and the wrinkles

around his mouth made him look another ten years older. 'Yeah, okay. I know.'

But he couldn't seem to start. I'd seen this with witnesses before.

'You left me a message on my office machine,' I prompted. 'You wanted me to meet you at the theater?'

'Yeah, but before that . . .' He got up and started pacing back and forth from one end of the caboose to the other. Rain drummed so noisily on the iron roof that I barely heard his words as he walked over to the doorway to watch water cascade off in silver sheets.

I felt like drumming my fingers on his head. 'Why was Michael there?' I prodded. 'Did you shoot him?'

'God, no! How can you even ask that?' He turned and for a moment I thought his face was splashed with rain. Then I realized that beneath his John Deere cap he was crying uncontrollably.

'I loved him. He was my life.' Tears streamed from his eyes and dropped in dark splotches on his vest. 'Now he's dead – and dear God in heaven, how can I – how *will* I live without him?'

I can't stand to see anybody cry uncomforted. Convulsive sobs wracked his thin body as the rain sluiced down all around us, and I held him like a child and went on holding him, listening to his incoherent grief, till the worst was over.

Yet, even after his emotions were back under shaky control and he'd used his handkerchief to wipe his eyes and blow his nose, it still took a few minutes before he could talk about anything except his enormous loss.

'I'd been with others by the time we met – hell, it was the

231

swinging sixties – of course I had. We both had. But after that, he was the only one,' said Denn. 'I never looked at another man after our first night together. After a year, he comes back down here and I think I've lost him forever . . . but then he sends for me and eighteen years, kiddo. Sounds soupy in this day and age, doesn't it?'

'No,' I said. 'Actually, it sounds lucky.'

'We were good together, too.' He sat down on the iron bench opposite me. 'Michael gave me security and I gave him warmth – someone he could be free with for the first time in his life.'

'My mother used to say that Dancys live behind glass walls,' I said.

He thought about it a minute, then nodded. 'Only Michael was always trying to get out. He was a good person. Too good sometimes. Too religious. The kind of religion that—' He fell silent again, twisting his handkerchief in his small clever hands. 'I'm not religious myself. But I always thought it ought to comfort and sustain. Not put you on a cross, too.'

The rain had slacked off. I glanced at my watch. Almost four.

'What happened Friday?' I asked again.

'We fought. Again. He's been so restless this spring.' His face threatened to crumple again, but he forced himself to stay calm. 'He says he's tired of me. Tired of the country, tired of making pots and being good, tired of me.' Denn's voice dropped. Became shamed. His head drooped until his face was obscured by the bill of his cap. 'He's seeing someone else. Someone younger than me over in Durham. Twenty years younger.'

Once more he resumed his pacing. 'But he'd have come back to me. I know that now. He *would* have.'

How many times I've sat in my office, filling in the blanks of a divorce petition, and heard tearful wives or brokenhearted husbands say those exact words: 'It's just a phase. A fling. The seven-year-itch. The other lover doesn't matter. It won't last. We have too much history together.'

Sometimes they did; more often they didn't.

'I pop off. I admit it. I say things I shouldn't. Make threats I don't really mean. But after all the things *he* says—' He blew his nose again to cover a choked gulp. 'This time's different and I see there's nothing to do but leave until he comes back to his senses.'

While Michael had gone stomping off to the creek with the dog to cool off, Denn had flung his most important possessions into the pickup.

'—because I can't get my Chinese chest in the Volvo and I don't want to leave it. Not that I expect to come back and find the locks changed—'

From his tone, I gathered that was exactly what he expected. It sounded as if there'd been an ultimatum: get out or be thrown out.

'So why was Michael at the theater?'

'Cathy must have heard me call you and told him. I don't know. Maybe he thinks I'm gonna keep the truck to make him mad. He's ashamed of being gay. Did you know that? That's why it was so brave of him. To come out down here – I mean even if it was self-punishment – which it wasn't. Not really. But he could be pure Primitive Baptist at times. Very moralistic. And, of course, the truck's part of it.'

He was chattering, lurching from one subject to another, barely making sense, and I said so.

'Well, it was like, okay, maybe he's gay, but that doesn't mean he's not a man like any of those other good ol' country boys. Pickup truck, dog in the flatbed, rifle on the gun rack, the whole goddamn *schmear*. Sitting up there in the cab of that truck, he can tell himself he's just like everybody else. I hate the fucking thing, but I need it to move my stuff to a friend's place over here. I was gonna see you and then take it back and get my car.'

While I was still curious about what he wanted to give me, I've learned not to interrupt witnesses when the narrative flow is upon them.

'It takes me longer to get my stuff unloaded than I think and it's a little past nine before I get back down to the theater. I drive around to the rear and the first thing I see is the Volvo. I drive right up to it and shine the headlights inside and – and—'

He nearly lost it again.

'Why didn't you call for help?'

'Okay, so it's dumb, but walk in my shoes for one minute, kiddo. I've just had a flaming fight with Michael, right? Everybody knows I've got a half-inch fuse. And there he sits, blown to hell before he can even get out of the car to talk to whoever's holding the gun. I'm gonna call the same deputy sheriff that comes out the day before and lectures me about shooting at people?'

He held up his hands.

'I know, I know. Some dumb *schmuck* from Long Island, right? Too stupid to remember that there's a test they can do to prove whether or not you've fired a gun, but God! I've just seen the man I've lived with eighteen years – I'm supposed to think straight?'

'Why *did* you shoot at him out at the mill?'

Without thinking, he blurted, 'I wasn't shooting at him. I—'

He looked at me guiltily.

I was incredulous. 'You were shooting at *me*?'

'Not *at* you. I just wanted you and the Whitehead kid to quit bugging Michael about Janie Whitehead and go away. That's why those flyers. To get your mind back on your campaign and off Michael.'

The rain had stopped entirely now. There were occasional drips from the trees above and I could hear the carousel's Wurlitzer again.

He was so outrageous that there was no point getting angry. I could only shake my head and marvel.

'You know something, Denn? You really are a piece of work. You take a shot at me. Spread lies about me. And then you expect me to hold your hand when you go talk to Dwight Bryant?'

The wrinkles around his mouth creased in an ironic grin. 'Yeah.'

20

Come On In, Stay A Little Longer

All the way down Forty-Eight, I berated myself for a fool.

'You don't need this,' fumed the pragmatist pacing up and down one side my mind.

'I'm not taking him to raise,' my Good Samaritan preacher soothed from his armchair on the other side. *'Just being a friend in need. As soon as I get Ambrose Daughtridge to take him off my hands . . .'*

'Ambrose Daughtridge's got more sense than you have. You heard what he said. He wants to stay in the Vickerys' good graces and Denn killed their son.'

'Did he?'

'Who knows? Okay, maybe not, but it's still none of your business.'

'Yeah? What ever happened to "Inasmuch as you have done it unto the least of these my brethren, you have done it unto me"?'

A cynical snort. 'Oh, well! If you're going to start quoting the Bible—'

'Yeah, that part always embarrasses me, too. Just the same . . .'

'I thought you wanted to be a judge.'

'I do! But not if it means—'

'Oh spare me any more Sunday school slogans.'

'Oh go to hell!'

A few miles out from Raleigh, Forty-Eight to Cotton Grove splits off to the right while Seventy goes on to Dobbs. It seemed so natural to head toward Cotton Grove that we were half a mile past the fork before I remembered that we'd agreed Denn was going to drive straight back to Dobbs and turn himself in to Dwight. I speeded up and honked my horn.

He waved and kept going.

Annoyed, I pulled out around him and signaled that we were going to stop. There was a church up ahead. I put on my turn signal and drove into the churchyard. (ASK ABOUT OUR SUMMER SALVATION PLAN, said the portable sign at the edge of the road.)

Denn sailed on past in the pickup.

What the hell was he pulling? I'd already cut him as much slack as I thought I could afford when I followed him through Raleigh earlier so he could return the license plate a friend of his had 'borrowed.' Instead of wasting my time calling Ambrose Daughtridge and getting his runaround, I should've called Dwight and had him waiting at the county line.

Another couple of miles and just as I'd decided he was going straight into Cotton Grove to tackle Ambrose himself, he put on his left turn signal, waited till oncoming traffic cleared, then turned into the gravel road that led to Possum Creek Theatre. The sun never had come back out and I followed him down the drive and around back under skies as gray as my mood.

By the time I switched off the engine, he was standing on the concrete loading pad fumbling with his keys, an ingratiating smile on his thin lips.

'I know, I know,' he said. 'This isn't part of our agreement, but I just remembered that this door was open when I found Michael. I want to check and see that everything's okay.'

'The police searched it Friday night,' I told him. 'And Dwight got Leslie Odum to come over, too.'

Leslie was his assistant stage manager who probably knew as much about the storerooms as Denn did. She'd walked through and seen nothing unusual about the backstage clutter and I told him so.

I could've saved my breath. He unlocked the door and slipped inside, as if my words were nothing more than so much wind wafting through the tall pines around us.

The hallway was dark and still. Denn knew the way, but I had to fumble for lights, and by the time I found them, he had already reached the prop room on the far side of the building.

'Hey, Denn, you never told me what you wanted to give me Friday night.'

'Hmm?'

He stood in the middle of the big cluttered room – props shelved all the way to the ceiling on one side, costumes hung in two tiers on the other, with worktables down the middle.

'The message you left. You said you had something special

239

for me.' I looked around for the red velvet cloak and didn't see it at first, even though the bedsheets that normally acted as dustcovers had been rucked up onto the top tier of hangers so that everything was exposed. I went over to the racks and started pushing garments aside.

'What the hell are you doing?' cried Denn.

'Looking for the Red Riding Hood's cloak. Wasn't that what you were going to give me?'

He rushed over and started rearranging the costumes I'd pushed aside. 'You're crushing things. Do you know how hard it is to iron taffeta? And no, it wasn't the cloak. Will you quit bugging me about the damn thing? You can have it when I'm dead. I'll will it to you, okay?'

He flipped the bedsheets down and tucked them protectively around the garments, as if I'd attacked them with muddy hands.

That was the final straw. To hell with Good Samaritanism. The pragmatist was right. 'I'll call Ambrose and tell him to meet you at the sheriff's office. See you around, Denn. Have a nice life.'

'Oh shit, Deborah, I'm sorry,' he said in instant contrition. 'It's just – my mind's going in a million different directions. Tell you what. If we don't use the cloak in *Bouncing Betty*, you can have it, okay? Look, I'll even make it official.'

He grabbed a loose sheet of paper from the worktable and printed in big capital letters I HEREBY GIVE DEBORAH KNOTT MY RED VELVET CLOAK NOW HANGING IN THE POSSUM CREEK PLAYERS THEATRE TO BE DELIVERED NO LATER THAN 60 DAYS FROM THIS DATE. Then he signed it Dennis Aloysius McCloy, dated it, and held the paper out to me with a flourish. 'Here you go, kiddo. Okay?'

I was still ticked but he noticed that my shoulder bag was unzipped and he deftly folded the paper and crammed it inside.

'No more stalling,' I said impatiently. 'Wait'll you see if you're going to be arrested before you start worrying about another production.'

'I'm ready.'

He flicked the light switches and the windowless prop room was plunged into darkness.

As we came down the hall, I thought I saw something move beyond the open outer door.

'See? What'd I tell you?' said the pragmatist.

'Oh dear!' sighed the preacher.

The patrol car was parked so that the pickup was completely blocked. A uniformed sheriff's deputy leaned against the truck's hood with a happy grin on his pudgy face and a meaty hand resting lightly on his holster. Deputy Jack Jamison.

'Major Bryant's on his way over,' he drawled. 'He said he'd 'preciate it if y'all'd wait on him.'

21

I Never Said It Would
Be Easy

Okay, so it turned out not to be as bad as it could have been.
The fact that I'd called Ambrose from Raleigh supported my
claim that I really was escorting Denn to the sheriff's office
even though, strictly speaking, Possum Creek Players Theatre
wasn't on the route.

Dwight arrived a little after six and took me off to one of
the side rooms to hear as much as I could tell without
compromising Denn's attorney-client privileges, even though
I hadn't formally said I'd represent him. We sat down at a
table across from each other; and starting off, it was Mr
Deputy Sheriff and Ms Lawyer as I described how I'd wound
up meeting Denn at Pullen Park. No meaningful glances, no
locked eyes this go-round, and soon he was back to treating
me like the Knott boys' kid sister.

'What's your gut feeling on him, Deb'rah?'

'Did he kill Michael Vickery?' I asked. 'No.'

'Well, who does he think?'

243

'I don't believe he has a clue. But if your next question's is he telling everything exactly like it happened, your guess is as good as mine. I keep trying to pin him down about why he wanted me to meet him out here, and he keeps prevaricating. You going to charge him?'

'Wouldn't you?'

'Why? Just because they fought? Lots of couples fight.'

'Oh, come on, Deb'rah. He took a gun out to the woods. He damn near killed Vickery right in front of your eyes last week. That's no little domestic squabble.'

'He was trying to scare Gayle and me from involving Michael in Janie's death again. He said Michael still had nightmares.'

'Yeah? Like a war vet's post-traumatic stress syndrome?' Dwight looked skeptical.

'I don't know. Denn keeps bringing up religion. Maybe Michael felt guilty because she lay over there so long and he didn't know, didn't help.'

He leaned back in his chair and propped one of his size elevens on the edge of the table as if he were back in my mother's kitchen, arguing with my brothers around the dinner table. He's big all over, Dwight is. Played basketball in high school and could have played at Carolina if he hadn't joined the army. Dean Smith liked the way he could handle a ball enough to send a scout over to some of his games. Big hands, bit feet, big shoulders.

And yeah, everything else in nice proportion, too.

The summer I was ten, to teach me patience and keep me out of trouble, my mother gave me a good little pair of binoculars and a bird book and told me to go find a sheltered place and just sit quietly without making sudden movements and I would see nature's wonderful secrets. There was a thick stand of grapevines and honeysuckle that overlooked the creek bank where the boys used to swim and horse around buck naked after their farm chores were done. I always came back to the house with chigger bites and scratches, but Mother was right. To this day, there's a whole bunch of men walking around Colleton County whose natural endowments are no secret to me.

Oblivious to my memories, Dwight was still laying out reasons to arrest Denn.

'—besides, you know as good as I do how many homicides come from domestic fights. If Denn was a woman whose husband'd been cheating on her, you know he'd be the prime suspect. How's this any different?'

'For one thing, I talked to his friend in Raleigh who swears Denn didn't leave his place till a quarter past nine. Say thirty-five minutes to get to the theater, you're talking what? Nine-fifty, almost ten?'

Dwight doodled a clock face on the yellow legal pad in front of him. 'It was nearly twenty-four hours before you found the body. The ME said everything was "consistent" with nine P.M. being when he died, but fifty minutes more or less don't make an alibi.'

He sat back, clicking and unclicking his ballpoint pen.

'Denn's friend also helped him unload the truck,' I said, 'and can swear categorically that there was no shotgun in it.'

Before Dwight could say the obvious, I beat him to it. 'Yeah, yeah, I know. He could have stashed it anywhere between here and Raleigh.'

Dwight grinned. 'Now you're starting to sound sensible. One drawback though: nobody at the Pot Shot ever saw a shotgun out there. Just the rifle.'

He took his foot off the table and the chair came down with a bang. 'I guess I'll just get his statement first and see what happens. You going to sit in and advise him?'

'If I can't get Ambrose to come over.'

'Is that a smart thing to do?'

'Somebody has to.'

'Yeah, but should it ought to be you?'

'Probably not,' I sighed. 'Is that all?'

'I reckon. For now anyhow.'

On the way out of the room, I remembered something and shut the door before I even had it open good.

'What?' he asked.

He's a lot taller than me, so I had to reach up to pull him down to my level. It wasn't mouth-to-mouth resuscitation or anything like that, but it was still a damn good kiss.

'Hey, wait a minute,' he said and stepped back, breathing heavily.

I laughed and fluttered my eyelashes outrageously. He was just Dwight again, only more so. 'Well, you wanted to know, didn't you?'

He was still looking dazed.

'Yeah,' he said. 'I guess I did.'

'Anything else?'

'Naah,' he grinned. 'I think that'll just about get it.'

Using the theater phone, I tried one last time to make Ambrose Daughtridge come over and sit in on the interrogation, but even after I told him that Dwight probably wouldn't book Denn, he still declined.

'I am not now and never have been Mr McCloy's attorney,' he said. 'I may've drawn up his will as a favor to Michael Vickery, but I do not consider him my client.'

Ambrose Daughtridge is silver haired and soft spoken and looks like he should be cataloguing rare books in a university library somewhere. Unlike a lot of us who are ham actors at heart, Ambrose avoids courtroom appearances when he can, prefers civil cases to criminal, and never defends anything more serious than a misdemeanor if he can help it, even though his courtroom skills are quite adequate.

'I hope you won't take this wrong, Deborah,' said Ambrose, misinterpreting my silence. 'It's not that I'm prejudiced against homosexuals or anything. I always got along just fine with Michael.'

'Because he didn't flaunt it and Denn's more obvious?' I asked caustically.

'Because he was a gentleman,' came the soft reply. 'Now I do appreciate your courtesy in calling me and your concern for the proprieties, so let me assure you, for the record, that there is nothing in my former dealings with Mr McCloy that would preclude your representing him, if you and he so choose.'

What could I say except, 'Thank you, Ambrose'?

Actually, as I walked back down the hall to tell Denn I'd look after his interests tonight if he still wanted me to, it occurred to me that I'd heard something else in that telephone conversation. Ambrose is always a perfect gentleman even when he's casting aspersions on a witness's testimony, but there'd been a conciliatory note in his voice. A definite attempt not to alienate me.

Well!

The first sign that maybe I didn't need to start drafting a concession letter to Luther Parker quite yet.

The interrogation went smoothly and quickly. Dwight set his tape recorder on the table in the green room. Denn answered all his questions calmly without breaking down again, and I had to interrupt and object to the phrasing of a question only two or three times.

When Dwight got to the specifics of Friday night, Denn said, 'You have to understand where I'm coming from, okay? Every time the Whitehead woman is mentioned, Michael freaks. So I know that if Deborah and Gayle Whitehead stir things up, Michael will start having nightmares again, right? So I think to myself that the best way to stop Deborah is to give her something else to worry about. If she's busy shoring up her campaign, she doesn't have time to bother Michael, okay? I couldn't think of any other way to stop her, so I cranked out those letters.'

He rubbed the back of his thin neck and gave me a sheepish smile. 'If I hadn't left Michael, I had this letter from Jesse I was going to doctor up. But I'm so angry Friday night that I decided nightmares serve him right, and now I'm sorry for the hard time I've given you, okay? This is a good place to meet. I'll confess. Do the sackcloth and ashes bit. Give you a pitcher – the prototype for a new line that I'll never get to produce since I'm leaving, maybe even going back to New York for a while.'

The rest I'd already heard: how he got to the theater around ten, how he found Michael dead, how he panicked and fled. He added nothing new to the telling.

When he'd finished, Dwight clicked off the tape recorder and sat looking at Denn a long moment. It was like a big brown Saint Bernard looking at a high-strung miniature poodle. Luckily for Denn, Dwight was no homophobe.

'Okay,' he said at last, 'I'm not arresting you tonight, but you don't leave the county without checking with the sheriff's department. I'll have somebody transcribe this and maybe you'll come in and sign it, say tomorrow afternoon?'

I started to shake my head silently, but before I could explain why, we heard a car horn. Deputy Jamison, who'd sat silently through the interrogation, went out to see who it was and returned a few moments later with one of the last people I expected to see that night. Dwight immediately stood up, and even though I'd heard Denn poke fun at Southern manners, he too was on his feet as Jack Jamison ushered in Michael Vickery's sister Faith, the Hollywood something or other.

She was the middle of the three Vickery children and had the same good looks. Like her mother her back was straight and her voice was cool as she addressed us after introductions had been made.

'I've come on behalf of my mother. Mr Daughtridge told her you were here, Major Bryant. Is Mr McCloy under arrest?'

'No, ma'am.'

She turned to Denn, who stood there small and gaunt in the unforgiving overhead light.

'Mother wanted you to know that Michael's wake is tonight.

At Aldcroft's. The visitation hours are from seven till nine if you wish to come?'

Denn nodded, for once inarticulate.

If there were rules of etiquette to cover a situation like this, I'd never read them; but trust Evelyn Dancy Vickery to do the correct thing. I could admire that and yet at the same time it seemed so unfair that Denn, who had loved Michael and had shared Michael's life, now had to wait on the sidelines until he was invited to participate in the rituals of Michael's death.

'The funeral will be tomorrow afternoon. At Sweetwater,' Faith Vickery concluded. 'Mother hopes you will sit with the family at tomorrow's services?'

Denn had been frozen into immobility, but as Michael's sister finished speaking, he went to her, took her hand and lifted it to his lips. A theatrical gesture, yet this time it seemed totally appropriate.

Faith squeezed his hand and for just an instant, her eyes seemed to tear. 'I *am* sorry,' she said quietly and then turned and left.

22

Lying Eyes

Denn McCloy had played the aging punk for so long that it really surprised me when he emerged from his bedroom. He couldn't do anything about the buzz cut on such short notice, but otherwise he might have been one of the middle-aged VPs over at First Federal: neat gray suit, white shirt, conservative tie, the works. He picked up on my surprise and shrugged. 'Church and Christmas dinner with his parents. Michael was pretty conventional about some things.'

I had come back to the barn with Denn because he wanted to go to the funeral home, but he didn't want to walk in alone. Even though it was stretching the attorney-client relationship, the whole situation was so bizarrely awkward that I couldn't help sympathizing. Dwight just shook his head when he heard me agree to go, but what else could I do?

There was a powder room at the top of the stairs. 'Make yourself at home,' Denn had said, so while he changed clothes in his bedroom, I'd taken a quick tour around the converted loft and decided to freshen my makeup in the master bathroom – Michael's evidently – where the light was better. Despite the long day, my slacks and silk cardigan still looked fresh. A skirt would have been more appropriate, but at least I wasn't wearing jeans.

Lily followed me in, flopped down on a towel that had been thrown on the floor, laid her muzzle on the cool tiles, and let out such a long sigh that I knelt and talked baby talk to her a minute. You always wonder how much they sense.

This was the first time I'd been upstairs at the Pot Shot, and I admit I was impressed with the quiet good taste and tidiness that permeated the whole apartment, especially Michael Vickery's bedroom, which was on the opposite side of the loft from Denn's quarters. In spite of the luxurious sand-colored carpet, the heavy handwoven beige coverlet on the king-sized bed, the expensive chests of blond oak, there was an austere feel to the room.

'Almost like a monk's cloistered cell,' said the preacher approvingly.

'Yeah, if the monk had a Dancy trust fund,' jeered the pragmatist. 'You don't find these fabrics or those custom-built chests in a thrift shop. And look at those wall hangings. Like medieval tapestries.'

'Exactly. I knew Michael was religious, but not that he was so devout.'

'May I point out that you don't have to be devout to hang works of art on your wall?'

'But look how they're arranged – almost like an altar in

a Gothic chapel. And I don't care what you think, that's certainly a cross.'

Pragmatist and preacher dissolved into pure curiosity as I righted the heavy ceramic cross that had fallen over on the chest top and looked closer at the wall hangings. There were two, approximately two feet wide by three and a half feet long; and each hung from its own heavy oak dowel that rested on inconspicuous oak pegs. Not strictly medieval now that I took another look. More a Pre-Raphaelite flavor to the figures woven into the scenes. The one on the left was a familiar-looking Madonna with long flowing brown hair, her luminous brown eyes fixed on the curly-haired infant in her lap. On the right was the woman taken in adultery, with the Christ figure pointing to a white stone in the foreground.

'He that is without sin among you, let him first cast a stone.'

Surely an odd choice of subjects?

Between the two was an empty space about four feet wide, and I realized it held a third pair of pegs positioned slightly higher on the wall. One peg was snapped off flush. And there was the third dowel itself, wedged between the back edge of the chest and the wall. Was that what had knocked over the cross?

Dwight's people had searched here, but they wouldn't have disturbed things more than necessary and they would have left all as they found it. Certainly they wouldn't have thrown a towel on the bathroom floor, nor dirtied the sink. Amid such disciplined tidiness, these anomalies leaped out at me.

I could almost see it happening: Michael had returned

from the creek, seen that his truck was gone, questioned Cathy King, who was on her way home, and learned about Denn's phone call to me. Cathy told Dwight that she'd left Michael loading one of the racks with greenware; and from the condition of the workshop, one of the other potters thought he must have put in at least an hour's work.

After that, for some reason, he'd suddenly rushed upstairs, into the bathroom to wash the clay dust from his face and hands, then back here where he'd yanked down the middle panel in such a hurry that he'd broken one of the pegs and knocked over the cross.

And then what? Driven over to the theater with it? Why? And where was it now?

No sooner had Lily and I returned to the living room than Denn entered, properly dressed for a funeral. There was a lost look in his eyes when he mentioned Michael's strong streak of conventionality, but I was too wired to be his comforter at that moment.

'Tell me, Denn, what was the middle tapestry in Michael's bedroom?'

His head jerked up and his eyes blazed. 'What the fuck were you doing in there?'

I stepped back involuntarily and he rushed past me toward Michael's room.

'And how'd you get in?' he cried. 'Pick the goddamned lock?'

'Who the hell do you think you're talking to like that?' I shouted and strode after him with matching anger. He was on his knees in the hall, examining the lock on the door, and I saw immediately that it was a heavy-duty Yale lock, not the

usual flimsy thing found on interior doors but one that required
a key both to lock and unlock it. For some reason, the open
door caused Denn to break down again and once more I was
disarmed.

'It's always locked,' he wept. 'Always. No one's allowed
in when Michael's not here. *No one!*'

'Not even you?' Surprise dissipated the rest of my anger.

'We each needed private space,' he said defensively as he
pulled out a white handkerchief and blew his nose. 'Michael
didn't go into my room uninvited either.'

Didn't go/no one's allowed. Where was Denn's choice in
the matter? I filed it in the back of my head.

'Dwight had a search warrant,' I said, 'but that lock
doesn't look forced. You sure Michael wouldn't have left it
open when he rushed out?'

I told him about the crumpled towel, the dirty sink, and
then the missing panel.

Denn stood as if dazed and uncomprehending.

'Why would he take it down?' I prodded. 'What was the
scene?'

'Scene?' he asked stupidly, staring at the empty wall a
long moment. Then he sighed and shrugged his shoulders. 'It
wasn't a scene. Just symbols of the Holy Ghost. You know –
a white dove. Lilies. That sort of thing.'

'We have to call Dwight,' I said.

'Why?'

'If it wasn't in the Volvo when I found Michael, that
might mean he either gave it to someone or his killer took it.
Either way, it could be important.'

We both looked at our watches.

'It's eight o'clock,' Denn said plaintively.

He was right. Too soon for Dwight to have gotten back to Dobbs and getting too late if we wanted to have much time at the funeral home.

'I'll call him from Aldcroft's,' I said.

As we passed back through the living room, Denn suddenly darted over to the open shelves that lined the stairwell and landing. Samples of the Pot Shot's products were displayed on lighted glass shelves like works of art.

'Here,' said Denn and presented me with a pitcher that had such subtle tones in the glazes that the colors seemed to glow with jewel-like intensity. I hated to think what it would cost in that expensive Atlanta store, but it felt good in my hands, with a nice balance and a well-designed lip. Just looking at it, I was positive this was one pitcher that would never let liquids drip or slop when I poured.

'It's not much compensation,' said Denn, 'but I really am sorry if I've damaged your campaign.'

'Sorry enough to let Linsey Thomas run a statement from you in the next *Ledger*?' I asked.

'I – yeah, okay. I guess I owe you that, too.'

Downstairs, he found a box, swathed the pitcher with tissues, and set it on the backseat of my little sports car. Lily watched with resignation as we drove off and left her sitting in the dooryard again.

Aldcrofts have been burying the dead of Cotton Grove and Colleton County from this location on Front Street for more than a hundred years; and with two Aldcroft sons recently graduated from mortuary school, it looked as if they were going to continue on into the twenty-first century.

When the first Aldcroft's burned down around 1910, they had replaced it with a stately white mansion reminiscent of Tara; and though the interior's been remodeled and modernized over the years, the exterior remains firmly antebellum. Across the front was a wide veranda graced by huge columns with Corinthian capitals. Inside were wide halls and three spacious viewing rooms furnished with comfortable sofas and soft chairs. Tall, gilt-framed mirrors on the wall reflected the subdued pink light cast by lamps with pale rose-colored glass shades.

The wide parking lot was so jammed when we arrived that I had to park on the street a half block away. Even though it was a quarter past eight, there was still a line of people that extended from the front door, across the veranda, and halfway down the broad front steps.

'Oh God!' moaned Denn as we drew near. 'I don't think I can do this.'

'Yes, you can,' I soothed. 'These are your friends, too.'

Taking his arm, we walked across the veranda and those who recognized Denn stepped back to let us pass up the shallow steps and into the crowded hall. It was just a little unnerving the way a point of silence preceded us, while a cone of low buzzing followed in our wake.

'Natural human solicitude,' whispered the preacher.

The pragmatist was too busy responding to solemn smiles and sober handshakes and trying to get a handle on the mood to remark on natural human gossips.

At most visitations, the recently deceased is the natural focal point. As a rule, collateral members of the family – cousins, nieces and nephews, or aunts and uncles – form a sort of receiving line on the right, just inside the doorway. You've come to pay your respects, so you're passed along the line till you arrive at the open coffin, where there is a moment of silence, a moment to gaze with good remembrances (often), or hungry curiosity (always), upon that still face forever silent till the trump of judgment calls it from the grave.

A closed coffin seems somehow almost antisocial. Even where there are compelling reasons for it, as with Michael, there's always a sense of something incomplete when one is confronted with nothing more than polished wood and a blanket of carnations and baby's breath.

Then the line moves again and now you are face-to-face with the immediate family.

I have been to wakes of unloved men that were like Sunday afternoon socials where folks caught up on their visiting and almost forgot the reason they'd come together. I've been to wakes for well-loved matriarchs of large families and seen such gladness for release from long or painful illnesses that the wakes often turned into bittersweet celebrations of their lives. Tragic are the wakes for toddlers, more tragic still for children and youths cut down in the morning of their lives with all those shining possibilities consigned to the grave. If I never attend another funeral for a teenager killed in a car crash, it will be too soon.

Until now though, Janie Whitehead's was the only wake for a murdered person that I'd attended and if there was a pattern, it lay in the numb disbelief of the victim's loved ones and in the low-voiced speculations of their friends.

Denn's presence exacerbated both.

Yet people were tactful and kind. Michael's two sisters and their husbands and three adolescent children were first in the family line beyond the coffin and they closed ranks around Denn as soon as we had found a pathway through the crush of mourners. Each sister squeezed his arm, each brother-in-law and Dr Vickery gave him a firm handclasp, and even Mrs Vickery held out her hands and lifted her ravaged face for a formal kiss. Then the sisters positioned themselves on each side of him, so as to minimize any remaining awkwardness.

And I had not been wrong when I reminded Denn that many of these people were his friends, too. Most were firmly against homosexuality in theory. Most were also firmly against atheism, secular humanism, adultery, alcoholism, kleptomania, and a whole range of other things people did or were that deviated from the perceived norm; and that didn't stop them from looking past all that if the person was basically decent and didn't do whatever it was in the middle of the road and scare the mules.

Michael and Denn had been liked for who they were and for their positive contributions to the community, and there were wreaths from both the volunteer fire department and the Possum Creek Players to prove it.

Nevertheless, I could feel an unusual electricity in the air, and I'm sure more than one person wondered when they murmured condolences and shook Denn's hand why Denn wasn't in jail or at least under heavy bond.

When I had been through the line and signed the register, I went down the rear hall to the business office and used their phone to call Dwight.

'A *what*?' he asked.

Patiently I described the tapestry wall hanging as Denn had described it to me.

'No,' said Dwight. 'There was nothing like that in the car. I'll get Fletcher to make a sketch of it tomorrow and we'll keep an eye out for it.'

23

This Ain't My First Rodeo

The next hour passed rapidly. The large outer hall ran the entire width of the funeral home and people who had already paid their respects to the family either lingered there to speak with those still waiting on line to go in, or, as I had done, broke off into quiet conversational groups.

In addition to friends and neighbors, there were also some prominent faces out from Raleigh. G. Hooks Talbert was accompanied by the current president of the bank that had bought out the Cotton Grove bank Mrs Vickery's family had founded. The Vickerys were not especially political, but they contributed generously to the Democratic Party and I recognized a member of a former governor's cabinet and some division heads.

Several of the people I spoke to were curious about my involvement with Michael's murder and were not shy about asking, including Sammy Junior Johnson and his wife, Helen, who lived a few miles out in the country, near Bethel Baptist.

Sammy's mother and mine had been best friends from girlhood, and Sammy Junior didn't mind telling me that he was worried about the effect all this could have on the runoff election. Both of them had campaigned for me in their community and Helen, too, was concerned.

'I mean, don't you think it's getting a little bizarre?' she asked. 'First there's Gray Talbert's letter to the editor supporting you – Gray *Talbert*? Whose daddy's one of the biggest Republicans in the state? Do you know how weird that sounds?'

Even though her voice was almost too low for me to hear, Sammy Junior shushed her. 'He's right over there.'

Helen ignored him. 'Then that story in the paper about those two phony letters, and more stories – on television even! – about you finding Michael Vickery's body, and now people are saying you're the only reason Denn McCloy's not reading about the funeral from the new jail over in Dobbs.'

'I can explain all that,' I protested.

'I'm sure you can, honey,' she said, 'but who's going to listen to the truth with such nice juicy rumors flying? You really ought to quit this messing around till after the election.'

'She's right,' said Minnie. She, Seth, and Haywood and their kids had joined our circle just as Helen launched into her indictment.

The teenagers soon splintered off to form their own circle with Sammy Junior and Helen's two, and when Minnie and Helen stopped lecturing me for things I mostly had no control over if they'd just stop and think about it, I stuck my head into the kids' circle to thank them for riding the *N&O* newsbox trail for me the past few nights.

'I'll fill you in later, but y'all can stop watching now,' I told them. 'There's not going to be any more of those letters.'

Haywood's Stevie and Seth's Jessica looked a bit disappointed that their night-riding was over so quickly, but I noticed that Stevie brightened up when Gayle Whitehead appeared on the line with Jed.

In the midst of death, we are in life.

It was after nine-thirty before the final visitors left. The three grandchildren and two sons-in-law had escaped twenty minutes earlier when the crowds first thinned. Dr Vickery was bearing up well, but Mrs Vickery looked absolutely at the point of collapse and her daughters hovered over her nervously. Even knowing how devoted she'd been to Michael, I couldn't help wondering how much of her exhaustion was from grief and how much from all the touching and hugging she'd had to endure since Saturday night.

I lingered discreetly on the veranda while Duck Aldcroft confirmed a few final details about the next day's arrangements. The service was going to be out at Sweetwater with interment among those Dancys who had first farmed the land where the Pot Shot now stood, and Duck needed to find out who was going to ride where. They fixed it that daughter Hope would ride in the lead car with her parents and that Denn would be taken in the second car with Faith and her family.

The Vickerys left, and Duck and I passed a few words while we waited on the veranda for Denn to have a final time alone with Michael. It was almost ten before he emerged, clutching his handkerchief, red blotches under his eyes.

'Thanks for waiting, kiddo,' he said and then didn't speak again until we crossed Possum Creek and headed south on Forty-Eight.

'I just wish Michael could somehow know how nice his family were tonight. Mrs Vickery . . . You know how much she hated it when Michael brought me down.'

'Yes, I do,' I said. 'People thought it would absolutely kill her to admit Michael was gay.'

I flicked my beams and the oncoming driver hastily dimmed his. On such a dark night, brights were even more dazzling than usual.

'Perversion is abomination unto the Lord,' said Denn. 'That's what she told Michael when she came up to New York and realized I wasn't just an ordinary roommate. She almost won, too, did you know that?'

Despite an emotionally draining day, he seemed keyed up and anxious to talk, as if he needed to put his years with Michael in perspective.

'How?'

'That time he left me and came home. She almost owned his soul. See, she comes to New York, finds out for sure her only son is gay and just about flips out. The abomination. The shame. She goes berserk and does such a head job on Michael that he gets schizoid about it; starts to think maybe she's right and New York *is* a bad influence. Lots of people are AC/DC and maybe he can be straight in an all-straight community. So he comes back, starts to date a debutante, takes over the barn, lays every brick of the kiln himself till he falls into bed exhausted every night.'

'And it didn't work?'

'Well, here I am, aren't I?' he said simply. 'Mrs V. hates it when he sends for me, but you know something? Once I get here, even though she never pretends to like me, every time I see her, she's always polite. But nothing like tonight. She's a real class act, isn't she?'

'Yes,' I said, turning into the Pot Shot's lane. 'She certainly is that.'

A minute or so later, I pulled up beside the pickup and Lily trotted over to greet us.

'I hate to drive this truck, but I sure don't want the Volvo back either,' Denn mused, as he opened the door and rubbed the dog's ears.

'Were you going out again tonight?' I asked.

'No, no,' he said hastily. 'Just thinking out loud. I guess I'll have to file an insurance claim on the car.' He sighed. 'Michael always took care of stuff like that. I never even had to balance a checkbook.'

He sighed again. 'Thanks for everything, Deborah. I'd invite you in, but I'm really beat. The only thing I want is to just go upstairs and fall into bed.'

I was thoughtful as I drove back down the lane, and the ceramic pitcher on the backseat only fueled my speculations. So many loose ends, so many unanswered questions, starting with did Denn think I maybe only scored a 380 on my SATs?

As I neared the intersection of New Forty-Eight and Old Forty-Eight, I met a sheriff's patrol car that passed and headed south. Too dark to recognize the driver, but Jack Jamison was probably home watching television at this hour.

The sensible thing was to go on home to bed myself.

'Better to confirm a suspicion than let it fester,' said the pragmatist.

'Right on!' said the preacher.

Back of Possum Creek Theatre, a rough drive circled down to the edge of the creek, and I stuck my car in amongst some tall bushes. There was friction tape in the glove compartment and I used it to tape the light button closed so the overhead wouldn't come on every time I opened the door, then I kicked off my leather sandals and put on the beat-up sneakers I always keep in the trunk next to the locked tool box.

Inside the box, on top of the usual screwdrivers and pliers, was the loaded .38 Daddy gave me when I told him I didn't need a man to take care of me. I checked to make sure the safety was in place, then strapped on the leg holster that I occasionally use when I'm out on the road late at night by myself. Carrying a concealed weapon without a license is against the law, of course, but one advantage of being a white, well-dressed female in this part of the country is that if you get stopped for a traffic violation, you're never going to have to submit to much of a pat down. Especially if you've made it clear up front that you're an attorney.

Putting penlight, pocketknife, and keys in my pocket, I locked my purse in the trunk and leaned against the car till my eyes got used to the darkness.

Darker than usual, too. The moon wasn't due up for another hour and there wasn't even any starlight with the sky still socked in. If it hadn't been for Raleigh's lights reflected off the low clouds, it would have been pitch black. I shivered in the clammy night air and wished I'd kept Denn's jacket.

Down here by the rain-swollen creek, I heard no sounds of traffic from the highway. A dog barked way off across the creek like he'd treed something, but mostly it was the insistent repetitive call of chuck-will's-widows in the near underbrush and cricket chirps from all around that filled my ears.

When my eyes were fully adjusted, I walked up the lane to the theater, now a bulky white shape against the darker pines. If I'd been thinking clearer earlier in the evening, I'd have left a window unlocked or slipped the bolt on the theater door so that it'd close without actually locking.

No cars and no movement. I slipped across the concrete loading area on the off-chance Jack Jamison might not've locked the door.

Fort Knox.

So it was to be breaking and entering? And me with nothing but a pocketknife to jigger a lock.

'Go home,' said the pragmatist. *'If Minnie and Helen think you've got troubles now, what're they going to think when you appear before Perry Byrd for burglary?'*

'Nothing ventured, nothing gained,' the preacher said *nervously.*

As I went around the old wooden building testing windows, I heard a snatch of human sound and froze. Silence. Wait. Cautiously circling the west side, I saw car lights flash back and forth on the highway and realized the noise must have been someone's loud radio.

An instant later, I got lucky. Like an invitation to a naughty world, not only was there an unlocked window on this side – the men's room, if I remembered rightly – it was already open a crack at the bottom. I wouldn't have to use a rock after all.

Standing on tiptoes, I gave a mighty push and cringed at the raucous squeak of wooden window against tight wooden sash. Once it was open, I was further chagrined to discover I couldn't swing myself up as nimbly as I'd once shinnied up trees and clambered around on rooftops. Evidently morning stretches weren't enough anymore. Going to take something more strenuous to get back my upper torso strength.

I wound up doing an undignified scramble over the window ledge and landed with a crash in a bank of urinals. Thank God, there was no one there to see.

Inside was blacker than Satan's unwashed soul, but I fumbled my way out into the windowless hall and closed the door before risking a quick flick of my penlight. Once I got my bearings, I went straight down to the prop room, every nerve taut, all my senses quivering.

As I opened the door, I heard a rustle somewhere near and every red corpuscle in my body ducked down behind the nearest white ones.

Remembering that the light switches were just inside the door, I reached down for my gun, flicked off the safety, and switched on the lights all in one fluid motion.

The big cluttered room sprang into sharp focus.

Empty.

I let out the breath I'd been holding for the last week. A mouse, no doubt, and here I was like Dirty Harry ready to blow it away. I put the pistol back in my leg holster. Time to quit scaring myself with imaginary goblins and look for a good hiding place. If I was right, I probably wouldn't have very long to wait.

The open shelves offered no cover. Behind the costumes?

Too Abbott and Costello. Besides, my sneakers were sure to be noticed beneath the hemlines.

Several pieces of furniture were stacked on top of one another at the far end of the long room, and off in the corner stood that one item indispensable to comic farce – a Chinese screen.

Perfect!

I turned off the lights and used my penlight to keep from banging into worktables or tripping over clutter as I worked my way back into the corner where the screen stood.

Suddenly, a sense of danger overwhelmed me and the closer I got to the corner, the stronger it was.

Just as I reached over to pull the screen out enough to slip behind, I heard an indrawn breath.

My penlight swept over big male boots, long male legs and I almost screamed when it touched his leering face.

'Boo!' said Dwight.

24

You Really Had Me Going

'You scared the holy shit out of me,' I raged.

'Well, how do you think I felt when I saw you waving that pistol around?' Dwight asked. 'Bo Poole give you a permit to carry that thing?'

Before I could think of a misleading answer, he thumbed his walkie-talkie and it crackled into staticky life. So much for a radio up on the highway.

'Blue Jay to Baby Bird,' he said. 'I'm back on the air. Over.'

'Blue Jay to Baby Bird?' I hooted.

'Shh!'

Immediately I heard Jack Jamison's voice. 'Baby Bird to Blue Jay. The Snowball's rolling. Just passed my position, heading north on Forty-Eight. Over.'

'Give him plenty of slack, Baby Bird. Out.'

Dwight flicked on his own flashlight and stepped from behind the screen. I followed and put on the overhead lights.

'Who thought up those names?' I teased.

Dwight just looked at me and shook his head. 'The first thing most women would ask is what I'm doing here.'

'Obvious,' I said. 'You're waiting for Denn McCloy. Soon as I called you about a tapestry panel missing off Michael Vickery's wall, you remembered how Denn stopped off here this afternoon. And then you figured that he'd probably sneak back tonight to get it.'

'You don't?'

I've got to start remembering that Dwight knows me too well.

'Oh, he's coming back for something,' I said, 'only I think it's something he left here himself Friday night.'

'Yeah?' He glanced at his watch and walked over to the door. 'Come on. Let's go where we can see him coming.'

Using our shielded flashlights, we walked through the aisles of the theater out to the front lobby where double glass doors overlooked the main drive in from the highway.

I didn't need to have Dwight draw me a picture to know that he'd stood right here and watched me drive in and hide my car down on the creek bank.

''Preciate the open window,' I said.

'I was afraid you were going to bust one before you found it. Hey, you know something? I always thought cat burglars were supposed to be quiet.' He was a dark shape against the white walls, but I saw his teeth flash in a mocking grin as I punched his shoulder.

'So what'd McCloy leave here?' he asked, turning serious.

'Whatever it was he was going to give me.'

'A pitcher?'

272

'Made a pretty story, didn't it?' I said sourly. 'Only when we walked upstairs together for him to change clothes for the funeral home, that particular pitcher was sitting on a shelf at the top of the stairs. He thought I wouldn't remember that he was supposed to've had it with him on Friday night when he drove out here to meet me. Kinda insulting, isn't it?'

The walkie-talkie burst into sound again. 'Baby Bird to Blue Jay. The Snowball should be in your view any minute now! Over.'

Up on the highway, headlights slowed, then turned into the drive. Instinctively I drew away from the door as Dwight said, 'I see him, Baby Bird. Proceed as planned. Out.'

As the pickup's headlights flashed through the pines, Dwight turned off the receiver and took my hand and we rushed down the aisle. He tried to get me to hide behind the curtains on stage, but I said no way, José, and there wasn't time for him to make me. As it was, we barely got ourselves stationed behind the screen again than we heard the outer door thump to. No hiding the truck or cautious reconnoiter for Denn.

A moment later, the prop room door opened and lights came on. The Chinese screen had four hinged panels, and Dwight and I both had our eyes up against the narrow cracks. We saw Denn framed in the doorway, still in his white shirt, but now wearing his usual black jeans and black leather cap.

'No!' he said sharply. 'Come on in here and behave yourself.'

A familiar clicking sound pattered along the hall and then, to my utter dismay, Lily trotted past him and began sniffing the air.

Dwight and I both froze.

'Good girl,' Denn said absently and walked over to the racks of costumes.

Lily quartered the room, poking her nose under the dust sheet, checking out the boxes under the worktables.

As Denn started to pull back a dust sheet, Lily suddenly caught our scent. Her hackles rose and a low rumble started in her chest.

'What's the matter, girl?' asked Denn, hesitating with the sheet in his hand.

Stiff legged, the dog slowly stalked across the room toward our hiding place. Her growl became a snarl and then she was barking fiercely and looking to Denn for instructions.

Without waiting to see who we were, Denn took off through the door.

'Stop!' Dwight roared as the screen fell over with a crash.

Confused, Lily didn't seem to know whether to run or attack and I used her hesitation to call out, 'Good girl, Lily. Come on, you know me. Right? There's a good girl.'

I don't know if it was because she did remember that I'd scratched her ears earlier in the evening or because she had always been more Michael's dog than Denn's, but she lowered her hackles and came over to me with her tail wagging while Dwight chased after Denn.

It wasn't much of a chase since Jack Jamison – ol' Baby Bird – had blocked the pickup's exit again.

Denn was brought back to the prop room where he tried to bluster it out.

'I have a right to be here. I have a key!' he stormed. 'Do you? Where's your warrant?'

274

He did a true double take when he saw me standing there with Lily. 'Deborah? You here, too? What's going on?'

'You want a minute alone with your client?' Dwight asked.

'He's no client of mine,' I said. 'I don't keep clients who lie to me.'

'*Lie?*' cried Denn.

'Lie,' I said coldly and gave him chapter and verse about the pitcher. 'You start telling the truth right this minute or I'm outta here and you can rot in jail for all I care. In fact, jail might be your best bet right now. Hasn't it sunk in yet that maybe it was supposed to be *you* lying in a closed coffin at Aldcroft's? Your car, *kiddo*, sitting right where *you* were supposed to be.'

His head came up and his eyes widened abruptly. Clearly this was the first time such an obvious – and terrifying – possibility had occurred to him.

'You've jerked me around all afternoon,' I snarled. 'I haven't had any supper, and I'm tired of holding your hand while you think up more lies. Why'd you really leave word for me to come here Friday?'

Denn's thin shoulders suddenly slumped in defeat. 'I was going to tell you who killed Janie Whitehead.'

25

It's Out Of My Hands

As soon as he'd said it, I think Denn wished he could take it back. The narrow brim of his black leather cap shadowed his eyes from the overhead lights, but I saw the wrenching pain there as he bit his lips.

'It feels like such a betrayal now,' he whimpered. 'He said we were through. There's someone in Durham he wanted to be with. I was hurt. And furious. All I could think of was how to hurt him back. If you'd answered the phone, Deborah, I'd have told you then and there what happened to Gayle's mother, but it was only because I was mad *then*. I knew before I left Raleigh that night that I wouldn't go through with it. That's why I was late getting back. I hoped you would have gotten tired of waiting and already left. How could I betray him after all these years?'

'He can't be hurt now by anything you tell us,' I said.

Dwight was less diplomatic. 'Talk,' he said, plunking the tape recorder down on the table in front of Denn.

Rattled by the emotional roller coaster he'd been on since Michael's death, Denn talked.

While Jack went off to try to find us some hamburgers or something, Denn sat hunched in a wicker peacock chair with a slipcover of gold satin – the throne from *Once upon a Mattress*, I believe – and told us how Janie Whitehead died.

'I explained about how Michael came back to Cotton Grove eighteen years ago and tried to lead a straight life?' he asked me.

I nodded. 'But you need to tell Dwight, too.'

Haltingly, Denn repeated the tale of how Mrs Vickery had worked on Michael's basically conservative nature and his sense of guilt to persuade him to come home and make an effort to be the manly son she and Dr Vickery could be proud of. He could do it if he tried. They would help him.

'You don't realize how much things have changed down here these last twenty years,' said Denn. 'I'm not saying gay marriages are ever going to make it in this county, but back then some people would rather have their kids dead than admit they were gay. Am I right?'

''Fraid so,' said Dwight, and I thought of Will. He'd still rather take a licking than have it come out about Trish.

'So Michael tells me good-bye and comes home in January. New year. New beginning. And from January to May, he tries to be straight. He prays, he paints, he piles bricks for a kiln, he even chases after pu' – glancing at me, Denn caught himself – 'pretty girls.'

He paused. 'Could I have some water?'

He and Dwight both looked at me.

278

'Why sure,' I said. 'I believe there's a water fountain down by the men's room. Y'all go right ahead. I'll just wait and drink whatever Jack brings me.'

Dwight laughed. Denn didn't seem to think it was particularly funny. He went over to the work sink, pulled a paper cup from the dispenser hanging on the wall, and ran himself a long drink.

'Not stalling, are you?' I asked.

'Now, Deborah,' Dwight said mildly, 'let the man wet his throat.'

Well, look at that, I thought to myself. *I get to play Bad Cop.*

The table was just a hair too wide for me to kick Dwight. Besides, I had on sneakers, not some pointy-toed pumps that would do a number on his shins. But at least my sharp question got Denn back on his fairy-tale throne and Dwight turned the tape recorder back on. He gave me a transcript later and I might as well put it in here, since the rest of Denn's story was pretty much a monologue.

TRANSCRIPT OF INTERROGATION CONDUCTED 15 MAY

Voices present on this tape:

DM = Dennis 'Denn' McCloy

DB = Maj. Dwight Bryant, deputy sheriff, Colleton County

DK = Deborah Knott, attorney at law

DM: As I was saying, Michael tries to do it Mrs

Vickery's way and he's miserable. Now, at the back of their grounds, that's where Janie Whitehead's living with her husband and new baby. She's nice. Friendly. Michael doesn't think twice about her because she's a married lady and a mother.

I told you that he was pretty conventional in a lot of ways, right?

Anyhow, on the day it happens, Michael's been working out at the barn all morning and he drives back into town and stops at Hardee's for a hamburger. As he gets back to his truck, it starts to rain again and about that time, Janie Whitehead pulls in beside him. She wants a Pepsi and she's got the baby with her and Michael, always a gentleman, goes back in and gets it for her. Well, the rain's really coming down now, and she pushes the car door open on the passenger side and tells him to get in and talk with her a minute. He eats his hamburger, she drinks her Pepsi, she asks him about how his remodeling's coming along out at the barn.

If he'd worked ten minutes longer or quit ten minutes sooner, it never would've happened.

DK: Wait a minute. They sat and talked at Hardee's? You sure? Somebody said it was at the old Dixie Motel.

DM: Yeah. Howard Grimes. Michael never understood how that old coot got the two parking lots mixed up. Turns out it was a good thing he did though.

See, Janie starts asking so many questions that somehow, before Michael knows how it happens, he asks her if she wants to see the barn. Of *course* she does. Then she acts like it's a done deal that they have to drive out together, and since she's got the baby and all in the backseat, she drives.

God, he's such an innocent, Michael. He's got no interest in women, so he forgets they might think he's the sexiest looking thing *they* ever saw.

DB: What'd you say, Deborah?

DK: Nothing. Denn's right though. Michael *was* a hunk in those days. I just never realized Janie was looking, too.

DM: She was looking, kiddo. They get out to the barn and she takes the baby upstairs with her to see how Michael's roughed in the partitions and laid out the baths. Marble slab for the hearth. And all the time, she's giving him this line about how it might surprise him to know that Cotton Grove's as sophisticated as New York in some ways. Right. And then she tries to kiss him. Takes him so off-balance that he blurts out something that makes her guess, and he's too flustered to deny it right away. And to show you how sophisticated she is, she totally freaks. I mean, she's bouncing off the goddamn walls, yelling what the fuck's happening to Cotton Grove? Is everybody in the whole fucking town queer as a three-dollar bill? When did Cotton Grove become the fag and dyke capitol of the county? I mean this lady's the homophobe from hell, right?

You want to hear the kicker? Seems *she's* been jumped by a couple of lesbians a couple of weeks earlier! She's decided she has to get it on with Michael to prove to herself that there's nothing queer about her, and damned if she hasn't hit on the only man in town who can't get it up for her!

DB: You wanted to say something, Deborah?

DK: No.

DM: Well, she starts screaming that she doesn't care who he is. Cotton Grove doesn't need his kind of filth. She's going to tell everybody in town. He'll be run out on a rail. His family disgraced. The whole schmear. She grabs her coat to go and—

Okay, he never says he actually pushes her, but he does panic. He sees this messy scandal, his mother totally wiped out with humiliation in front of the whole town, his father shamed. He can't let her do it. I don't know how it happens, but suddenly she falls over backwards and cracks her head open on the sharp edge of the marble hearth. There's blood all over everything. Now he *really* panics. It's bad enough she was going to tell the world he's gay; now he's a gay who's assaulted a sweet young mother.

He knows he ought to drive into town for help, but he's too scared of what'll happen when she regains consciousness. He thinks, What if she never wakes up? His secret will be safe. She almost quits breathing. He's sure she's going to die any minute and he's paralyzed. It's like a bad dream with no way out and he sits there for hours till it's past dark and he realizes that he's waited too long. There's no way he can call for help now. And soon somebody's liable to notice how long his truck's parked at Hardee's.

The baby's screaming. He runs down and finds a bottle of milk and the baby drinks it and goes off to sleep. He's not thinking clear at this point or he'd put the baby in the car and leave her, but he's afraid no one'll find the car before she gets a heat stroke and dies. Anyhow, he drives Janie's car back to Cotton Grove, leaves it behind her father-in-law's office, and walks over to Hardee's about a block away, where he picks up his truck and goes on home to his parents' house, like nothing's happened.

When he gets there, he hears that Janie and the baby have been missed and that half the town's turned out by this time to look for them. He hardly closes his eyes that night, and next morning, he's almost afraid to go back out to the barn.

He finally does. Janie's still alive and the baby's screaming like crazy till he can't stand it. He picks Janie up and carries her down to the creek. It's still cool and rainy. At first he thinks maybe he'll put her in the water and let the creek take her away. But he just can't do it. He keeps walking on down the creek bank. When he gets opposite the mill, he's talked himself into believing that even if she's found now, she's too far gone to ever regain consciousness. He'll just put her and the baby in the mill loft and soon somebody's bound to check it out.

DK: But they already had. My brothers were there that Thursday morning.

DM: Yeah? Was that why it took 'em so long to find her? I wondered about that.

DK: But Michael *knew* my brothers were there, Denn. He told Gayle and me that he'd met them coming out of the lane and that's why he didn't search the mill himself.

DM: Yeah? Well, he probably said that to throw you off, keep you from wondering why he didn't go over himself. Anyhow, he spends Thursday cleaning up the blood till there was no trace of it. Every minute he expects the sheriff or somebody to drive into the barnyard and ask if he knows anything about how Janie got in the mill, but nothing. Another awful night. The tension's killing him. He stays away Friday. Doesn't come back till early Saturday morning and they *still* haven't found Janie. So now he decides that she's never going to be found. It's over with. He just has to carry on normally. He's arranged for a couple of guys to work that morning, so he goes and gets them and drives them out to the barn. I guess you know the rest after that? How they found her. And Michael had to go over and look at her. It was awful for him. Just awful.

DK: When did he shoot her?

DB: And what did he do with the pistol?

DK: Come on, Denn. Finish it up.

DM: That's the part he never wants to talk about. In fact, I don't find out for months that that's how she finally dies. He tells me all that I've just told you when he comes for me. How it was an accident, but he can't ever tell anyone. But he doesn't mention the shot and there's not that many people around here talking to me yet. It's on into next spring and somebody says something about Janie Whitehead being shot and it surprises the hell out of me. He wouldn't tell me any of the details. 'It had to be done,' he says. 'She suffered too long as it was. I was a coward not to do it the first night.'

DB: If he was so afraid to have Cotton Grove know he was gay . . .

DM: Why'd he come out of the closet and bring me down?

DB: Yeah.

DM: He tried it straight and look where it got him. He's in total despair. Can't sleep. Can't eat. It's like he has to do something major to make up for hurting Janie. He talks about atoning.

Gives up art. Or thinks he does. He says the fine arts are a snare and a delusion and from now on he's just going to be a simple artisan and make plain utilitarian things. Like the Shakers. Only he really is an artist, and even when he's trying to be plain, it's plain with a spin on it, right?

And it's still not enough. He's like one of those strange desert monks from early Christian times, those guys that sit inside hollow trees or on top of pillars. Michael really loved me, I know he did, but at the same time, coming out of the closet was sort of like a hair shirt.

Okay, okay, I know it sounds strange, but it sort of makes a crazy sense – Janie gets hurt because he denies what he is, right? Even though I tell him it's not really his fault. And when you think about it, she's as much to blame for what happened as he is. It's not him who goes looking for her, is it? But Michael can't see it like that, and so to punish himself, he admits to the world that he's gay.

DB: He gets to be himself and this is punishment?

DK: It's weird, but Denn's right, Dwight. Go take another look at that altar he set up in his bedroom. I thought the Madonna and child looked familiar. They could be Janie and Gayle. They *were* Janie and Gayle to him, weren't they, Denn?

DM: Yes.

DB: So who killed him, McCloy?

DM: I don't know. Honest.

At this point, Baby Bird Jamison returned with a bag of hamburgers, fries, and four chocolate shakes. Denn wasn't hungry and merely picked at his, but just the aroma made me shaky. It'd been nearly twelve hours since I'd had anything more than a stale Nabs cracker I'd found in the bottom of my purse before locking it in my trunk. I was so ravenous that I'd gobbled down all my fries and was ready to start on Denn's when Dwight remembered the missing panel.

'Why do you think Michael took it down, and where is it now?' he asked.

Again Denn shook his head. 'I just can't figure it.'

He unwrapped his hamburger and began feeding it to Lily, who acted almost as hungry as me. When she'd finished it, he leaned back wearily in the golden chair. 'I'm dead.'

That brought an ironic smile to his lips. 'Look, could we please call it a day? Any minute now, all my systems are going to crash.' He took a deep breath. 'And tomorrow doesn't look to be any easier.'

Dwight looked as disappointed as any man with a mouthful of dill pickle could manage. 'I was hoping I could get you to draw me a picture of what that panel looked like. The Holy Ghost, I believe you told Deb'rah?'

Denn yawned without bothering to hide it. 'Yeah. A dove and some lilies. Can't it wait till tomorrow?'

'Okay,' Dwight said. 'You want Deputy Jamison to run you back?'

'No,' he answered wearily. 'I'll be okay. Come on, Lily. Let's go home.'

Jack Jamison looked after them so longingly that Dwight took pity on him, too.

'The Pot Shot's on your way home, isn't it?'

'Yes, sir,' said Jamison.

'Well, if Miss Knott here will drop me off in Dobbs—'

'Consider yourself dropped,' I said.

'You can head on home then,' said Dwight. 'Just follow along behind McCloy and see he doesn't run off the road.'

We munched in companionable silence for a few minutes after we heard the two vehicles drive off, then Dwight said, 'Oh, damn!'

'What?'

'I never asked him what he was looking for in amongst the costumes.'

I finished my hamburger and walked over to the racks. 'You reckon it was Michael's panel?'

I hitched up the dust sheet and started flipping through the costumes one by one. 'It would be easy to slip a piece of fabric like that on one of the hangers, wouldn't it?'

Interested, Dwight pulled a chair over and started working through the upper rack from the other end.

It took longer than I thought it would since some hangers held two garments, one inside the other. We passed each other in the middle and, after about ten minutes, had reached the ends of our respective racks without finding the panel.

I glanced up and saw Dwight with his hand on red velvet. 'My cloak,' I said.

'Huh?'

'Denn's going to give me that cloak soon as the next production's finished. Isn't it gorgeous? Hand it down a minute.'

He lifted it off the rack, hanger and all. 'Thing weighs a ton.'

'Why do you think Victorian women were called the weaker sex?' I said. 'They must have been worn out before they began, just lugging that much cloth around on their bodies all day. No wonder they were always fainting.'

'I always thought it was those whalebone corsets.'

I undid the clasp to free the hanger and then realized there was another garment underneath.

One that was stiff and red and shiny.

'Oh my *God*!'

'What?' Alarmed by my tone, Dwight quickly stepped down from the chair and came to me. 'What is it?'

'Janie's raincoat,' I whispered. 'The one she was wearing the day she disappeared.'

26

Hell Stays Open All
Night Long

Dwight had read through the files on Janie Whitehead's death when he took over the detective division at the sheriff's department, but he'd been in the army both when she died and when the SBI reworked the case seven years ago. Even if he'd been here, the SBI wouldn't have let him read *their* files, so I had to explain the significance of Janie's slicker.

By this time, I was getting a little confused myself. 'What makes it crazy is that Howard Grimes was so right about seeing Janie wearing this, yet got it mixed up about where they were parked.'

'Howard Grimes . . . he any kin to Amos and Petey Grimes?'

I wasn't sure. 'Their uncle, maybe?'

Dwight shook his head. 'Their daddy's the only one I knew. Howard Grimes. He died a few years back, didn't he?'

'Yes, just about the time the SBI reworked the murder. I

asked Dr Vickery about him last week and he said Grimes really did have a bad heart.'

Even as we talked about him, we were both being real careful not to touch the slicker Howard Grimes had described any more than we could help. Such a shiny surface would hold fingerprints. Dwight lifted off the heavy cloak and I hung the coat, still on its hanger, on a nearby hook.

It was cheaply made and unlined. Slick red vinyl backed with some sort of white cheesecloth to give it shape. Dwight was interested in an ugly brown splotch on the inside and he used the eraser ends of two pencils to hold the front open.

'No fold marks,' I said.

'Hmm?'

'If this had been folded up in a box for eighteen years, it'd have deep creases. It's already starting to have some from being squashed inside the cloak. See?' It was an A-line garment and I pointed to some longitudinal folds where the skirt part had been constricted. 'But look at the shoulders. That's odd. Permanent wrinkles across the upper sleeves?'

Dwight stepped back and watched as I lifted a sleeve with his pencil until it was extended straight out horizontally from the shoulder. The wrinkles fell into place naturally.

'It was stored flat?' Dwight asked.

Despite the warm evening, I felt the hair on my arms stand up. 'You could say that. I bet if you turn the hanger around though, you'd see a deep little dent at each elbow.'

Dwight reached out and turned it.

I was right.

'Picture this hanging on a wall,' I told him, 'with a three-foot oak dowel running through the sleeves to hold them out, and the dowel resting on two pegs. It would look like a cross, wouldn't it?'

'Crimson as the blood of Christ,' he said. 'Splashed with Janie Whitehead's blood. Jesus! Was he crazy?'

'Define crazy,' I said, feeling infinitely weary. 'Only north-northwest, probably. Every time I ever saw him, he could tell a hawk from a handsaw.'

Dwight smiled. 'Tired?'

'A little. What time is it?' I looked at my watch. Not yet midnight. It felt much later. 'I guess it's too late to call Terry Wilson?'

He scowled.

'Don't be like that,' I said. 'You know you're going to have to sooner or later. Scotty Underhill, too.'

'Yeah, I know. I guess I was thinking it might be nice to let the Vickerys get their son buried before we tell everybody he was a killer.' He went back to the table and sat down on the edge with his milkshake. 'Still got a lot of unanswered questions. Who killed Michael? Why'd he bring the raincoat over here and hide it?'

'That wasn't Michael, that was Denn.'

'How do you figure?'

'Because when I thought it was a tapestry panel missing, he very obligingly made up a dove and some lilies, remember?'

'Oh, yeah.'

He held out his empty cup as I uncapped the chocolate milkshake Denn hadn't touched. I poured him half and took the rest for myself. Most of the ice cream had melted, but it was still cool and sweet on the tongue.

'There must have been a spare key to Michael's room, so when Denn called me, he knew he was going to bring the slicker as proof. And I bet he stopped off here first on his way to Raleigh because he wouldn't have wanted his friend to see it.'

'Makes sense.' Dwight slurped his straw and tossed the cardboard cup into the wastebasket. 'Three points,' he crowed, and I saw a lanky teenager in his grin.

'Two,' I said. 'Your foot was inside the circle.'

He stood and stretched with his hands clasped over his head so that the thin fabric of his summer jacket tightened across his chest. Then he shook himself out and finished summing up.

'So Michael goes upstairs, suddenly realizes the thing's missing. He can see his whole life hitting the fan. He might not know where Denn's gone with his truck, but Cathy King's told him where he's going to be at nine o'clock. And who's McCloy planning to meet? The same little ol' busybody lawyer who's been poking around about Janie Whitehead's murder.'

'Michael lied to Denn about the mill, you know. Will and Seth did meet him at the end of the lane that morning.' I was suddenly sobered. 'Was I a catalyst, Dwight? Did I cause somebody else to figure it out first and is that why Michael was killed?'

'You can't start second-guessing everything you do, shug,' he said. 'Anyhow, Janie's got no brothers to avenge her and her daddy's dead. 'Course, Jed's still living.'

And Will, I thought.

And who knew who else might've had reason?

'Doesn't have to be a man,' I said. 'There's her sister, for instance.'

'Well, it sure enough doesn't take much skill to hit somebody with a shotgun,' Dwight agreed.

'Chauvinist. A lot of women shoot as good as a man. You taking the slicker now?'

He nodded. I found a hanger for the red velvet cloak and he put it back on the top rack. Then we turned out the lights, he locked up, and we walked down the slope to my car. As he carefully laid the raincoat on the backseat, Dwight said, 'I know you're tired and it's out of the way, but you reckon we could run by the Pot Shot a few minutes? I'd like to see where this was hanging and maybe get that dowel before it goes missing.'

'You sure it can't wait till morning?' I grumbled. 'I'm really not up to another session with Denn.'

Dwight unclipped his walkie-talkie from his belt. 'Well, I suppose I could call Jack to come back.'

'Oh, get in,' I said crossly. 'You know good and well you're not going to haul any baby birds out of bed when I'm here to cart you around.'

At that hour, most of Cotton Grove was sleeping and Front Street was deserted. We headed south on Forty-Eight, and in less than ten minutes, I was turning in at the Pot Shot sign, then through the narrow lane, past the shrubbery, and into the farmyard. Lily met us at the gate, barking loud enough to wake the dead.

Well, no, actually, it wasn't quite that loud.

'Stop!' Dwight yelled, but I was already stomping on the brakes.

Denn lay right where he must have stepped out of the pickup. The door on the driver's side was still open and the cab light was still on.

This time, the killer had aimed the shotgun at Denn's chest.

Baby Bird got hauled out of bed after all.

So did Terry Wilson.

I didn't get to go home till almost four.

27

I Could Be Persuaded

Michael Vickery's funeral was one of the largest ever held out at Sweetwater Missionary Baptist Church. They opened up the Sunday school classrooms on either side of the main auditorium and brought in extra chairs and still the church was too full to hold all who wanted to attend.

Those who couldn't get in took up positions outside around the open grave, and Duck Aldcroft and his two sons had their hands full trying to keep reporters and television cameramen out of the way of the pallbearers. I later heard that he'd actually raised his voice at one point, but I put that down to sensationalism.

I didn't go.

I didn't go to Denn McCloy's funeral either, mostly because it was a private ceremony held on Long Island. His next of kin was a brother up there, a claims investigator for a national insurance company, I believe; and as soon as Denn's body was released by the medical examiner, it was shipped north.

* * *

After only an hour's sleep, I got up again Wednesday morning, showered, and drove back to Cotton Grove. Jed had just put on a pot of coffee when I knocked on the kitchen door.

'Deborah?' Except for his jacket and tie, he was already dressed for work and he smelled of fresh aftershave. It was still Old Spice, after all these years. He looked rested and untroubled.

'Can I come in, Jed? I need to see you and Gayle.'

'Sure. What's wrong?'

Gayle came down the hallway, sleepy-eyed and still in her nightgown. 'Hey, Deborah. What's up?'

'I wanted to tell you about Denn McCloy before you read about it in the paper or see it on TV,' I said.

'What about him?' asked Jed as Gayle smothered a yawn with the back of her hand. Her brown hair was rumpled and her soft cheek still held the impression of her pillow.

'He was killed last night,' I said. 'Shot. Just like Michael Vickery.'

Gayle's brown eyes widened and she sat down on a stool at the breakfast counter. 'Murdered?' Her small toes curled around the stool rungs.

'Who did it?' asked Jed.

'They don't know yet. It only happened around midnight.' I glanced at the blue wall clock over the sink. 'Six hours ago.'

'Sit down,' said Jed, pulling a chair out at the breakfast table. He poured me a cup of coffee and he remembered that I liked it black.

'You look like you had a rough night,' he said gently. 'Were you there?'

'Not when it happened. A few minutes later.' The coffee was too hot to drink but I drank it anyhow. 'There's no easy way to say this, Jed.'

I turned to Gayle. 'You wanted to know what happened to your mother, honey? Apparently Michael Vickery killed her. I don't think he meant to or wanted to, but all the same, he did.'

'Michael?'

First they were incredulous and then they peppered me with questions. In the early morning hours while technicians measured and charted, photographed and videotaped, I'd thought about what I was going to say.

At one point, I'd asked Dwight, 'Do you *have* to speculate about who those two Cotton Grove lesbians in Denn's story were?'

He acted embarrassed and wouldn't meet my eyes. 'Terry Wilson has to get a true copy of the tape. And if it ever comes to trial—' He shrugged. 'We don't tell the media every little thing we know.'

I knew then it'd be safe to slide past the reason Janie reacted so violently when she found out Michael was gay.

For Gayle, hearing that her mother had tried to seduce Michael Vickery seemed to confirm something that she'd already half-assumed.

For Jed, it was a sudden unexpected betrayal from the grave, and I found myself trying to shore up his feelings. 'It was nothing to do with you, Jed. She knew you loved her, but lots of new mothers – especially when they've always been as pretty as Janie . . . I mean, she probably just wanted to see if she was still attractive. I'm sure she didn't mean to endanger your marriage.'

I had a feeling I wasn't getting anywhere. The stricken look on his handsome face was turning to—

'Oh Christ!' groaned the pragmatist. 'After all these years, don't tell me he's going to be humiliated because he wasn't sexy enough to satisfy his pretty little wife?'

'You always forget to remember where the male ego's centered,' scolded the preacher.

When I finally left, Gayle followed me out to the kitchen patio, still barefooted. 'Thanks, Deborah,' she said and gave me a warm hug. 'Dad'll be glad to finally know, too, once his feelings quit being hurt.' She hesitated. 'You won't ever tell him, will you?'

'Tell him what, honey?'

'About – you know. About me thinking maybe he hired somebody to—'

I put my finger on her lips. 'You never said a word,' I promised.

Dwight later told me that his interview with the Vickerys was one of the worst experiences of his entire life.

'I played the second tape for them,' he said, 'and they just sat there watching my tape player like two hypnotized birds watching a blacksnake. Dr Vickery groaned a couple of times, but I swear if Michael Vickery was cracked on the subject of religion, his mother's the one who did it to him. I mean, I know you admire Mrs Vickery, but dammit, Deb'rah, when that tape ended, you know what her only comment was? "God's will be done on earth, as it is in heaven."'

* * *

Terry Wilson and Scotty Underhill dropped by my office two days later. I'd already talked to them, of course, given my opinion that Denn had told the truth on those tapes Dwight made of both interrogations. 'Or at least as much of the truth as Michael had told him,' I amended.

The slicker was a cornucopia of information. The blood was definitely Janie's, most of the fingerprints were Michael's and Denn's and Janie's, but of the several others that might never be identified, all were probably there quite innocently. Even my own teenager prints had been found under the collar from where I'd once hung it up for Janie.

'You see the problem though, don't you?' Terry asked.

'Problem?'

Scotty Underhill looked a lot fresher than the night we first talked. He'd been slightly obsessed with Janie Whitehead's murder and had begun to think he'd go to his grave without knowing for sure what happened. Ever since Terry woke him up early Wednesday morning to tell him, he'd been quietly pleased.

'There's still a question as to who pulled the trigger,' he said. 'On the tape, Denn still has Michael over in Chapel Hill all night, Friday.'

'Obviously Michael lied. Denn either forgot that Friday night was when Janie was shot or maybe he never even knew,' I said. 'After all, it was several months before he learned she was shot. Don't forget how Michael lied to Denn about not knowing the mill had already been searched *before* he dumped Janie there to finish dying.'

(Seth and Will had again been questioned on that point,

and both confirmed that they'd met Michael at the head of the lane the day after Janie disappeared.)

'He must have lied about his alibi. Anyhow, wasn't he just one of many back then? How carefully did you really verify it?'

'True,' Scotty said.

Terry was satisfied. 'One more unsolved murder off the books,' he said complacently.

'One off, two on, isn't it?'

'Naah. This one we'll get. Vickery's new boyfriend doesn't have a watertight alibi for either night. And neither does the new boyfriend's old boyfriend, if you take my meaning. Plus, we've already checked the phone records and learned that Vickery called the new one early enough Friday night that either of 'em could have been sitting at that theater when Vickery drove up. He *says* Vickery just called to say McCloy had moved out, but we'll see.'

'Sounds awfully thin to me,' I said skeptically.

Terry and Scotty exchanged glances. Then Terry sighed. 'I told you she wouldn't buy it.'

'Buy what?' I asked.

'And she's nosey as hell, too,' said Terry, shaking his head.

'*What?*' I demanded.

'Look, Deborah, what I'm about to say goes no further, okay? We haven't run all the tests yet, but the lab's trying to work us up a hopper pattern on those shotgun pellets.'

'I didn't know you could trace shotgun pellets,' I said.

'You can't. Not like bullets. But you know how they're made?'

302

Interested, I shook my head.

'Not to go into too much detail, what it amounts to is that you melt a bunch of lead ingots in a vat and then you make the melted lead into pellets. Each vat's got a slightly different metallurgic composition, so when the pellets are poured into a giant hopper to load the shells, each day's production means a distinctive pattern effect in the hopper. More than likely, when somebody buys a box of shells, they all came out of the same hopper. When you analyze all the pellets in a single shotgun blast, you can say whether or not they match the metallurgic composition of another shotgun blast. Got it?'

'Sounds awfully complicated and not terribly accurate,' I said.

Scotty shrugged. 'Sometimes it's all we've got to go on.'

'The point is,' said Terry, 'the new boyfriend may or may not be involved in some other mess that's going on, but these are not the first two guys that've been blown away with shotguns in the last six weeks.'

I looked at them, flabbergasted, remembering that shooting down near Fort Bragg a few weeks back. '*Drugs?*'

'Well, think about it,' Terry said, his homely face dead serious. 'Who had a motive to kill them? Jed Whitehead? Maybe. *If* he'd known that Vickery killed his wife and McCloy helped cover it up. But how could he've known? Besides, he was at a schoolboard meeting that night till almost ten.

'The Pot Shot's fifteen minutes from I-95 that ties Miami to New York. Every two or three weeks, Vickery ships a load of pottery to Atlanta. Maybe the pottery didn't always travel empty. You hear what I'm saying?'

I heard, and oddly enough, it was more believable than their first solution. Just last week, one of the businessmen in Makely, an ex-police captain in fact and a man I'd have sworn was above reproach, was arrested for laundering drug money.

'Just cool it for a while, okay?' asked Terry. 'I don't want to be doing a pattern analysis on pellets we dig out of you, okay?'

'You got it,' I said, trying to assimilate all they'd given me to think about.

As the two agents stood to leave, Terry cut his eyes at me in a familiar flash of droll amusement. 'Guess I'll see you next week.'

I was confused. 'You will?'

'Yeah, Stanton and me. Kezzie's invited us to your pig picking.'

'He's really giving one?'

Terry grinned. 'You mean he forgot to invite you? Hell, girl, it's gonna be the social event of the political year. I hear Jim Hunt's coming, and they're even trying to get Terry Sanford – all the biggies.'

A week later, Ambrose Daughtridge stopped by for a heart-to-heart after court adjourned and began by telling me that Denn and Michael had indeed written mutually beneficial wills.

Each named the other as executor of his estate and, failing that, I was named substitute executor, he said.

That Michael had intended to rewrite his will carried no legal weight, of course, and his original instrument would be probated as written: everything to Denn. Denn's left everything to Michael as primary legatee and, should Michael die first, to his own brother's sons, two teenage boys.

Ambrose leaned closer and, in a softer than usual tone that meant this was to go no further, confided that Mrs Vickery intended to try to have the ninety-nine-year lease on her Dancy property set aside.

'If she just could've brought herself to tell me about Michael back then, I'd have sure made some different provisions in that reversion clause,' he said.

To look after his sons' interests, Denn's brother had retained the legal services of a high-powered law firm in Raleigh. For starters, they were claiming that the lease alone was worth over a million dollars; and the court fight was shaping up to be every bit as complicated as John Claude had anticipated.

I wanted no part of the battle, and it gave me great satisfaction to tell Ambrose, 'I really do appreciate your courtesy in consulting me and your concern for the properties, so let me assure you, for the record, Ambrose, that there was nothing in my dealings with Mr McCloy that would preclude your settling his affairs any way you choose.'

Without the least hint of irony, he said, 'Thank you, Deborah. Now you be sure and bill his estate for services rendered, you hear?'

A rainy afternoon in a Pullen Park caboose? An arm to lean on, the night of his lover's wake?

Sure.

28

I Will Arise And Go Back To
My Father's House

My mother had been such a sociable and hospitable person that people loved to come visit almost as much as she loved having them come. Daddy might grumble over the upset and inconvenience, but he enjoyed being a patriarch and acting the host to all the far-flung friends and family who trekked back to the farm. No matter how full the house, floor space for one more sleeping bag or pallet could always be found. Her favorite parties were big ones. Not the 'cocktails from seven to nine' type, but big sprawling affairs that might go on for days.

The summer that one of the little twins decided to get married at the farm, Mother brought home a stack of etiquette books from the library. I remember that when Daddy started to fuss about the size of the guest list at breakfast one morning, Mother opened one of the books and said, 'Now, Kezzie, listen to this: "Whether or not you have included a request to RSVP, once invitations are extended beyond the bride and groom's immediate family, you may safely assume that at least twenty-five percent of your guest list will not attend.'''

Daddy shook his head at that. 'That stuff's written for New York City, not down here,' he said pessimistically. 'Everybody'll come and bring along their friends.'

In the end, formal invitations were mailed to 220 people, Mother rented 250 folding chairs just to be on the safe side, but Daddy was right: at least twenty-five people had to stand through the ceremony.

The year before she got sick, Mother threw a Saturday birthday party for Daddy that had people coming in from seven states up and down the eastern seaboard. The first guests arrived on a Tuesday, the last didn't depart till the following Wednesday week. At one point, the old farmhouse slept eight extra adults and two babies, and Daddy threatened to have the boys dig a three-holer in the backyard so he wouldn't have to stand in line for a bathroom.

She would have loved the pig picking Daddy put on for me: three pigs, an iron wash pot full of real Brunswick stew ('It ain't real Brunswick stew if it ain't got at least one squirrel in it'), wooden tubs of lemonade and iced tea for children and teetotalers, and kegs of beer discreetly off to one side for those who liked their liquids a little wetter.

The pigs weren't due to come off the cookers till six-thirty, but by the time I got there a little after two, cars were already lining the lane and one of my nephews had begun directing guests into the near pasture. 'But I saved you a place right at the front door, Aunt Deb'rah,' grinned his snaggle-toothed eight-year-old sister who was helping out.

A volleyball game was in sweaty progress in the side yard and the clank of iron against iron drew me past the cookers and on down to a stretch of open space beside the potato house, where horseshoes were flying back and forth. I got there just in time to see Minnie win her game with a ringer. 'Come and take my place,' she said. 'I've got to get back to the kitchen and see if they've got enough cabbage chopped up.'

Ostensibly she and Seth and three of my other brothers and their wives were hosting this party. Even though it was Daddy's idea, Minnie had done most of the planning and she was the one who coordinated all the details. If Minnie had organized the flight out of Egypt, it wouldn't have taken forty years to reach the Promised Land.

My brother Will and I paired up against an agricultural extension agent and her boyfriend, the principal of a Widdington high school. We'd have taken them, too, if my leaner at the end hadn't been knocked flying by the principal's second shot. They easily fended off Dwight Bryant and his sister-in-law Kate, a couple of tobacco lobbyists from over in Widdington, and two attorneys from Makely, only to be done in finally by Terry Wilson's son Stanton and Linsey Thomas.

'Y'all hear 'bout Perry Byrd?' Linsey boomed from behind his bushy moustache as he and Stanton waited to see who their challengers would be.

'Hear what?'

'He had a stroke this morning.'

'What?'

'Yep. Went out after breakfast this morning to cut his

grass, leaned over to crank his lawnmower, and never came back up.'

The two attorneys from Makely chimed in with more details about the rescue squad's arrival, its resuscitation attempts, and the rush to Dobbs Memorial.

'Is he going to be okay?'

They shrugged. In that near-shout that was his normal speaking voice, Linsey said, 'I called over to the hospital right before I came out here and they said he's critical but stable, whatever that means.'

'Wonder who Hardison'll appoint if Byrd has to resign?' asked one of the attorneys.

'Oh Lord,' I grinned. 'You don't suppose this is where Hector Woodlief finally gets a public office?'

They reminded me that the governor would have to pick another Democrat, since Perry Byrd was one.

'Maybe I'll have to rethink my editorial policy,' said Linsey as Haywood and Seth banged their horseshoes together and wanted to know if he was there to talk or play.

Linsey may have endorsed Luther Parker, but after running a brief story about how it'd been Denn McCloy who'd written those flyers, he'd quietly decided that the *Ledger* would have no further comment on the race for judge.

He also had enough of his grandmother in him that he'd refrained from sensationalizing Denn's allegations against Michael Vickery, and the *N&O* was so surprisingly restrained in its coverage that I wondered if maybe some behind-the-scenes personal plea hadn't persuaded the publisher to back off. Terry's speculation that the two men had been involved in drug trafficking had not found its way into print; even so, a lot of people around the county had come up with a similar explanation for their violent deaths.

By now, it was two weeks since I'd discovered Michael's body, and talk had begun to die down as life returned to normal for almost everyone involved.

Since the Vickerys were such faithful Democrats, kind-hearted Minnie told me that an invitation had been sent to them – out of courtesy for their position in Cotton Grove, not because she actually expected them to attend. 'Of course, you can't predict what Dr Vickery'll do,' she'd said.

Indeed, Dr Vickery had played golf the Sunday before, causing some raised eyebrows; but Mrs Vickery hadn't yet been seen in public, not even in church. Their daughter Faith had stayed on after the funeral and was said to be concerned about her mother's health.

By six o'clock, the luscious aroma of hickory-cooked pork well seasoned with Daddy's 'secret sauce' had a lot of people circling the cookers like buzzards. Over two hundred people had been invited and while I tried to act nonchalant about it, I was gratified by the number of dignitaries who had accepted Minnie's low-keyed invitation to attend a pig picking 'in honor of Deborah Knott, candidate for district judge,' even though I knew that several of them had also accepted invitations to a fish fry for Luther Parker the previous weekend.

Among the state's movers and shakers were Thad Eure, former secretary of state and self-proclaimed 'oldest rat in the Democratic barn,' there in his trademark red bow tie, and Bill Friday, former president of the state's university system, who everyone regarded as a shoo-in for senator or governor if he could only be persuaded to run.

I had a cryptic conversation with a black female judge from the third division, who gave me some good advice and told me to feel free to call if I won and ever needed somebody to unload on about the way the system worked. She was nearing the end of her first term and sounded cynical about certain aspects. 'I thought my big problem was going to be race. Honey, race is *nothing* compared to being a woman in a good ol' boy system.'

As the afternoon wore on and the sun began to set, Gray Talbert came driving through the back lanes in his black Porsche and parked at the edge of the orchard. I went over to welcome him and to thank him for his earlier letter to the *Ledger*.

'You didn't change parties, did you?' I asked.

'Nope,' he grinned.

'So?'

'So why not?' he drawled with a supercilious smile that sort of got my back up. 'Was I wrong? Aren't you the best candidate? That's what your daddy told me.'

'Oh? And what about *your* daddy?' I cooed sweetly. 'Doesn't he mind about you supporting Democrats?'

He shrugged indifferently. 'I'm sure you know my daddy doesn't give a damn what I do long as it doesn't make the six o'clock news.' He spotted Morgan Slavin's long blonde hair and ambled off to make her acquaintance.

I wasn't sure which rankled more: that he'd written that letter to the editor to ingratiate himself with my father or that he'd opted to flirt with Morgan instead of me.

Soon Minnie sent one of her children to locate me and bring me up to the side porch where Daddy waited with Barry

Blackman and my brothers and sisters-in-law. Minnie made a graceful speech of welcome, acknowledged the notables, spoke of Democratic unity, then introduced Daddy, who welcomed everybody again and said he hoped they'd forgive him for being partial to one particular candidate.

Laughter.

'Now some of y'all've seen her hold her own against all the menfolk in this family, so you know she can handle anything they throw at her. The only thing against her is that she's my daughter, and there ain't much she can do about that. I just hope y'all'll vote for her anyhow.'

Laughter and applause.

Next, Minnie introduced Porter Creech, the most colorful official in the Department of Agriculture and one of Daddy's old hunting buddies. He began with a couple of sly remarks about how much it pleasured him to speak on behalf of the daughter of a farmer who'd done so much for agriculture: 'A man, ladies and gentlemen, who single-handedly increased the production of corn in this county by twenty-seven percent all during the thirties and forties. And when he quit raising corn – least he *says* he's quit?'

('Just enough for the cows,' Daddy said amid more laughter from the crowd.)

'When he quit raising cain, he started turning out a bumper crop of fine upstanding citizens, including this young lady here, who brings it back full circle. I've known her since she was nothing but a twinkle in Kezzie Knott's eye and a blush on Susan Knott's cheeks. I've watched her grow. I know what kind of intelligence and integrity she will bring to the bench if she's elected.'

My three *h*'s of public speaking are be *b*right, be *b*rainy, be *b*rief; and since the first two would only undercut Porter Creech's remarks, I limited myself to a few words of welcome, thanked them for their support, and concluded by turning to Barry as I said, 'Preacher Barry Blackman has kindly agreed to ask the Lord's blessing on us all.'

Barry delivered an eloquent prayer of thanksgiving for food and fellowship, then folks headed for the cookers, where the three master cooks had sliced the meat from the bone, deftly mixed some of the dry meat from the hams with the juicier shoulders, chopped it together a little, and were now prepared to start serving. Good servers can eyeball a crowd and tell whether to load the plates or stretch the meat out a little further to make sure everybody gets some.

At the head of the double-sided table were bowls of additional sauce labeled HOT, HOTTER and THE DEVIL MADE ME DO IT. There were huge platters of deep-fried onion-flavored hush puppies, bowls of cole slaw, and more bowls of Brunswick stew. A dozen or more round tables, each with ten chairs, dotted the grass, but many people either sat in lawn chairs they'd thought to bring or perched on a low stonewall that had defined Mother's iris border.

I stood with my brothers and sisters-in-law for another thirty minutes or so, shaking hands with late arrivals, accepting their words of encouragement, and telling them, 'Now y'all be sure and get you some of that pig before it's all gone.'

We'd already used a host's privilege and fixed ourselves a sandwich a couple of hours earlier when the pigs were turned, so we were in no hurry to fill a plate.

I was surprised to see Faith Vickery near the end of the line.

'So pleased y'all could come,' Minnie said, clasping her hand warmly.

'Well, Mama thought it would be good to get out of the house,' Faith said. She'd lived in California so long that there was no Southern accent left. Only the 'Mama' betrayed her. She looked a little worried though as she said, 'I just hope she isn't overdoing. I haven't seen her in the last half-hour.'

'Maybe down by the shelter?' said Will's wife, Amy. 'I thought I saw her going that way a little while ago.'

'Thanks,' said Faith and set out to find her.

'Is Dr Vickery here, too?' I asked, not having noticed either of them.

'Faith and Mrs Vickery are the only ones I've seen,' said Seth, and Haywood's wife added, 'If he's here, he came by himself because he wasn't in the car with them that I saw.'

Our reception line disintegrated as the others drifted off to eat or socialize. I lingered a moment to savor the relative quiet.

Stars were coming out and bats were graceful silhouettes as they swooped and darted overhead for night-flying insects.

Lights had been strung through the trees, and as twilight deepened, the fiddlers started tuning up down at the potato house, a warehouse-sized structure where hundreds of crates of sweet potatoes were cured out each fall. Tonight, the big space had been cleared except for a makeshift musicians' platform at the far end. The sliding metal doors had been shoved up onto their overhead tracks, and strings of small clear lights turned the place into an open-air dance hall.

Uncle Ash was back from South America, and he and Aunt Zell were already following the teenagers down the slope for some serious square dancing.

I was surprised to see that people were still arriving and hoped it omened something for the runoff. The side pasture was lined three deep in cars, but the snaggle-toothed child who'd been helping her brother direct traffic had wandered down to the shelter. I saw her talking to Gayle Whitehead and pointing back through the crowd.

I hadn't had much opportunity to talk to Gayle since Denn's death and indeed, I'd almost tried to avoid her because she kept wanting to talk about the SBI's failure to find Denn and Michael's killer, and I couldn't really comment on the drug-connection theory making the rounds because Terry Wilson had sworn me to silence.

On the other hand, there was still such a ragged and unfinished feeling that I couldn't quite put it behind me either. Usually when I hear a murder case unraveled in front of a jury, I'm left with a satisfied sense of understanding how and why. This time, some of Michael's actions still weren't clear, and I knew Gayle had begun to pick up on my frustration.

Stevie came past. 'Neat party, huh?' he said. 'I'm ready to boogie. You seen Gayle?'

'Right over—' I started to point, then realized Gayle was no longer there. 'Well, she was right over there.'

As he headed off to look for her in the growing darkness, I had one quick surge of envy that there wasn't somebody special here for me, too. Before the night was over I'd probably dance with Jed Whitehead, Terry Wilson, Dwight Bryant, maybe even Gray Talbert, but none of them would quicken my pulse the way Gayle quickened Stevie's.

More people were drifting down toward the music and dancing now, though there were animated huddles around several tables with brisk political discussions and bursts of raucous laughter here, some quiet lapel-pulling there. I saw the tobacco lobbyists in earnest conversation with one of our state assemblymen. There was such a shortfall in revenues that for the first time in years there was serious talk that the state assembly might actually consider raising the three-cents-a-pack cigarette tax.

Bo Poole was in earnest conversation with the vice president of the Democratic Women as I passed.

Daddy and Dwight had their heads together talking fishing with Terry – 'that sucker fought me all the way across the lake, heading for them root snags and—' Out on the dance floor, Reid had made up a square with Fitzi, Will, and Amy, and some others I didn't recognize. Will looked as if he might've visited the beer keg a little more than he should've. Stevie still hadn't located Gayle and was scanning the crowded floor for her.

L.V. Pruitt, Colleton County's coroner, had stepped up to the front of the platform to call the figures. A small spare man who normally spoke in hushed funereal tones, he had a lively inventive talent for spontaneous rhyme and could make himself heard above the fiddles: 'Now you swing your partner out the back door, then you promenade all around the floor! Ladyfolks left and the gentlemen right; see who goes home with who tonight.'

Out beyond the circle of light, as many people were talking in tight clusters as were dancing.

'—like a drowned puppy that needed to be put out of its misery!'

'—so I said, well, if that's the way the rest of the pulpit committee felt, I'd go along with their decision and just go home and pray on my own failings because—'

'—'cause the main thing to remember is that integration's been a bigger success in the South than it could ever hope to be in the North and the reason—'

'Still didn't find your mother?' I asked Faith Vickery, who was standing on tiptoes to see across the crowd.

She came down on her heels and looked at me blankly for a moment, almost as if she didn't recognize me. 'Oh. Deborah. No, and I'm concerned. She really isn't well, you know. She really shouldn't have come.'

'Why don't I go look up at the house?' I offered. 'Maybe she's sitting with some of the older women on the porch.'

'No, I already looked there.'

Some of Faith's concern began to transfer itself to me. What if she'd stumbled and fallen out here in the dark? 'Do you want me to stop the music and ask if anyone's seen her?'

Faith looked undecided. 'You know how Mother is,' she said. 'If she's just off in a quiet corner somewhere in conversation with a friend, she'll be so annoyed at me for making a fuss.'

It occurred to me that perhaps she might have been too overwhelmed by too many sympathetic well-wishers and had gone on back to the car to wait for Faith.

'I'll bet that's it!' Faith exclaimed. 'I'll go right now and

---

check and if she's there, I'll just take her on home. Please thank your brothers for inviting us.'

She cut across the side yard and headed for the part of the pasture where she'd parked.

Up by the house, where the pasture gate actually entered the lane, a departing guest struggled to maneuver a car into the lane without scraping any of those parked on either side. As I neared the gate, I realized it was Gayle behind the steering wheel of an elderly Mercedes. She seemed to be having difficulty driving the large car.

'Gayle?' I called.

She didn't hear, and as I hurried over, I saw Mrs Vickery on the seat beside her. I thumped on the window, and when Gayle rolled it down after a quick glance at Mrs Vickery, I bent down to look inside.

'Faith's been looking for you everywhere, Mrs Vickery.'

'I'm afraid I'm not feeling at all well,' she said, 'and Gayle has kindly agreed to drive me home.' She sat erectly in the passenger seat with her large purse in her lap. Her left hand was on top of the shapeless purse, her right hand was inside it, and I felt as if I were looking at a copperhead moccasin.

'But Faith—'

'I'm quite sorry,' Mrs Vickery said politely, 'but we truly must go now.'

'Then why not let *me* drive you?' I said. 'Gayle's father's looking for her, and anyhow, I'm more familiar with a straight drive than Gayle is.'

'You mustn't leave your guests, Miss Knott. I'm sure she can manage. Drive on, Gayle.'

Helplessly, Gayle shifted into first and lurched slowly down the lane.

Equally helpless, I looked around and saw no one but the child who must have delivered Mrs Vickery's message that had lured Gayle out to her car.

'Melissa, listen!' I said as I ran back to my own car, pulled my revolver from the trunk, and slipped it in the pocket of my jacket. 'Do you know Dwight Bryant?'

Large-eyed at the sight of my gun, she shook her head.

'Okay, then, run find Granddaddy or Uncle Seth and tell them Mrs Vickery's trying to hurt Gayle and that I've gone after them to make her stop. Scoot!'

She darted off and I jumped in the car just as Faith Vickery came through the pasture gate, looking frantic. 'Mama's car's gone.'

I flung open the door and cried, 'Get in! She's got Gayle Whitehead.'

Faith hesitated and I revved the motor. 'Dammit, either get in or get out of my way!'

Quickly, she hurried around to the side and half-fell in as I'd already started moving.

'Your mother's flipped out, hasn't she?' I said.

No answer.

'She's holding a gun on Gayle. Why?'

Faith let out a half-strangled sob.

'*Why?*'

'Because she thinks Michael would still be alive if Gayle hadn't asked you to look into her mother's death.'

In the distance, red taillights glowed briefly, then turned right toward Cotton Grove. I hadn't yet turned on my lights because I could have driven the lane blindfolded.

As the ramifications of what she'd said sunk in, I was seized with horror. 'Your mother shot Michael!'

'No!' Faith cried.

'And Denn, too? Oh God, I *told* Denn that first blast was meant for him and it was! Michael was in Denn's car, sitting where she expected to find Denn.'

Faith had begun to cry with low hopeless sobs. 'No, no, no,' she moaned.

I barely heard, for I was trying to remember what Daddy had said about Mrs Vickery when she was a teenager and used to come out to the old Dancy place with her brother to go hunting. Of course, she'd know how to handle guns. Any guns.

'Denn and Michael were splitting up, and Denn grabbed Janie's slicker to give me that night,' I said aloud, working it out as I spoke. 'When Michael realized, he must have called your mother. Why? Unless – *yes*! She must have known. He must have told her all those years ago. He probably blamed *her* for Janie's death, since he'd tried to be straight to please her. That's what Denn said: he'd tried to deny his own nature and look what happened. That's why she held her head high when he brought Denn down here. He didn't give her any choice, did he? What'd he do, say let me be gay or I'll tell the world I'm a killer?'

Faith was still into heavy denial. Ahead, the taillights had reached the stop sign at Old Forty-Eight and turned left. I let two cars go by, then finally put on my lights and pulled onto the highway. Maybe the normal Saturday night traffic would keep her from noticing me.

'My nieces and nephews were out watching the town the night Michael was killed,' I told Faith. 'They kept logs, too. If she was out in that Mercedes, one of them may well remember seeing her.'

'She always adored Michael,' Faith said dully. 'He was the Prince of Light for her. It nearly killed her when she learned he was gay. I could never understand how she could be so – so *accepting*. And all these years, she's loathed Denn McCloy. I never realized till after my brother's wake. She made me go invite him to the funeral home. I was so proud of her for that. And all the time—' She broke off and fumbled in her purse until she found a tissue. 'We were exhausted when we came home that night. Everyone fell into bed. But I couldn't sleep. I got up and went downstairs around midnight for a book. A few minutes later, I heard the garage door open and her car drive in. I slipped to the side door, opened it just wide enough to see her take the shotgun out of the car and hide it up on the garage rafters. I was so frightened. And then the next morning when we heard – When I saw her eyes—'

'She murdered your brother!' I burst out.

'She thought it was Denn,' Faith protested. 'Don't you understand? She thought she had to protect Michael.'

The two cars ahead of me abruptly swung out to pass the slower Mercedes. What was going on? And how could I avoid passing, too, without giving us away? But what – ?

Then I realized that they were slowing down for the entrance lane to Ridley's Mill. 'It's blocked,' I muttered and was forced to pass as the Mercedes turned off the road.

There was a driveway a few hundred feet down, and I cut my lights and coasted to a stop without touching the brakes.

322

The cable across the mill lane gleamed dully in the lights of the other car.

As I hesitated over whether to go back, the Mercedes suddenly backed out onto the highway and swept past us, once again headed for town.

'Where's she taking Gayle?' I asked as I fell in one car behind.

'Maybe they're going home,' Faith said with hope in her voice.

The hope died as we entered the town limits. Instead of turning onto the Vickerys' street, the Mercedes continued north on Forty-Eight, right through town.

'The theater!' I exclaimed. 'She wanted to go to the mill, and since she can't, she's going to take Gayle to where she killed Michael. And then what, Faith? Kill her, too?'

'I don't know,' Faith moaned. 'I don't know!'

If I was right, there'd be no way in hell I could follow down that winding drive to the theater without Mrs Vickery noticing. I had the feeling that some warped sense of divine retribution would require that Gayle be standing on the spot where Michael had died, but if I spooked Mrs Vickery, she might go ahead and pull the trigger.

With a prayer to God and fingers crossed, I stepped on the gas, passed the Mercedes as if it were standing still, and zoomed out of town doing seventy as I wove in and out of the four-lane traffic. If I got stopped by a patrol car, well and good. If not –

'What are you doing?' gasped Faith.

'We're going to get there first,' I told her. It was another three minutes to the theater entrance and I took the turn on two wheels. The first production of the new season was due to open the next weekend, but the theater was as dark as ever.

I zipped down the graveled drive, cut my headlights as I drove through the rear lot, and used my parking lights to fumble past the loading area and around to the far side of the building. I winced as bushes tore at the paint job and the housing of the universal joint hit a rock.

'We'll get out,' I told Faith, 'and wait at the corner here till they get out of the car.'

The overhead light came on as we opened our doors, and she protested when she saw the gun in my hand.

'You're not going to—? She's my mother!'

'She's a killer, Faith, and I'll be damned if I'll let her kill Gayle, too. You try to warn her or stop me from doing whatever has to be done and I swear to God I'll shoot you where you stand! You understand?'

She stood gaping at me in the starlight.

'That's not a rhetorical question, dammit! Do you understand?'

'Y-yes.'

Not knowing if she could be trusted, I pushed her in front of me and we waited without talking.

Two weeks ago I had waited like this with Dwight. If only I had his comforting bulk beside me now!

Headlights swept across the side of the theater and traveled steadily down the graveled road. As they disappeared around the front, I flicked off the safety and held my breath until I saw them wash over the bushes at the rear. Then there was only a reflected glow as the lights shone directly on the rear door of the theater. Abruptly, the engine died and silence flooded in.

I put my left hand on the small of Faith's back.

'Not a sound,' I whispered and nudged her forward.

She stumbled, caught herself, and then we were peeking around the corner, straight across the loading platform and into Evelyn Dancy Vickery's ravaged, maniacal face.

Gayle was a dark silhouette between us, and I cursed myself for not thinking far enough ahead to have circled around to the other side of the theater as they drove in.

Too late.

'On your knees!' cried Mrs Vickery, waving the pistol at Gayle.

'Mama, *no*!' Faith screamed as I pushed her out of my way.

Instinctively, Gayle ducked behind the car as Mrs Vickery's first shot slammed into a board beside my head. The next one ricocheted off the roof of her car. I fell to the ground, took a two-handed grip on my gun, and fired. The bullet spun her around and I heard her pistol hit the hood of the Mercedes.

Instantly, I was on my feet, found the gun, and flung it into the far bushes.

Then Gayle was in my arms, sobbing hysterically. 'She was going to kill me! To make up for Michael. Sh-she said she should have done it in the first place instead of leaving me to grow up. Oh, Deborah! She shot my mother!'

I held her tightly. 'Sh-h. It's okay, honey. You're safe now. It's all over.'

'I was so scared.' Her teeth were chattering as reaction set in. 'I thought you didn't know she had a gun. I kept looking to see if anybody was following. How—?'

Faith was kneeling beside her mother's unconscious form. Blood drenched the lower right side of her white cotton shirtdress.

'There's a phone inside,' I said. 'Gayle and I'll go call.'

This time there was no open window and I had to use a rock.

It was one of the best-attended crime scenes in the county's history: one sheriff, one deputy sheriff, three SBI agents, and a coroner arrived in a dead heat with an ambulance and two patrol cars.

Gayle had calmed down some by then, and she listened quietly while I told Dwight and Terry that Mrs Vickery had killed Michael by mistake, Denn on purpose, and that she was the one who'd actually fired the bullet that killed Janie. 'All three of them,' I concluded.

'Four,' said Gayle. 'Howard Grimes, too. He saw Michael parked with my mother at Hardee's that day, and he'd been blackmailing her. When the SBI came back, she thought he was going to tell, so she substituted stronger heart pills for the ones Dr Vickery prescribed and everybody thought he died naturally.'

29

That Just About Does It,
Don't It?

After all that, the runoff election was anticlimactic. There were so many rumors, so many wild tales. It took some backing and hauling but eventually the media got it all perfectly straight and within three days had revised and emended until the absolute truth was told. Nevertheless, the electorate seemed to feel it had two choices.

Judicial candidate (a), the daughter of a known bootlegger, had shot and seriously wounded one of the most respected citizens of Colleton County after running around the district befriending and defending drug pushers, homosexuals, murderers, and God knows what else.

Judicial candidate (b) hadn't.

The electorate went to the polls that Tuesday and cast fifty-nine percent of its votes for (b).

30

Daddy's Hands

Okay, it was childish and immature, but I couldn't go to the office on Wednesday as if nothing had happened. To have to endure everybody's condolences and attempts to buck me up? To have to hear 'better luck next time'? To have to say, 'Luther Parker's going to be a fine judge'?

In yer ear, Norton.

Luther Parker *was* going to be a fine judge and I'd played the gracious loser and told him so two hours after the polls closed. That Harrison Hobart's seat wasn't going to be filled by a Perry Byrd clone was the only lily among the bouquet of nettles and bitter herbs I'd been handed.

(But *I* would have been a fine judge too, dammit.)

I wanted to stay in bed with my head under the covers and the air conditioner turned down to sixty. I wanted to fly to New York City and stand in the middle of Times Square surrounded by twelve million people who'd never heard of Colleton County or anybody in it. I wanted to buy a pound of chocolate truffles and go sit through three screenings of *Random Harvest* where nobody would notice if I bawled my head off, because everybody cries for Greer Garson and Ronald Colman.

Instead, I drove out to the country, parked my car up a deserted lane, and walked out into a twenty-acre field that bordered the western edge of Possum Creek. The tobacco was waist high, and scattered here and there were plants that had already begun to top out too early with pink tuberoses – the end of the plant's dedication to leaf growth and the beginning of its desire to make seeds.

I found a sturdy stick at the edge of the field, and for the next fifteen or twenty minutes I walked up and down the rows slashing tops off every flowering hill like Lash LaRue flicking guns out of outlaws' hands. *Whack!* for those lying letters Denn sent. *This* for Linsey Thomas's endorsement of Luther Parker. Luther Parker? *Whack!* Fifty-nine percent? *Whack!* Every Vickery that ever walked the face of the earth? *Whack-whack-whack!*

Eventually my fury and humiliation abated and instead of slashing at tobacco tops, I found myself using the stick to poke at stone flakes and flip bits of quartz out of the dirt as I walked along.

The woodland Indians that lived here before Columbus arrived usually built their villages and camps on the west side of rivers, and my brothers and I had picked up hundreds of their projectile points when we were children.

As had my aunts and uncles.

As do my nieces and nephews.

As will their children and their children's children if the land abides with us.

Yet no matter how many we carry away, each spring plowing turns up more. The oldest go back more than eight thousand years, the newest are less than two hundred, each point shaped by a human hand.

There's something innately soothing about walking slowly up and down rows of growing plants, your mind drifting across consciousness like a cloud across the blue sky overhead, only your eyes alert to leaf green flint or white quartz.

A front had passed through during the night and the air was cool and dry. The tobacco was just high enough that whenever I lifted my eyes from the dirt, I was an island in the middle of a fresh green lake that rippled in the soft June breeze.

Yet I was not alone. A hundred eyes watched my passage up and down the long rows. Grasshoppers fled before me, lizards skittered, a toad sat passive and immobile. In the next furrow over, a young snake with rusty blotches gave me a turn until the shape of the head and patterns along its length let me see that it was a harmless corn snake and not a poisonous copperhead. I'm not afraid of any snake once I know it's there, yet, like Emily Dickinson, I never come across one unexpectedly without that involuntary 'tighter breathing and Zero at the bone.' Desmond Morris says that's because we're descended from apes, and snakes were the only natural predator that could follow us up into the trees. The Bible says it's because we're descended from Eve and lost Eden through the serpent's guile.

Upon thy belly shalt thou go, and dust shalt thou eat all

the days of thy life. And I will put enmity between thee and the woman.

Poor snakes.

I found chips and flakes and broken points with missing bases and then a piece of pottery half as big as my hand, the outside textured in an even pattern, the inside smoothed by clever fingers gone to dust two thousand years ago. Was it enough for the maker, this simple grace of common work done well? If she'd known that she would live and die and all that would survive to mark her passage would be these few square inches of sand-colored bowl, would it have troubled her?

Man is born unto trouble, as the sparks fly upward.

I could see her sitting before campfires on cold autumn nights. Did she watch the red and gold sparks fly upward and merge with the stars until her mind stretched into the vastness of the cosmos? To know and believe absolutely and without doubt that God – whatever god – created the universe and all that is in it is to stand with a shield against the outer darkness; and yet always comes a still, small, the-emperor-has-no-clothes voice that asks, 'But then who created God?'

And what is the universe that it is mindful of – wait, wait, *wait*! There on the ground lay the tip of a beautifully flaked point, its base hidden by the dirt. Holding my breath, I stooped and picked it up. Lovely! No missing base, no broken corner. It was a Kirk Corner Notched point, as whole and perfectly formed as the day it came from its maker's hand, two thousand years before the first pyramid.

As I smoothed away the last few grains that clung to this gift from the past, I suddenly realized that I'd begun whistling a syncopated version of *It's me, it's me, it's me, O Lord, standing in the need of prayer.*

Okay, so Luther Parker won this time. No matter who finished out Perry Byrd's term, that seat was up for election in two years. I'd learned a lot this go-round and next time . . . a cluster of small chips drew me forward.

I saw the cloud of dust kicked up by the wheels before I heard the pickup. I had wondered how long it would take him. Though I hadn't noticed anyone, I wasn't fool enough to believe no human eyes had seen me down here in this back field.

By the time Daddy's battered red Chevrolet made its circuitous way around the edge of the fields, I was waiting at the end of the rows where cultivated land gave way to creek brush. He pulled up beside me and spoke through the open window.

'If you don't want no company, I can get on back to the house, but Maidie thought you might like some dinner.'

A tip of his head indicated a soft blue cloth tucked into a cardboard box on the seat beside him.

'She send enough for you?' I asked, knowing well and good who thought I might be ready to eat lunch.

'I reckon.'

He cut off the engine and handed over a jug of sweet and strong iced tea, and we walked down a path to a big flat rock beside the water. Trees overhung this stretch, but sunlight still dappled the brown water. We spread the blue cloth on the rock and I set out a platter of crispy fried chicken, warm spinach salad, and deviled eggs. The biscuits were still hot from Maidie's oven.

As we ate from paper plates, perched on the rocks, I showed him the arrowhead and the piece of pottery and we talked about bonfires and Indians, about family and tenants, until finally he said, 'You're doing okay then?'

I reached for my father's gnarled and workworn hand. 'Yes, I really am.'

'Them crows sure put a pecking on you, didn't they, shug? You still sorry you didn't win?'

'Yes,' I said honestly. 'I can live with it, but yes.'

'You know something, daughter? You never once told me how come you wanted to make a run for it.'

I picked up some nearby pebbles and began plunking them into the creek. 'You never asked.'

'I'm asking now.'

So I told him about how it'd all come to a head that rainy January day when a black plumber was charged with drunk driving and Perry Byrd had mean-mindedly piled the whole weight of the law onto his shoulders.

'You'd've turned him loose?'

'No, sir. He did go out on the highway after drinking; he did, for whatever reason, refuse to take the Breathalyzer. Those two things are against the law and the law *does* save lives. But justice could've been tempered with mercy. Maybe one night in jail to think it over, but on the weekend, when it wouldn't interfere with his livelihood. Instead of taking away his license altogether for a year, I'd've kept him off the road when he wasn't working. How can a plumber keep his business going if he can't make house calls? Punishment's supposed to deter a person from doing it again, not crush his spirit.

And it shouldn't depend on what color his skin is, what sex he happens to be, or what social class he's from.

'White-collar embezzlers should get at least as much time as a blue-collar worker who steals a TV; if a mayor's daughter gets to do community service for a hit and run, so should the mayor's cook's son. The Perry Byrds can be bigots, snobs, and toadies in their personal lives, but when they put on that black robe and sit on that high seat, they should be like priests administering law like a sacrament of Justice. For all the people. It'll never be an exact science, but it doesn't have to be a crap shoot either.'

Frustrated, I took another handful of pebbles and plunked them one by one into the slow-moving creek while Daddy lit another cigarette and watched the little splashes without speaking. Silence rippled out around us. A brown thrasher swooped past, as if we were only a couple of fellow creatures come down to drink, too. I lobbed the last pebble and said, 'When you were bootlegging, did you ever kill anybody?'

He tipped his hat back on the crown of his silver head and looked at me steadily with those piercing blue eyes. 'No. Wanted to a couple of times, meant to once, but never did.'

Something that had been coiled tightly within me for years suddenly relaxed. 'What was prison like?'

'It didn't crush me.'

'No,' I said. 'You're a hawk.'

'You are, too, shug.'

'Am I?'

He flicked his cigarette into the creek.

'Let's you and me go find out,' he said, and pushed himself upright with such purpose that I didn't question.

I packed up the box and folded the blue cloth over it again and followed my tall father back up the path. Tree roots had pulled themselves out of the ground, loose pebbles crunched underfoot, yet his thin back was straight as ever and his feet didn't stumble.

I climbed into the passenger side of the old pickup – part of Daddy's 'I'm just a plain ol' dirt farmer' window dressing – and we drove along the edge of fields till we came to a homemade bridge spanning the creek. As soon as we drove across, we were on Talbert land.

'Gray Talbert know about this bridge?' I asked as we rattled across the loose boards.

'He furnished the boards. Shorty and B.R. and Leonard asked him if it was all right and he said fine.'

Shorty, B.R., and Leonard all lived rent-free on Daddy's land, but they worked for wages with Gray Talbert. Coming across the creek like this instead of going around by the roads probably saved them six or eight miles each trip.

'Is he expecting us?'

'Well, no, I can't say he is. I believe he had to go to Raleigh this evening. They don't expect him back much before five.'

I glanced at my watch. It was a little after two.

We drove on up the lane and approached Gray Talbert's nursery business from the rear. As we neared the greenhouses, Shorty Avery appeared, hitched up his jeans, and motioned for Daddy to pull in under the willow tree.

'A willow tree's like a nice big umbrella,' said Daddy. 'Hard to see under from the air.'

'Howdy, Mr Kezzie, Miss Deb'rah,' said Shorty Avery as

we got out of the truck. He was maybe midfifties and had farmed with Daddy all his life, one of those wiry little white men that look like tuberculosis would take them away the very next winter, but who go on till ninety.

'Hey, Shorty,' I said. 'How's Barbara May these days?'

Barbara May was his daughter and a high school classmate of mine.

'She's doing fine. Her oldest is fixin' to start high school in September.'

We agreed that time flies, then Daddy said, 'Everything okay here?'

'Just fine,' said Shorty. 'You want to show her around, you just go right on ahead.'

Daddy'd evidently been here before, and he pointed out some interesting features that Gray had instituted. 'See how all these newer greenhouses are dug into the ground three feet? Lets you take advantage of the natural insulation of dirt. Easier to heat, easier to cool. And these here evergreens. Now, they make a good windbreak, don't they? So thick you can't even see through 'em, can you?'

I nodded and agreed and wondered what the point of this tour was. Whatever it was, Gray's other employees seemed to know about it. No one came over to greet us, no one asked why we were there.

'How many greenhouses you reckon Gray's got here?' Daddy said.

I looked around and began to count. It was difficult to tell because the windbreaks were almost like a maze. Daddy waited till I'd walked to the front of the business and back again. 'Fourteen,' I said.

'You missed two.' The evergreens were laid out in interlocking L-shaped patterns, he told me. 'Real pretty looking from the air, I bet. And real easy to make a USDA inspector on the ground get turned around. Maybe look at the same greenhouse twice.'

As he spoke, he led me around the corner of a windbreak, and sure enough, there were two more identical greenhouses. This time of year Gray wouldn't need to use the growing lights that ran the length of the arched plastic roof. The hundreds of knee-high marijuana plants seemed to be flourishing nicely on natural sunlight.

'I heard somewhere that every stalk of this stuff is worth about a thousand dollars,' said Daddy.

'Enough to buy a new Porsche every year?'

'With a little bit of pocket change left over,' he agreed dryly.

We walked back to the truck and Daddy thanked Shorty for his hospitality.

'Any time, Mr Kezzie. Nice seeing you, Miss Deb'rah.'

We drove back across Possum Creek and parked near my car.

'As I see it,' said Daddy, 'we got us a little gray area here. We can tell Terry Wilson or Bo Poole and they'll close young Gray down and put him in jail maybe and that'll leave Shorty and Leonard and B.R. and the rest of 'em out of work.'

'Or?'

'Or I can send G. Hooks a copy of the videotape I had somebody make back there last week. One of them tapes that has the date and time running through the whole thing? G. Hooks is a right big contributor to the Republican Party. I figure he can have a little talk with the governor.'

I began to see where Daddy was going on this.

'How's it gonna look,' he asked rhetorically, 'if people find out that one of Hardison's biggest backers is growing this stuff?'

'Even though it's Gray—?'

'It's G. Hooks's name on the deed, same man as said he didn't care to deal with bootleggers.' He cut his eyes at me. 'Been saving this for just the right time. Sure would love to see his face when he finds out he'd got a bigger mess fouling his own nest. Not too smart to do stuff on your own land. Don't leave you much of what they call deniability.'

I scrunched down on my spine and rested my sneakered feet on the ancient dashboard. 'So you're going to squeeze G. Hooks's balls and he's going to squeeze Hardison's?'

Daddy frowned. 'I never did like to hear a lady talk dirty. Besides, Hardison's never cottoned to G. Hooks. He's gonna like it that Talbert has to beg *him* for a favor.'

'Will I still be a lady if I let you blackmail G. Hooks into getting me appointed to fill Perry Byrd's unexpired term?'

'Why not?'

'There's a small matter of ethics,' I said stiffly, even as the shameless pragmatist inside my head began to raise himself hopefully from the floor of yesterday's defeat and despair.

'You want this. You know you do.'

'Think of the price,' warned the preacher. *'You can live with defeat. Can you live with this?'*

'Ethics make mighty thin eating to a man hungry for that justice you were talking about,' said Daddy. 'Besides, you don't take it, who you reckon Hardison's likely to appoint?

Another nigger-hating, lickspittle mossback like Perry Byrd who'll keep trying to undo all the progress the South's made these last twenty years?'

Afterwards, I liked to think I wrestled long and hard over my answer, weighing the good I might do against the certain knowledge that this was a tainted appointment.

In reality, it was only a moment or two before I nodded and said, 'Just make sure G. Hooks understands that one week after I'm appointed, Terry Wilson's going to be told about those greenhouses.'

Daddy looked a mite uncomfortable. 'Well, now, shug, I thought ten days. Give him time to get 'em all cleaned out good and planted with real nursery stock.'

I bolted upright. 'You already sent him that video? Then what the hell was all that back there?'

'Thought you ought to know what's involved. Make the choice yourself.'

'See if I was a hawk?' I asked sardonically.

'No. I already figured you were. Just wasn't sure you knew it yet.'

P. C. DOHERTY

AN ANCIENT EVIL

The Knight's Tale of mystery and murder as he goes on pilgrimage from London to Canterbury

As the travellers gather in the Tabard Inn at the start of a pilgrimage to pray before the blessed bones of St Thomas à Becket in Canterbury, they agree eagerly to mine host Harry's suggestion of amusing themselves on each day of their journey with one tale and each evening with another – but the latter to be of mystery, terror and murder. The Knight begins that evening: his tale opens with the destruction of a sinister cult at its stronghold in the wilds of Oxfordshire by Sir Hugo Mortimer during the reign of William the Conqueror and then moves to Oxford some two hundred years later where strange crimes and terrible murders are being committed. The authorities seem powerless but Lady Constance, Abbess of the Convent of St Anne's, believes the murders are connected with the legends of the cult and she petitions the King for help.

As the murders continue unabated, special commissioner Sir Godfrey Evesden and royal clerk Alexander MacBain uncover clues that lead to a macabre world sect, which worships the dark lord. But they can find no solution to a series of increasingly baffling questions and matters are not helped by the growing rift between Sir Godfrey and McBain for the hand and favour of the fair Lady Emily.

FICTION/CRIME   0 7472 4356 5

More Thrilling Crime Fiction from Headline:

MARTHA GRIMES

THE HORSE YOU CAME IN ON

Richard Jury is supposed to be on holiday when the telephone call comes. And in any case, what has sudden death on American soil to do with an English police superintendent? But when the victim turns out to be British by birth, and to have a distant connection with Jury's old acquaintance, Lady Cray, he reluctantly acknowledges that his marker is being called in. Enlisting the aid of reluctant peer Melrose Plant, and accompanied by the irrepressibly lugubrious Sergeant Wiggins, Jury crosses the Atlantic to see what he can find out.

Baltimore turns out to have many attractions – not least that it is the home of avant garde novelist Ellen Taylor, last encountered at The Old Silent inn. Ellen is painfully engaged upon finishing her new book, but takes time out to introduce the trio to the delights of the city – football, Edgar Allen Poe, Bromo-Seltzer and a bar called The Horse You Came In On.

A case of plagiarism, a blind and deaf street-dweller, an engaging child who bears a strong resemblance to Scarlett O'Hara – these are just some of the elements in a complex puzzle whose solution looks set to defy the combined talents of the visiting team and put an end to a very promising writing career...

FICTION/CRIME   0 7472 4221 6

TAKEOUT DOUBLE

A CASSIE SWANN MYSTERY

SUSAN MOODY

Two years of teaching biology had been enough. Two years of dissecting frogs and reeking of formaldehyde had finally persuaded Cassie Swann to set up as a bridge professional instead. So far, she has managed to make a reasonable living, operating from her Cotswold cottage.

And then, during a Winter Bridge Weekend at a country-house hotel, she finds three of her punters dead around the green-baize table. And at least one of them is indisputably the victim of murder.

Nothing to do with Cassie – or is it?

When she realises that her livelihood is now threatened by the unwanted notoriety, she is forced to undertake some investigations of her own.

Set amid the eccentricities of English village life, *Takeout Double* is the first in a marvellous series featuring an amateur sleuth in the obsessive world of bridge players.

FICTION/CRIME 0 7472 3946 0

A selection of bestsellers from Headline

MONSIEUR PAMPLEMOUSSE ON LOCATION	Michael Bond	£4.50 ☐
THE CAT WHO WENT INTO THE CLOSET	Lilian Jackson Braun	£4.50 ☐
MURDER WEARS A COWL	P C Doherty	£4.50 ☐
CURTAINS FOR THE CARDINAL	Elizabeth Eyre	£4.99 ☐
ROUGH RIDE	John Francome	£4.99 ☐
MURDER AMONG US	Ann Granger	£4.99 ☐
DEADLY ERRAND	Christine Green	£4.99 ☐
IDOL BONES	D M Greenwood	£4.50 ☐
THE END OF THE PIER	Martha Grimes	£4.50 ☐
COPY KAT	Karen Kijewski	£4.99 ☐
CLOSE UP ON DEATH	Maureen O'Brien	£5.99 ☐
THE LATE LADY	Staynes & Storey	£4.50 ☐
SWEET DEATH COME SOFTLY	Barbara Whitehead	£4.99 ☐

All Headline books are available at your local bookshop or newsagent, or can be ordered direct from the publisher. Just tick the titles you want and fill in the form below. Prices and availability subject to change without notice.

Headline Book Publishing PLC, Cash Sales Department, Bookpoint, 39 Milton Park, Abingdon, OXON, OX14 4TD, UK. If you have a credit card you may order by telephone – 0235 831700.

Please enclose a cheque or postal order made payable to Bookpoint Ltd to the value of the cover price and allow the following for postage and packing:
UK & BFPO: £1.00 for the first book, 50p for the second book and 30p for each additional book ordered up to a maximum charge of £3.00.
OVERSEAS & EIRE: £2.00 for the first book, £1.00 for the second book and 50p for each additional book.

Name ....

Address ....

....

....

If you would prefer to pay by credit card, please complete:
Please debit my Visa/Access/Diner's Card/American Express (delete as applicable) card no:

Signature .... Expiry Date ....